MW01225447

Alan Duff was born in Rotorua in 1950. He has published six previous novels (*Once Were Warriors, One Night Out Stealing, What Becomes of the Broken Hearted?, Both Sides of the Moon, Szabad* and *Jake's Long Shadow*), a novella (*State Ward*) and three non-fiction works (*Maori: The Crisis and the Challenge, Out of the Mist and Steam* and *Alan Duff's Maori Heroes*). *Once Were Warriors* won the PEN Best First Book Award for Fiction. This and *What Becomes of the Broken Hearted?* were made into internationally acclaimed films for which he wrote the original screenplays. He works as a full-time writer.

Dreamboat Dad

ALAN DUFF

v

National Library of New Zealand Cataloguing-in-Publication Data

Duff, Alan, 1950-
Dreamboat Dad / Alan Duff.
ISBN 978-1-86979-024-0
I. Title.
NZ823.2—dc 22

A VINTAGE BOOK
published by
Random House New Zealand
18 Poland Road, Glenfield, Auckland, New Zealand
For more information about our titles go to www.randomhouse.co.nz

Random House International Random House 20 Vauxhall Bridge Road, London, SW1V
2SA, United Kingdom; **Random House Australia Pty Ltd** Level 3, 100 Pacific Highway, North
Sydney 2060, Australia; **Random House South Africa Pty Ltd** Isle of Houghton, Corner
Boundary Road and Carse O'Gowrie, Houghton 2198, South Africa; **Random House Publishers
India Private Ltd** 301 World Trade Tower, Hotel Intercontinental Grand Complex, Barakhamba
Lane, New Delhi 110 001, India

First published 2008

© 2008 Alan Duff

The moral rights of the author have been asserted

ISBN 978 1 86979 024 0

This book is copyright. Except for the purposes of fair reviewing no part of this publication may
be reproduced or transmitted in any form or by any means, electronic or mechanical, including
photocopying, recording or any information storage and retrieval system, without permission in
writing from the publisher.

Richard Wright's poem 'Between the World and Me' on page 251–2, and the extract on page 238,
are reproduced with the kind permission of the Estate of Richard Wright, by special arrangement
with Julia Wright. Abel Meeropol's poem 'Strange Fruit', on pages 125 and 130, is reproduced with
the kind permission of J Albert & Son.

Random House New Zealand uses non chlorine-bleached papers from sustainably managed
plantation forests.

Text design: Elin Bruhn Termannsen
Cover illustration: Diving for Pennies, Whaka, Rotorua, 40456: 2007.98.15, Rotorua Museum of
Art and History, Te Whare Taonga o Te Arawa
Cover design: Matthew Trbuhovic
Printed in Australia by Griffin Press

In celebration of my African son, Makhosonke Ntokozo Zulu, 1982–2008, who showed us what determination is.

This one is for Harriet Allan, my editor, friend and harshest critic, to let readers know the line is often blurred between writer and editor. So, with my huge thanks.

Thanks to Claire Gummer, with her sharp eye and great suggestions.

To my father Gowan for giving his children a love of the written word.

My two youngest kids, Virginia and Rosy, who never get a mention.

To David Moore and Bruce Plested, two friends who backed me.

The people of Whaka whom I grew up with and will always love.

Every African American whose sufferings gifted the world with musical genius and a whole lot more besides.

PART ONE

CHAPTER ONE

IT TOOK A FEW TIMES and a few years before it registered what had been said about my mother, that she was a slut and why did I think my name was Yank, surely I would've figured that out? But I hadn't given it much thought, hearing comment of my mother's lowly status to do with sex and somehow linked to the only name I knew and liked.

A kid doesn't think about his name he just is it, like Chud, Hopscotch, Lulu, Beebop, Manu, Kaipara, Heretini, Ngawai. They're just names aren't they?

At the time of this revelation I'm a ten-year-old boy called Yank — so what? Is Boyman both a boy and a man? Honeygirl, is she a girl made from honey? My mother calls my best mate Boyboy, does that make him twins? We call him Chud, from the chewing gum we call chuddy. They're all just names. Except when I hear Chud's name, it's like a bell chiming confirmation he's a brother.

My surname is Takahe, it's official on the school roll. A wonder Henry allowed me to use his name, unless it saved embarrassment with my sisters being his daughters. My siblings are true Takahes, the name of a native bird and a man whose house I live in but who doesn't like me, even though I have a secret liking for him. Sometimes.

Until I was five and started school, I thought he was my real father who just happened not to like me. Even though my big sister had told me early I wasn't his son. A little kid believes what he wants to believe. How could he be my sister's father and not mine, when we shared the same mother?

Henry hardly said a word to me, not good morning, not have something to eat, not anything — if you don't count grunts and him using sign language. I never saw his teeth revealed to me in a smile. Not once. I still would have died of joy if he had dropped all that and become a father.

Mum promised she'd explain: *when you're old enough*. When five is already too old not to know the reason why. I mean, kids hurt more because they lack understanding.

Ten years on this earth before my selective ears will let the word take on meaning. The way the person's mouth forms is enough. Sl–ut. When no mother is supposed to be one of those. Till I woke up I truly believed Mum was Mary, the Holy Mother statue at the Catholic Church up the road. Not Lena, her real name. Not the statue. But the real Mary the statue was modelled on.

When I was young enough to believe in ghosts and God, I would picture the Virgin Mary in my mind when thinking about my mother: with a glow–ring round her head, a presence full of promise, not a lie to her name, and really beautiful.

Mary, who kissed me not just goodnight but good morning and hello during the day and just anytime. When she lifted me up I truly believed I played with the glow–ring above her head, that it was shiny, sparkling silver gold and was warm like a tricycle handlebar you've held on to a while.

I'd hear the word muttered over the years, from older kids, adults. But it was like a fuzzy signal on our crackly old valve radio.

A slut can't be a wonderful mother. I find out it's a woman who sleeps around, which means taking off her clothes and going at it with a man and his stiff cock in her vagina. Going at what? Well, down there, what every kid has growing but shocked awareness about.

When they're saying this about your mother you want to die, or kill, or a hole to open in the steaming thermal ground and boil you and your shame away.

A slut?

Yeah, didn't you know that, boy?

A slut? My mother?

Where your name came from. She did it with a Yank.

As bad as Chud's mother who's a pisshead and beats her kids up?

Just as bad. Some men would rather have a drunken missus like Shirl Kohu than a slut.

I slunk around for a bit, thinking everyone had been laughing at me all these years. Relieved when I found out only the nastier ones in our little village called her that, those with long memories or their imitators. But Mum was never Mother Mary again. Gone was her halo. Though I still adored her.

CHAPTER TWO

SHORT OF MY MOTHER BEING confirmed to be a lifetime slut, just about nothing could ruin the joy of living here in Waiwera, Two Lakes. Not in one of the world's — the *world's* — most unique places. And we don't have to have visited countless places to compare. We just know there is only one village in the world sited on a thermally active area the way ours is, the river and the bridge crossing it a big introductory part, our thermal baths, the steaming landscape and fact we're the native people of this country: Maori.

Our village is a one-off, which is why the tourists come from overseas to gape in awe at our steaming, erupting, boiling acres, and experience our Maori culture groups putting on our songs and dances in a highly professional way. Pay a fee to our women guides to tour them over our amazing landscape; guides who give a well-practised commentary on the different thermal manifestations. Tell of victims over the years who have fallen into pools and been boiled alive; inform of the tribal history and how an eruption in 1886 of a mountain twenty-five miles away brought the survivors to take up residence here, on the same fault line that the huge Tarawera eruption broke through, completely destroyed what was called the Eighth Wonder of the World, the Pink and White Terraces. A lot of the houses here have framed pictures of paintings of those stunning thermal creations created by nature and claimed by her too. What a waste. Why would God destroy what people say only He could make?

On certain nights, when cloud has stolen the stars and ghosts are on the loose, the thermal noising can sound like someone weeping, an anguished soul crying out in pain as his flesh boils off his bones, crying out for a second chance. You might be heading for a soak in one of our built concrete bath tubs and get stopped in your tracks at a sound as if someone is being throttled, a baby strangled to death, as thermal pressure forces a way through a narrow gap. Can sound like a noisy whistle kettle too.

Or you'll hear one of the old people singing half-note waiata and older kids tell you it's a death chant and listen out for the final death rattle. You'll know when a final blast of rotten stinking air comes out of the old person, and if you breathe it in you're either dead or you will catch a terrible disease.

All over are different coloured little lakes, cobalt blue, emerald green, sulphur yellow, mud grey, crystal clear. I'm taking this from any of our guides' spoken commentaries; every local kid knows them off by heart: we mimic, make fun, add to them. And I've mentioned but a fraction of what is on visual offer at Waiwera.

Now where would a slut fit in a place like this? They'd have booted her out long ago. But as I adjust to the idea I get to thinking — hoping more like it — one of those Yank tourists could be my father come back to search for me. He could be any one of those I'd shown copycat contempt, to impress the older boys. Could be rich, live in a huge mansion in — where? California somewhere. New York. He could live anywhere in that vast country . . . soon my atlas at school becomes a much studied work.

One day I might hear a voice call out, Mark? I've come to take you home.

What would I say? How would he know me, would my mother point me out swimming in the river, bring him to me lolling about in one of the hot pools? Would he recognise me instantly? Do I look like him? Is he kind? Will he ever turn on me, let me down? Will he love me no matter what I do?

Unlike my sisters' grandmother whose house I go past every day, to her dirty look if she's outside on the veranda, in her vege garden. Old bat never comes to our house because of me and she gives lollies and food to my sisters, Mata and Wiki, and especially *my little Manu* — her *real* grandson — right in front of me. Says hello, gives them a kiss, not one word or treat my way. Just like her ignorant son. How will my father make up for suffering that?

Takes a little while longer before everything falls into place: a couple of years pass. It's like a series of curtains being pulled back — if you are born of a mind to pull them open. Must be from my father to have this curious mind wanting answers, even enlightenment. Not that I know of the word then.

Old Merita, one of our oldest residents and respected villagers with time for anyone. Not a kid in the village who hasn't taken a morning newspaper up to her house up on the ridge, nor any who hasn't confided in her, or just listened.

With tattooed lips and chin etched and chiselled in the old way, Merita yet has a keen interest in the wider, modern world. Older people say if she had been a man she would be the chief of our village, maybe the whole sub-tribe. Women have different rights and status to men, though in a kids' world we seem about the same — if it wasn't for the sexual interest boys spill over with and girls don't.

Merita *loves* the newspapers, morning and evening editions; wants to discuss what she's read. Kids don't get most things, but I have an ear for words as I do music, how they're both like dough you can shape in your hands. Early on I made the discovery of letting go with music and, funny thing, it was by watching Henry sing, how he just gets glazed eyes and launches his voice. Same way I learned to dive off the bridge top rail — just let go. I'm one of the best dancers in the village too, age regardless.

So while not understanding most of what she's saying, I do learn things. When I was little she'd take me up and let me run fingers in her chin tattoo done in the old style and she'd say, feels like a corn cob, eh? Sometimes she'd be cuddling me pretending to be passive then suddenly break out with a scary noise. Give a cackling laugh and her thermal-bath warm eyes and say, orrr, you're a scaredy-cat.

Her view looks down on the main tourist area. House has a dirt floor that's warm from the thermal underneath. Like every house the furnishings are basic. Framed photographs adorn every Waiwera house wall, as do prints of Her Majesty, Queen Elizabeth, and some of her father, King George. British royalty doesn't mean the same to us kids. Though at the picture theatres we have to stand up for *God Save the Queen* or get chucked out, or get a whack from an usher's torch.

Merita sweeps her dirt floor with a manuka broom, can break off a bit from a tree right out her back door when the old switch wears out. Her husband died before he could install a proper wooden floor, but he lives on in her memory as a good husband and good father to their eleven children, all but two moved to other towns at her encouragement. Same as she encourages me: move away when you're old enough, learn how beautiful the wider world and yet how lovely this place too. Open your mind up, closed if you stay here.

She tells me, I miss the old times, Yank. Everyone knew their place. We had order, a structure in which our society and culture was strong. Sure, we had the tourists to help give us a living. Our male elders who only thought they ran the place when, behind the scenes, it has always been us women. But we held together. I worry it won't hold for much longer, not unless we have strong leadership like Henry. You won't understand me saying this, not now, but you will.

. . . What you here for this time, boy? Your mother? Well, for starters, don't be listening to this nonsense your mother is that word. She's not. Just some people are cruel because that's how they are. Because we're in a village and all related doesn't mean we're pure as milk and sweet as honey. Your mother is a good woman and you make sure you always respect her. She's the one going to give you strength.

CHAPTER THREE

HERE HE COMES, THE YOUNG man who left as a private and returned with an officer's prouder posture. He's hardly looking at the throngs of adoring, joyful villagers, not like his fellow returned servicemen breaking out in smiles and shaking heads in disbelief that the five-plus years' ordeal is over; it didn't feel that long, now they are back walking on home territory.

Fingers and arms of steam rise up from the thermal ground like tossed white streamers. Great billows of steam from a pool surging with activity like a regular, slow-pulse puffing of the Earth's heart. Cauldrons of mud simmer and bubbles burst releasing pungent sulphur and gas smell, and look there, the mighty Potaka Geyser blasts welcome up on the nearby rise, a hundred feet and more high, and all around voices have risen in song and call and crying in joy and grief.

Nor does he appear to notice the glances and looks trying to convey to him, *Captain* Henry Takahe now, that all is not well. She is not here to welcome you, Henry. She waits no doubt trembling with the boy to explain, when you only expected to see for the first time the daughter born of your loins, in your absence.

Poor Henry: no soldier deserves such news. Though if truth be known, it is happening in other Maori villages, and European households, imparted as the exact same shock news all over the country now the boys are home. The Yanks were here.

She waits, Henry, but not as you have every right to expect of your wife — untainted, saved only for you. No. She has another man's child to introduce, a child she could have adopted out. Everyone would have understood; she could have applied the Maori custom of whangai: given the kid to a relation, a close friend, let them bring it up. Poor shamed, humiliated Henry, war hero. A half-sibling to your daughter you've yet to see.

The women are all in black with leafy garlands in their hair, weeping and laughing and singing at the same time. Up ahead a young warrior charges towards the returned warriors of modern times, wearing only muscle armour and a flax piupiu skirt clacking and flinging its hard dried strands to his violently choreographed motion in a traditional challenge, asking are you friend or foe? Asking even of their own, since it is age-old custom from when the challenge was real and directed at visitors.

His prancing is complex and perfectly executed; he must maintain this standard or else the mana of the challenge is reduced or even lost. This is the greatest occasion of his life: every staged movement of this muscled, sweating warrior must reflect respect for these heroes and a millennium of warriors in the proud past.

He twirls the long-bladed taiaha with magnificent dexterity, at such speed it is a blur and it does not seem possible he will not drop the weapon as it flashes this way and that, stabbed, prodded, feinted, spun, action reversed, ripped from below when the emphasis was at the apex, his tongue stabbing, sunlight catching the spittle leaping from his teeth-bared mouth, all over with ceremonial hatred, a *dare any take up my challenge* stance, grunts and short shrieks like he is trying to convulse and vomit up objects from his insides.

On he comes this muscled warrior from another time, to the halted group of demobbed soldiers, taiaha spinning, bare feet on the hot earth, backed by the steam making its different sounds, not many clouds in the blue of a warm summer day, back-heeling, kicking up small puffs of dust, a delicate dancing designed to fool the eyes, while clouds of steam and heat belch up from nearby hot pools and drift across the warrior like the past trying to claim him back.

Then he emerges from its vapoury grasp running right up close to the lead man, Henry Takahe, who wipes not at the spit spotting his face, flinches not at the blur of deadly weapon cut across inches from his face; this is a fine challenge, one befitting returning heroes and remembering the fallen in faraway foreign soil. The people reduced to silent admiration.

Nothing though can stop them wondering: what is to follow this heroes' welcome? What will happen when Henry is informed of the illicit child, his wife's ultimate insult? Woe is she who broke her marriage vows.

Behind the warrior's back the weapon goes, makes his chest and rigid arm muscles stand out, neck sinews become taut strings, eyes bulge as last threat. Last grunts warn there be no tricks no false move as he goes to one knee, removes from his waistband a leafy twig, lays it on the thermally warmed ground not for a moment taking eyes off Henry, who in turn bends and takes up the offering, brings it to his belly to say he — they — come in peace, of course in peace for they are one people and the real war has ended in victory, the foreign enemy lies crushed, in ruins in his own invaded land. Freedom has triumphed, a majority have made it back home.

A last furious look then the warrior stands up, dances backwards, turns and prances back to a large group of similarly flax-skirted warriors young and old, the village all, ready to haka.

The mass war dance, carefully configured and much rehearsed to bring down the curtain on this momentous event, is tribute and conclusion and reminder to these returnees, you are of us we are of you. We pull you back with glad hearts into our embrace.

And yet, villagers, and yet . . .

Yet there is change in our boys. Look how their faces are different, see the dark around the eyes, the gaunt cheeks, stains of disillusion and disbelief; there's a haunting in too many eyes, a couple clearly brain-damaged. Look at the deep-furrowed brows, twitches and tics that weren't there before, see how some look disoriented, unsure of where they are, even here, back home at this unforgettable place. They may have come home the victors but a price was paid.

Now, most of the soldiers are crying, though not Henry who maintains his officer's posture, a leader of men who must set example. His outbreaks of smile have died, replaced by confusion perhaps suspicion. But maybe he has known for some time, maybe she wrote to him. His people observe closely, like plotting palace subjects keeping careful eye on their ruler, positioning themselves for his fury, his wrath to come and, one day, his favour.

Ah, but look at poor Nathan Kururangi, who left here in 1939, the searing late summer light of eager youth, brain blind to what lay ahead, and came home with the darkness forever drawn over his eyes.

Look at Barney Mutu's lips moving, yet no words issue. Fine looking still, he is reduced of the man he was, words unable to get out.

In alphabetical order Henry has committed twenty names to memory, a brother, cousins, close friends, sons, grandsons from families he knows so well, whom he played with as a child; schooled and fought with and against on the rugby fields; at school athletics; swum in the river, bathed with.

Every spoken name makes for outbreak of grief. Henry has to pause each time. Barney starts staring and people realise Henry is nearing the letter M.

Mutu, Henry says. Harold.

Barney's eyes bore into Henry; his mouth opens and closes. Henry meets Barney's stare. Barney holds his captain's gaze for a moment then closes eyes and weeps for his late brother.

The feast will become local legend: crayfish by the score, shellfish by the sack, lamb, pork, beef, chicken, all cooked in the big steam boxes built beside the communal dining room. In a country six years rationed somehow food has been procured. The beer comes in kegs, whisky and rum by the case.

Inside a large hall set with groaning tables, individuals get up and sing, mighty natural-born tenors and baritones, big of build and raw personalities formed from growing up in this tiny community and yet influenced, subtly and without knowing it, by the host of international visitors and their broader outlook. For the Waiwera Maori boys gained renown for their excellent singing voices in that war.

The soldiers show off the Italian arias picked up while fighting, first in Egypt then in the Eyties' own backyard. More than a few could have had opera careers, with training. But mostly the whole community sings, harmonised and powerful with emotion and that part of the warrior breed's personality which turns soft and tearful on occasions like this.

The males young and old break out in haka after stirring haka, shake the ground like the tremor before a geyser erupts, as they erupt into choreographed display of chest- and thigh-slapping fury screaming the words to the enemy of days a hundred years gone but alive in their minds that they are coming for them, the hated foe.

Women take turns to sing harmonised songs. Individuals confidently do solos and miss not a note nor falter with a phrase. Love and lust shine openly in female eyes.

All day and into the night the celebrations go.

My mother could hardly turn up at proceedings with me in tow, just had to sit at home and wait for Henry.

My big sister told me he called Mum a slut that night. A fucken slut. And gave her a hell of a hiding which Mata said she'd never forget nor forgive. Mata remembered him using the word Yank quite a few times. That would be my father.

Growing up we read comics with pictures of Jap soldiers with buck teeth, wearing thick-lens spectacles, depicted as little slit-eyed monsters getting whipped by our giant, good-looking, white American ally soldiers. I presumed my father — my real father — to be one of those Jap-killing heroes. Tall and handsome, muscular, with shining white teeth and of paler complexion than my olive. He'd have a chest adorned with medals won in the war and the proud bearing of a soldier who'd served his country well.

I imagined him confronting Henry over beating up my mother and saying, try me for size, buster. Swelled my chest to bursting with pride thinking of my dad righting that wrong. But I had times of thinking what might in fact be wrong was a man's wife having a baby to another man while he was away fighting a war for his country.

CHAPTER FOUR

MY HUSBAND. HE'S HOME — if this can be called home, the place he returns expecting a loving wife who missed him terribly, expecting to meet his daughter for the first time. Thinking soon we will fall into each other's arms, weep and laugh and claw one another's clothes off, make urgent love. I can understand how he's seeing it. He can't even smile. I don't blame him.

He's never been what you would call handsome, but he has a presence and I think it's physical, not to do with intelligence though he has that too. Something chiefly about him even though he is not of high-born lineage. His presence is more like a slab of timber than an intricate carved piece. He is strength and powerful personality in one, quite dark of complexion as if his blood line has not been diluted by white blood that runs in most Maori veins of today.

Growing up a year younger I saw him fight boys several years older and win more than he lost — the fury he fought with, even when he was only nine or ten, was a scary sight to behold. Doubtless the man fought his enemies the same.

My husband is home, and he has five years of war in his eyes and a war of right now. His hearing cannot grasp that it is two children's voices out that back door, not one.

Poor Henry, he is confused at why I was not there: what possible calamity could have happened for his wife and child to be absent from the homecoming? This day is local history, part of our nation's history, of world history. Yet where was his wife?

I am not such a hypocrite I will go to his arms. I just say hello, Henry. I'm sorry. I couldn't tell you in front of everyone. Tears won't come.

Tell me what? You should have been there to welcome me home. Where the hell were you? Jesus, these are not the first words I should be speaking to my wife after five years apart.

I take a long time to answer, realising I have not rehearsed this, it's not the sort of thing you can go over in your mind, much too big of too much moment, will happen when it does and now the moment has arrived. My God, the moment is here.

I went with another man, Henry.

You what? What did you just say?

He advances towards me, all stunned disbelief, more hurt than a man deserves to expect. I don't blame him.

I want to tell him, it didn't feel like betrayal, not in the circumstances. I want to sit down and discuss with my husband now returned to me nearly six years older with seemingly a lifetime's war experiences that things don't stay the same back home either. The candle might well still be burning in the home window but a woman — women everywhere — get lonely and we change too. We find things out about ourselves that we would never have if our husbands had not gone away and for so long. A woman learns independence, how to keep her own counsel. With time mostly to herself her thoughts change. Might be the idea of marital love has changed too.

He's gone, Henry. Three years gone and for all I know killed.

So he's a soldier?

Yes.

What, a soldier boy home on feigned injury leave? Did you and him lie in our marital bed and laugh at my letters sent from different places after or before you screwed?

Nothing happened here in this house. I would never have done that.

He has hardly blinked. I can hear Mata and Yank outside; Yank is squealing at being chased by his big sister. Their sound does not —

cannot — register to the father of one of them. Rage will soon have him completely in its grip.

He better not be from here. Henry means mortal threat in those glistening eyes.

I shake my head, bizarrely relieved. No, not from here. Not even from this country. And I can see the relief in his face, too: he does not have to go to war again against my lover, against a fellow citizen.

He's American.

Except it swings back at me, my lover's nationality, like a heavy pendulum since it has already slammed into my husband's face.

He's what?

Can't repeat it. Henry heard clear enough, he's trying to adjust.

I'm sorry. It just . . . happened.

You're sorry? For being a married woman going with a Yank while I was fighting for your country, for the honour of our family, our village, our Maori race, our nation? And you say sorry, like you spilled the fucken milk or something?

I had his child.

His what? To a Yank? You have a kid . . . here . . . in this house? No? You adopted it out? Where is it?

In the thunderstruck features I see another man I don't know. Not a monster, who will come soon enough; this is a confused child, like a bullying kid who finds the tables have been turned on him so now he's hurt and confused and knows not what to do next.

Can he be blamed for feeling like this? For what I have done is an outrage. But not, as Father O'Sullivan up the road tried to insist, a sin needing time in the confession box owning up to a God I don't believe in. For surely sin is wicked intent or a deliberate ignoring of moral responsibility?

I committed no sin, even though I broke the marriage vow of fidelity. There was a war going on. And I was caught by surprise, finding deep dissatisfaction I had no idea existed within me.

All this way, thirteen thousand miles he's sailed. He's gone through the unimaginable, taking countless enemy lives, seeing indescribable things, just surviving the war a miracle when millions were killed. He has so looked forward to coming home to me — the pure me, who has known no other man — to see his daughter for the first time; he never stopped saying so in his letters.

If he'd first asked to see his daughter, who is peeping through a gap in the door in fear at this her first sight of her father; if he'd put his anger aside for long enough to embrace her, sit her on his knee, I might just accept him ignoring my son.

Not when he marches up and grabs a handful of my carefully brushed hair and drives his fist into my face and throws me all over the room he and his father laboured to build, for us, the newly married couple, a home for our children. Hitting me, hitting me, when he must know his child and my child are present.

I am not wearing a German uniform: I am in civilian clothes of 1945, a skirt seven years old of tiny floral pattern in but two colours, hardly worn because it has been saved for special occasions though of ordinary material and cheap price.

So why would a husband, on his first day home after more than five years, be beating his wife black and blue with two children right outside the door?

Welcome home, husband. How wonderful to have you back. This is your daughter. We called her Mata, after your grandmother. And when this beating is over you'll meet the kid the village call Yank, the reason why you're doing this to us.

Welcome home, husband, to your unfaithful wife, your first-born child. And the child of a soldier just like you.

CHAPTER FIVE

MUM HAD TOLD ME FOR as long as I remembered: you get used to anything.

I told her for just as long, I didn't want to live in the house with a man who never spoke to me yet smothered my two sisters with love. And why don't you leave, Mum? You and me can live near town, you can take Mata and Wiki. We can come and play here on weekends.

Where will I work? Not many jobs your mother can do, just factory work and the wages are too low to support a family on my own. Besides, we just live different lives under the same roof. You should be grateful he hasn't kicked us out.

Henry would rise early to get the coal range going, liked the kitchen to himself to cook breakfast for everyone including me. A big eater in the mornings, he sometimes roasted a piece of mutton and the family enjoyed plates of hot meat slices with roast potatoes and slices of white bread. I didn't eat at the table same time as him and so mornings my mother separated herself out to eat with me; Henry ate with his two daughters, later on Manu too when he got old enough. If it was roast mutton we were allowed to have what we wanted of it but not the knuckle, that was his.

Pig-headed man of pride against an innocent child — I never stopped seething inside.

At nights he arrived late, around eight or nine o'clock, almost always partly or totally drunk, we became a wider family at the meal table before he got home. Talked and laughed and joked as a normal family. So not as if I was isolated out on my lonely little island. But still, it would always hurt. Mum was wrong, you don't get used to it.

Every morning Henry would go for a bath up at the row of concrete tubs. Our house had a bath but we never used it, not when just a few yards from our house was Falls Bath, named for its waterfall feed from a larger and hotter pool at a higher level. On weekends, no matter what the weather, he and the girls would go to the top baths, where most of the community bathed.

How I used to envy them, the trio in winter morning dark huddled under two large umbrellas. I would watch them out the bedroom window wanting to be with them, feeling my life had been predestined differently to my sisters'. And I did very much wish Henry would talk to me. Didn't even have to treat me like a son, just say something normal. Say anything. A hug wouldn't have gone astray either, must admit.

Mum said he'd get over it, one day. But he never did. The years of silence between us just kept rolling by. I learned to keep my own company, to go into my imagination, discover my musical bent; I tried out dance steps to music either on the radio or in my head. Dancing came naturally to me. I could have hours of conversation with myself as I practised roles and conversational styles, like the women guides, like different American tourists, adopted the voices and attitudes of older kids. I lived where Henry could not hurt me with his ignoring: in my head. Or else in my mother's all-embracing love.

Mum and I ate breakfast while Henry was at the baths. Mum wasn't a big eater and she said her people ate far too much.

In winter the coal range heat drew us to the kitchen. Our sitting room had an open fire, but if Henry was around then I went elsewhere in the house. Our bedrooms were freezing. I'd get under the blankets and lose myself in imagination's landscape and settings. Sometimes Mum and I would go and soak in Falls, relishing the bitter cold air as we sweated in the wet heat. Henry and Barney had built a shelter so bathers could change and keep clothes dry. They were war mates and Henry was very protective of him: no kid dared tease Barney.

I'd walk into the sitting room or kitchen to Henry laughing or talking to my sisters, my entrance causing a sudden, awkward silence. Mata just stared straight ahead and would talk about anything to fill the silence. Wiki looked down and said nothing, a bit like the child who closes his eyes to make people disappear. Manu too young to understand. Boy, I hated those times.

He was gone before we went to school; my family knew I relaxed and became my cheeky self then: I loved to play tricks on my sisters, or if I was feeling thoughtful I liked to be buried in a book and say nothing till we walked to school.

Chud waited for me every school day and weekend mornings too. Often he'd have the marks of a beating but we learned not to say anything. Chud liked the talk to be about anything but himself and his terrible father and mother. If my sisters went to school with their pals, Chud and I did sometimes share what he went through at home, but not too much. We'd rather talk about what we'd do by way of revenge when we grew up, the versions of accidentally on purpose throwing them into a boiling pool, poisoning their food with a special plant old Merita would tell us where to find in the forest up on Totara Hill, how to prepare it. Mostly we were just boys living in our childhood.

As for bullying, no one, not even boys much older, dared touch Chud as he had a nasty temper and would use anything as a weapon to defend himself. He let others know that no one could touch me either.

School was different. Chud had no interest but I found it exciting and challenging and the teachers liked me in their classes. I took books home from the library. Not that I was a bookworm, I just liked words and what the imagination could do. Chud loved nothing better than throwing and kicking a rugby ball; he tackled young tree trunks, tackled me from behind if we were walking on grass, crawled all over me like a laughing big cat and would tell me, one day I'll be a rugby star.

The evenings were ours, to gather round the radio or play cards or games. We could be ourselves as we knew Henry's pattern to drink with his boss and their mates after work, often go to a party that didn't finish till after we were in bed. Rarely was Mum invited out socially with him.

At our make-believe parties in the sitting room Mum would dance to different songs, teach us steps to the waltz, the jitterbug, tango. Mata would warn, better not let Dad catch you teaching us dance steps from the war. Meaning learned from a certain American. We all sang along to the songs played regularly on the radio. Mata had a great memory for lyrics and she could sing. Like her father. My family encouraged my singing too; I could imitate well once my voice got a bit older. Mum promised puberty would bring the best change. I couldn't wait. Nor could I wait for other kinds of change: even thought of running away from home.

Maybe Henry would get ill and die. Yet the thought made me sad, sometimes overwhelmingly so. Maybe I loved him, even though he never loved me back.

Two, three times a year Henry would come home with a mission: my mother. Punish her for the crime of bringing me into this world and, I later figured, the act that led to it. Something about sex that gets to men. All men, according to Merita. Not that the old lady called it that, she called it the business.

He'd bring it up, in front of us if we happened to be there. Asking did she miss him. Not saying who. We knew. We'd try and melt away at first opportunity but feared getting his attention, especially me, Mrs Sinner's living piece of damning evidence resident in the victim's home.

Our mother had her pattern of reaction too: she would sigh and look away, then back at him and say, how many times do I have to tell you, I never give the past a thought? It's behind us.

Henry would say, oh, yes you do. Just that he's dead. But if he was alive?

If he walked into this house, Henry, I'd tell him to get out. He's dead, like I wish the subject was. How long you going to hold a grudge? And didn't you sleep with anyone when you were away?

He'd say, you were a married woman. How could you do this?

She'd say, why don't we cut the talk and you just hit me?

And Henry would march up to her, teeth gritted, fists bunched. You humiliated me. I'm a respected man and you humiliated me.

I've said sorry over and over. Just do it, Henry. But not in front of the kids. Please?

His finger would prod her chest — hard. You did your slut thing while your own kid was back here being looked after by your parents. Did you think about my daughter?

Kids, go to bed.

Mata would beg her father, please, Dad? Please don't hurt Mum. I love you, Dad.

Go to bed, I said.

We'd hear him yelling. The thump of her being struck, slammed against the wall. We'd hear Mata and Wiki's names yelled at him. But never mine. I wanted to hear my name spoken, to feel I existed too as someone who breathed and talked. But Mum never spoke my name to Henry and nor did he utter it. I got guilty that when he beat Mum it was my fault. I'd cry in private, as a boy crying in front of anyone is shameful. Weeping with guilt that my very existence was a permanent reason for harm done to my mother.

But mostly, once I learned to see it more objectively, Henry was a passive man who truly loved his daughters. He was very popular in the village, people looked up to him. I wondered why he didn't toss me and Mum out, get another wife, rid of me.

I heard him say to Mum, there is not a day in my life I am not reminded of what you did with that Yank piece of shit, and his damn kid living with us.

I wanted to rush out and say, my father is not a piece of shit — *you* are. Where will Mum and I live — in a cave?

I heard Mum tell Mata, because she was older, that Henry tortured himself about what happened. Mata said tell me about it. Us while he's at it. I'm sick of it, Mum. You didn't *murder* anyone. You gave life to my brother.

A brother who liked hearing that. Loved her too.

He did a lot of work for the village, at no charge. He said responsibility was thrust upon him by the elders and he must live up to it. I wondered if they minded him hitting my mother several times a year. Guess they didn't, probably hit their own wives. A lot of men did. Did the villagers know Henry never spoke a word to me? Probably wouldn't care, he was their favourite son.

Henry was in a constant battle with the town council and with the government for taking Waiwera land and, to add salt to the wound, taking most of the entry fee charged to tourists. He called it arrogance of white people.

At the hotel he fought with trouble-maker patrons. They said he'd never lost a fight, but never did he pick them. Which made me proud, even though he didn't like me. Something about an undefeated man that stirs a boy, even if man and boy don't talk.

Mum and Henry didn't talk a lot either. Though Mata said obviously with Wiki being born they must do the other. Only meant something when I found out what the other was. And then I felt like throwing up. Manu's birth when I was nine felt like a generation between us. Soon I was old enough to imagine the act that created him and I was disgusted. How could my mum let Henry? Or did he force himself on her?

But my life was a joy compared with my best pal Chud's. Which was what my mother kept reminding me of: there are others worse off no matter what your situation is.

CHAPTER SIX

FROM MERITA'S VERANDAH I CALL out to the few local humans below: *Shamed warriors who have been captured and enslaved, I own you!*

Slaves! Former warriors who took capture rather than honourable death, so shall you bury our sewage, do the heavy tasks. I despise you!

Merita's told me all the great Maori chiefs had slaves, some destined for the cooking ovens. Our school books tell us Egyptian slaves built the pyramids. The lowest of the low who laboured on every great world monument, like the Taj Mahal — and who remembers their names? Slaves are to be held in contempt. Better to be dead.

Go and build something to honour me, slave dogs! A castle, a huge mansion built atop Totara Hill, so all my subjects can adore me. But you shall be forbidden to cast your lowly eyes upon my person — look down, slaves! Do not ever gaze upon me lest you foul my presence.

Suddenly I mean something in this place dominated by Henry: *This is I, your great warrior chief! Dare look me in the eye and I will hurl you into a boiling pool!*

Merita tells me not to talk like that or someone will give me a biff round the ear. But she has told me my mother is of a high-born family, so that makes me high-born. Merita's spiral tattoo design says she herself is high-born. No ordinary woman is given such honour. The high-born endure pain as a mark of their superior status. This high-born kid endures the pain of living in Henry's house.

One day I'll make you one of my slaves, Henry Takahe. One day my father is going to arrive and then we'll see you tremble in front of a real man. Kneel, slave, my father will say. And you will kneel. Then he will behead you for how you treated his son.

CHAPTER SEVEN

THIS SIDE OF THE BRIDGE a rock face spills down to the water from a dirt road alongside, where early starters mill around, waiting for the decision on what to do first, hit the cold river or warm up in any one of four selections of baths. A complex process, not one you can rush. Boys and girls shuffle bare feet in the dust, swish a foot in a puddle, look down, look up, at the river, over the main thermal area, at the sky, down at the Smith house that lost two sons in the war, at each other, away somewhere on their own; each has his and her own best hope but not theirs to say, not anyone's, it just happens, the moment you join with a group you become owned by its mysterious will. Even the strong personalities don't always decide on where the day starts.

Not that Yank has a preference; he loves all and any of it in no particular order.

It's the river. Boys move down and spread over the rock face like goats ready to leap, shed of all but shorts, girls in tee-shirts as well, even those with but a hint of breasts, shivering even if it's summer warm, arms clutched around bodies, grinning and giving little giggles, eyes only between the steady flowing water and each other.

Then someone jumps, letting out a cry as he goes, a big belly-flop splash to begin the day. The other goats leap through the air after him.

That shock of hitting the cold wet; sweet immersion in a liquid playground. No time to muck around, there are games to play, old tried contests to engage in, swimming races above or below the surface, horseplay, tickling of someone's body parts, a wrestle.

It's called rattling. The money-hungry ones start immediately, diving down and whipping up sand and grit till a jingle is heard and up he or she comes, two joined hand-scoops of material to wash like panning for gold, so the coin edge emerges like a fulfilled promise especially if it's the largest denomination, a half crown: feels like God Himself placed it. Puts the coin find in his mouth, nature's purse, a perfect pouch for holding real cash treasure and down he and she goes, into the murk if rain has muddied it, or it's clear and they see each other and smile or glare, predators hunting down the money prey but friends too.

A half crown is the silver nugget supreme, two shillings and sixpence, two and six, with endless buying power as well as certain human drawing power, kids hoping the luck will rub off or they'll get some of the sweets and food purchases; a sibling a cousin might buy a ticket to the pictures, pay the bus fare. Kicking feet protrude from several kids rattling down there against the rock face where coins have nowhere else to go but sink deeper into the sand and fine pebbles, waiting for lucky kids to find them.

Yank today with another purpose moves quite a way upstream, quite a struggle wading against the flow. Reaches a spot out of the others' sight, turns, breathes deep, slips beneath the waters. Gone.

To his own private galaxy: it could be the heavens he races across — he's found a means to position his body forward in a crouch and run as if sprinting, the current speeds him across the watery sky, he becomes a comic-book hero, his own person none can see or witness, picking up speed; he can see bodies ahead so he can avoid them as he sweeps downriver, swift, a hero with power of flight, mind taken somewhere none can know, for he is alone in this discovery with no intention of sharing it; his mates think he just swims underwater like they all do, but this is different.

He's doing it for his father. For the grinning Yank in the cowboy outfit looking down from that bridge, waiting for his son to pop up. Or he's John Wayne in US marine uniform, as he must have appeared to the boy's mother, in dry-cleaned clothes (an American custom they brought here). Man of perfect features and perfect grooming looking out for his boy.

Up Yank comes, to the surface grinning up at the imaginary figure beaming back at him. Father throws his son a half crown. For you, son. Don't let anyone else get it. And down Yank goes, into the clear water, can see the biggest coin of all looping its way down: propels at it with feet driving off the sand. Gotcha!

Up he comes. Thanks, Pops!

The first coach-loads of tourists are dropped at the spot near the memorial archway where local women guides wait to take them on their thermal wonderland tour. Soon the first group appears on the bridge above, many nationalities, Americans dominating, Australians, English, Canadians, those from different European countries but not former foes — Germany, Italy, Japan.

Throwapennyplease! Throwapennyplease! When really, they want the silver coins thrown, especially a half crown. And Yank just wants to see the face of the father come back to take him home — to America!

The others are fierce competitors now, relation or no, this is treats in their bellies, entrance to the pictures, status and confirmation, affirmation, acquired by charm and begging, beauty, grace and courage: just watch them sail down twenty feet from the bridge into less than their height of water. Lady, I'll jump off for sixpence. Sir, I'll dive off the top rail for a shilling, do a toe-touch dive, mister, for two bob. Ma'am, you should see my swan dive. Two and six for a somersault and pay after you've seen it.

Yank clambers up the rock face on to the bridge. Asks his Yank father in his mind does he want his son to jump or dive? Naturally Pops wants to see a dive. Which is a lot more scary and difficult than jumping. But if he doesn't do it then his father will just disappear.

So he steps up on to the rail, the water so far below he wants to die. For Pops, Yank. Do it for your father.

The American tourists call out encouragement, a local kid asks who is he diving for, meaning he didn't see Yank put a coin in his mouth.

Yank focuses on the place his body will break apart in front of his father's eyes, wishing there was another way to impress. There isn't. Not at Waiwera. It's what kids do. What the son of the American must do.

Takes some time before he can find the courage. Several Yank women suggest he step down: it's too dangerous and we can see you don't want to do it. But he must do it. For his daddy.

Okay, ready now, Dad. Watch this.

Throws himself into the air and all fear departs, legs held together, arms out, feels like falling forever. Fingers slice into the water, he bends his back to break the descent, hears a snatch of cheering above him before the water encloses him and so does pride at showing his father what a bold son he has.

Surfaces to sight of his handsome father laughing proudly, pointing and telling his fellow Americans, that's my son you just saw! Isn't he something! Yank waves that he'll see his father later, there's money to be earned. Joins the others in real time.

Following a threepenny piece as it dances and flits like a butterfly, the larger shilling makes broader arcs, a two shilling coin short and fast falling, the prize half crown its own zigzag loop. Bodies clash and fuse and break loose under the water, it's another world, another dimension. The winner breaks the surface triumphant, holding the prize aloft.

Kids stay in the river as long as bodies will stand then head for the other blessing of warm baths. To the social warmth of touching bodies. Water as if with a slight oil content soft to the touch, slippery on the skin, all around sky and steaming wet.

Talking, jabbering, laughing, spit-squirting, food-smacking mouths, the mouths just on the surface blowing bubbles, mischief brewing in the eyes, smiles breaking white against a deep brown backdrop of complexion and uniform black hair, heads that sink beneath and hold breath for an impossible time and break free sucking air spitting laughter, triumph at a record broken. Hard truth of those who surpass the record and no one cares.

Still, this is their place all: those of weak personality, the strong, bland, boring, the lame the limited the dumb the mentally defective, the numbed of too harsh a home life too early, it cannot be discussed, quite a few suffer it, just know every kid feels for you, just stay close and stay loyal, die for us if asked and we'll give you comfort in return and die for you.

There are the ones born angry even furious, at something or just nothing, they're in too, the social cripples, the retarded of body and mind, the ugly, hideous, plain, the lucky gloriously lovely, the handsome, beautiful, gorgeous of feature and body, you're the better part of it but you owe too, everyone owes. Chud, you're one of us, you too, we don't care your stink parents. Yank, you're in too, don't care your name its origin, what some call your mother, none of that here, you're with us, of us.

Growing up in paradise like an underground garden sprouting a thousand steaming manifestations. And one day a father, come all the way from America here to claim his son.

CHAPTER EIGHT

HENRY AND HIS FATHER SAW into our future and built a four-bedroom house of basic design on family land, on ground not likely to have thermal break-outs. Hardly moved in as a young married couple, Henry about to start work as barman at the local hotel, I got pregnant, then war was declared.

Became a too-large place of lonely residence in the years of Henry's absence, even with frequent visitors and living in a close-knit village. I felt a nagging need for something else, something more than village gossip and petty gripe. But I was born here too, looking in the same mirror giving reflection of life unchanging back. Maybe I should have fallen into line, gone with the flow.

Having the baby made a difference, kept me busy and in that blissful state of motherly joyfulness. I particularly liked having a hot bath with her, surrounded by our relatives, the villagers. The custom was to share the child around, with two sets of grandparents, uncles and aunties, even cousins. Once past the breastfeeding stage little Mata might stay overnight with a relative. The house would feel too big and lonely again then. Wondered if my discomfort was a premonition of the future, that I would never really belong in this house.

When Henry's father died in 1943 my mother-in-law gave me the task of writing to inform her son. Took several months before Henry's reply journeyed back, expressing sadness of course at not being able to say farewell, the usual. But between us, he wrote that his father had been an ordinary man of no great note, other than building Henry's house with his son's energetic help. In the meantime three Waiwera boys' lives had been lost in a recent battle in Italy.

My own father took off with a Pakeha woman in his late forties, not long after Yank was born. I'd wondered why he had no strong words of disapproval for my fling, my secret revealed by the growing pregnancy. Dad's leaving shattered Mum — killed her, some said — and shocked and disgusted us his children; even I had the cheek to feel moral outrage. I guess because we had a mother totally dedicated to her family. My two older sisters moved away, in shame they said and at our mother dying of a broken heart. My two older brothers both had children and lived in a new suburb in town and I didn't see a lot of them. Locals said maybe it was the teasing of Dad's pale skin, or could be his preference for white flesh like his own was why he did what he did.

I started seeing that living in a village had its price. Same time it wrapped you in communal embrace, they were ready with poison tongues and hatred at the smallest transgression.

How my own transgression took place? Perhaps my father's daughter, I had vivid sexual dreams and woke up quite disturbed.

You can't control your dreams. Nor the body, though it refused to let me know its secrets.

Not in our reserved culture to talk about intimate matters. They skirted it by saying so-and-so is hot, warned men jocularly to look out she'll eat him for breakfast. But having a sexual climax? God forbid.

Then one of the tourist guides got sick, I got called in, and my life changed. I met an American marine called Jess.

Daring to follow him to the town near their camp outside of Wellington, I left my baby with my parents. Two weeks of unimaginable bliss, a great big door opened to find another Lena waiting. Gay, carefree, and abandoned in every way. Back home I couldn't care less the wagging tongues, even my mother-in-law's evil looks, silently demanding an explanation. I offered no excuse, simply said I'd been away and got caught up with friends.

I suppose I was in love. Difficult to tell with my head in the clouds, amazed at what I had discovered within myself — with his help. It might be freedom I was in love with, being liberated. Sexually unchained.

I missed a menstrual period. Then another. Please don't let it be. A third month and still no period, and no denying the slight bulge in my tummy. How the tongues went from behind my back to openly asking, what the hell was I doing carrying a baby? A married mother? You better hope your husband is killed because he's sure going to kill you when he comes home.

No choice but to become a bit of a recluse, difficult in a small village with everyone related and knowing one another's business and the communal baths being one of the social gathering places. I only bathed at home or at Falls Bath right next door to our house.

My own mother was in attendance at Yank's birth. I named him Mark, after one of Mum's brothers I was fond of. My baby distracted me too much to pick up on my father's detachment, his late nights. When Dad ran off with his Pakeha lover it hurt Mum more that she was white, as she had a thing about Maoris being considered a lesser, more primitive race than our white New Zealand counterparts. She wasn't the only one.

Mum died of despondency, I am certain, though people knew she was inclined to melancholia.

With brothers and sisters moved away and with little inclination to make friends given my own reduced status, I just focused on my two children till my husband's return.

My poor Yank, having to accept that Henry had no interest in him. Painful watching a little boy try and figure out why the man of the house does not say one word to him, answers none of the questions an innocent kid naturally asks. He believed Henry was his father till about age five.

Though Henry said I had caused him *lifelong humiliation,* at least he had his hotel job and community work to lose himself in. And in over two years of us sleeping in separate bedrooms, I know, just by the sniggers of the village's nastier types, that he had other women.

One day, though, he walked into my bedroom to find me undressed and he had his selfish — but exciting — way with me.

Things changed for the better after that; he was more his old self. Not that his sexual interest was for any but his own pleasure. Confirmed the saying that the beast is tamed when a man has sex, even one-sided.

His late father had left him a few hundred pounds so there was money to furnish the house, including a miracle called a refrigerator. We were among the first in the village to own one, and I felt quite proud. His good salary meant we didn't have to struggle like other families. We fell into a routine that seemed to satisfy each of us, as long as I suppressed my thoughts.

Our kitchen had a coal range, a small Formica-topped dining table and six matching chairs, rough-hewn timber shelves stacked with pots and pans, crockery, a few framed photos on the wall (none featuring me or my son). Windows looked straight into tall manuka trees, the back door opened out on to a small lawn that steamed in one corner over which Henry had built a wooden steam box; this I used daily for cooking.

The bedrooms were simply furnished with two sets of bunk beds in two, double beds in the others, chest of drawers, and in our resumed main bedroom the walls had several photos of Henry's brother killed in the war and Henry in army uniform. He'd taken down our wedding photos. How could I object?

Another Waiwera soldier's photo featured in our sitting room. He was Barney's younger brother, Harold, whose eyes followed you wherever you went in the room. Henry's close mate; they grew up together. Killed in a skirmish: Henry and Barney were witness to his death.

In the sitting room three walls were festooned with more photographs of Henry pre-war and in soldier's uniform, from ordinary private to beaming captain with shined shoulder pips on his broad shoulders. And post-war shots of a different, more serious Henry in civilian clothes. There were his family members, a few of different age-group rugby teams, some framed postcards of Egyptian pyramids, a castle in Italy, and in the centre right above the fireplace a print of parched, hilly Greek landscape with a smiling Greek peasant. A figure young Yank had got to know as a friend in his mind. I would come across my little boy talking to the man, he called him Geekgeek. Photographic studies of Waiwera at different times made its steamy presence known. There was a print of the Pink and White Terraces, that fabulous thermal creation. As Mata got older more framed photographs of her appeared, as did our other children Wiki and Manu gain admittance to the family photographic gallery. There were no images of mother or son.

CHAPTER NINE

RUNNING BARE FEET ON THE dirt road close to the house. Yank can feel the slight tremor, perhaps indicating how unstable the ground in these parts; by the speed of the footsteps he can hear it's either a sprint race or someone's fleeing from something.

Out the bedroom window Chud pulls to a halt on the patch of front lawn, sucking in breath. For twelve years old he's big, muscles already formed where other kids same age are still potentials waiting to happen. In his swim shorts and that's it.

His dark skin shows no less of the blood everywhere, source being his face. Mouth. Nose. One eye swollen shut.

Yank out in a flash. In Chud's one seeing eye Yank sees all he needs to know: words won't do it. Both boys fighting against crying. Chud doesn't know where to look, keeps trying to open the swollen eye.

Your old lady home, Yank?

Yeah. But don't call her that. You should go and talk to her — come on.

They make a sight in the kitchen, Chud sobbing in Lena's arms and Yank standing near the back door, hurting for his pal; she's running a hand over Chud's head, the other clasps him tight to her breasts like a baby. She's not saying much except calling him Boyboy, the name she gave him years ago when he first came to her for comfort after a hiding. Had just started school.

Come on, she says now, let's go and buy ice-creams.

They go the long way to avoid Chud's parents. Lena says you're going to enjoy your ice-cream, Boyboy, not get put off by those drunks. Local kids stare at his injuries, older ones snarl in the direction of the Kohu house whence sounds of a full-scale party come, hardly past noon of a Sunday. A teenage boy spits so Chud can see he's on his side.

A couple of dozen loud American tourists fall silent at seeing Chud with his injuries, a woman asks is he okay. Lena answers yes on his behalf, tells him to lift his head and *smile.*

Chud finds something of a smile. Yank his habitual quick look at the American men. In case.

Lena slips an arm around Chud and he walks at a slight angle leaned into her, taking hope from her kindness.

Going back, when Lena deliberately turns down the short cut track to her house, Chud leaves himself behind like a small boat cut itself adrift. Lena and Yank several steps away. Come on, Lena says. This is part of showing the world you might be hurt but yet you're not. And she comes back and takes Chud under her arm once more. We're walking past them, you hear?

First Lena's mother-in-law's house to pass. She doesn't show herself, could be peeping behind the curtains at the two people she hates most in this world, mother and son.

Now past the party. Could be a pack of apes acting on instinct, jabbering and cackling as they spill out the front of the Kohu house, roars of drunken statement and mindless laughter clashing between competing primates. The women chatter and break forth with leery laughter and each attempts a different dance or suggestive movement and looks nothing other than drunk, no class. All under a warm midday sun.

One starts to fall backwards, grabbed by a male hand, yanked to the man so he can plant a kiss and spray her with beery laughter. She falls anyway, when he lets go her hand, and everyone laughs. On the ground she kicks like a cast animal.

Over a woman comes and tips beer out of a bottle in measured stream to the one on the ground, her open laughing mouth. That gets the apes laughing and jumping.

But not so of their own species they are blind to the three passers-by.

A man calls out, hey? Ain't you her?

It's her all right, says another. The slut.

So now Lena's turn to ignore and give back with a smiling disposition, not just face. She positively waves. Not her son, though, who gives the man hatred with narrowed eyes.

Since Chud won't dare look their way it's Yank who asks, Mum, why are you putting up with that?

She doesn't answer, just checks if Chud is okay. Just keep looking ahead, Chud.

Chud! Hey, you — Chud!

Keep walking, Chud. Not far to go.

Ted Kohu comes swinging down the lawn like a male baboon claiming one of his brood. When I say your name you answer, boy.

Ted's pack gone pretty well silent except for the moaners and broken song singers too drunk to notice or care.

Lena brings her little party to a halt.

You talking to the boy, Ted?

I sure as hell ain't talking to the dog. Or maybe I am.

He's staying with us tonight.

Is he just? Got news for him — you're not! Get your black arse here right now.

Chud says to Lena rather than Yank, I have to go.

Lena says, no, you don't. Removes her arm from Chud and turns full on to Ted who has advanced to the edge of the weed spot supposed to be a front lawn.

There's a lot of men in this village who won't like being shown this boy's injuries. Henry included.

Ted laughs. What, when he couldn't even care less about you? We know how things are in your house, missus. So don't you be threatening me with Henry. Grinning at her.

He doesn't like children being abused. And the cops will be interested.

Ted needs to take that in. Cops? A dismissive gesture at Lena and turns back to the others.

Hate them, Chud says out the side of his mouth to Yank. Who doesn't?

CHAPTER TEN

THEY SING AS IF WITH something that can never be resolved, and yet as if all is at peace at least for the duration of their singing together. Returned servicemen, too many back changed for the worse, yet singing the songs learned before they went, the Western-adapted songs and melodies to Maori lyrics, just as they break out with songs in Italian learned from fighting that people as an enemy. Funny how not one German song was learned.

In the years of being home, the group of twelve has gained a town reputation, with five-part harmony and voices of natural pitch and power, along with the gusto of a warrior race who were also the war victors.

Lena is one of over a hundred people standing outside the Waiwera Hotel public bar, in raptures at the strains of a hymn in Maori heard through opened windows; not a whisper from the audience, inside and out, or something sacrosanct would be broken.

Lena thinking of the man whose voice rings out above the others that he could come home this evening and hurl the meal she has cooked for him to the floor, bring up again the subject of her sleeping with the Yank.

The sun is still high as it nears six o'clock of a hot December Saturday; children play under the shade of old oak trees on the forecourt of the sprawling weatherboard hotel, the tourists are back, there is a little more money in their community, though the government takes the lion's share.

The hotel gleams whiter in the sun from a fresh coat of paint and seems to have extra sheen with the massed song issuing from that public bar, as if from a spell cast by the former fighting men singing their hearts out inside. The oak trees put shade and cool on the kids playing beneath them. Flies and bees a background drone.

Hotel guests are stood outside listening in the same amazement. By appearance alone most are American, in their loud dress and confident manner. Some of the American tourist men are sure to be inside the bar, shocked at the beer-swilling. Though the singers won't be so drunk or it would spoil their performance.

Outsiders from the suburbs have come on bicycles, men of all ages have walked, driven in mainly old cars and battered small work trucks, older children have trekked, couples have made it an evening destination, kids from outside the area are drawn to the excitement, local kids check them out to ensure respect is shown, but only a few kids appreciate the singing. Yank is one of them, even if the main voice is Henry's.

A police car pulls up, a black Humber Super Snipe. Out get a constable and a sergeant pretending sternness, as the sergeant shakes his head that it's past six o'clock legal closing time. After the closing bell clangs the patrons have fifteen minutes to vacate the premises. But this is different: the Waiwera returned servicemen have widespread renown.

People break out in expressions of appreciation, admiration. Someone near Lena says, thank the good Lord they came home to us safely so our town didn't lose such voices. Of course Lena feels the same, even if with other thoughts on the distinctive voice standing out from the rest.

Enrapturing though the song is and yes her husband's voice, Lena keeps one eye out for her children, especially Yank engaged now in a conversation with an American. She doesn't ask about his engaging the Yankee tourists; a mother knows why. Though what questions he asks are a mystery as she has never spoken one word of the man she knows he is on a hopeless mission to find.

The cops then adopt an official posture, put on their helmets and head into the bar, same time the closing bell erupts and soon men are spilling out to sunlight and sober wives and children, responsibility to which they're now oblivious.

Henry the bar manager stands at the top of the concrete ramp firmly ushering them out. The cops have left. Every man wants to shake Henry's hand; most are drunk.

Yank and Chud sidle up beside Lena. Time to go, get the evening meal on the table by seven latest, even if Henry chooses not to come home till late. Those are the rules. A woman more or less resigned to it.

Then she sees Henry and Yank find each other's eyes, it happens every once in a rare while. Like magnets drawn to each other. Of course Henry's gaze is strong; clearly Yank would rather not be looking into Henry's eyes.

But nor can he unlock from the big man's stare.

Yank? His mother prepared to break it. Sees he's trembling ever so slightly. Then he turns and goes round to Chud's far side, further from his mother and even more from Henry.

Time to go home.

CHAPTER ELEVEN

I GOT A FEW PAID hours after school doing odd jobs at the Waiwera Post Office, because the manager Mrs McDowell took a shine to me. The post office was one place kids hung around; for some reason she singled me out, asked did I want a few hours' work a week.

Knowing every villager's business she wanted to call me by the name on my birth certificate, Mark. Said the name Yank isolated me when I felt no such thing. I couldn't tell her of my mild obsession with looking at father-age Yank tourists, accosting each with questions about the war and had he been here in Two Lakes back then. Found six who returned to relive old memories but, as I have no details to identify my father, could only ask if they remembered a woman called Lena.

Mrs Mac, not that attractive, believed she was. She thought my mother one of the most beautiful she'd ever seen and yet shook her head that she did not appear to believe it of herself. Guess she was saying my mother should stand taller. I did know I felt pretty lucky in the looks area, from a mum who told me every day how handsome I was. Maybe like Mrs Mac, though, I wasn't in fact good looking?

She gave me books to read, when our house had few and none but a handful of Waiwera homes had any books at all. When you live in a place like Waiwera reading is not the activity you think of and anyway, as Mrs

Mac said, Maori culture is oral. We did not have the written word until it was introduced by the Europeans.

The post office handled not just mail but banking, post office savings accounts, foreign currency exchanges for the tourists, and the staff took added responsibility for the gossip and private affairs of every Waiwera inhabitant worth talking about.

Like when the letter addressed to Lena Takahe came, bearing a United States of America postmark and Mrs Mac herself phoned my mother on the party line knowing eavesdropping was common practice, told Mum there was a letter she should collect in person, or would she rather her son bring it home this evening?

I was there when Mum turned up, a bit breathless in that way of hers that says why would anyone write to me, or even give me one thought? (Henry had taken something vital out of her, I was certain. I wanted her to walk around being *proud* of herself. Not this unassuming, modest woman who most of our village said was still one of our finer-looking specimens. Disgusting how some of the men, when they were drunk, tried to chat my mother up and got angry when she ignored them, called her a bag, a slut, said they know she turned it up for more than the Yank while Henry was away. Cruel hypocrites: knew she won't run to Henry. On my enslavement list too. My American father and I were going to have quite a few people to confront on Judgement Day.)

For you, Lena. Mrs McDowell handed over the letter. The staff whispering it had been sent from America. America! With all that that meant. My mother occasionally filled in for guides; often tourists not just from America but other countries were so impressed they sent a postcard, or started regular correspondence with the guides or locals they'd met. There could be no other possible explanation, not even to the person of greatest hoping, me.

From my father? Impossible. Never mind the years of fantasising he'd one day turn up in our lives. Absolutely impossible.

I saw Mum look at the letter, glance up, back down, up again — her face transformed.

She was white. Trying to speak but words wouldn't come.

I heard Mrs Mac say, why don't you go and find somewhere on your own and read it without interruption, dear?

I knew not to go after her to see who the letter was from.

Mum told me much later she clutched the letter and just started walking into town, three miles away. On through town and down to the lake to end up in Marsden Gardens, walking aimlessly round and round the big spread of well-kept park. Ended on a park bench sitting there stunned in the manicured surround.

All week she refused to say anything about the letter other than it was just from a tourist who remembered. I knew she was holding back and I thought it might be possible she had heard from him, my dad. But he would have written years earlier, not waited till I was thirteen. Still, he might not know of my existence; why would he? So many thoughts going through my mind.

The following day, Saturday, was our money-earning day in the river to go to the afternoon pictures. Mum said, go to the eleven o'clock picture and I'll meet you at two thirty at the park by the big pool. Don't tell a soul, not your best mate, not your big sister or Wiki. And don't ask me why. It figured this was to do with the letter and yet I saw no sign in her face to say it was epic news like that, of my dreamboat dad suddenly popped into existence.

I don't remember anything of the flick. Came out blinking in the sunlight, told Chud I had to go somewhere and he wanted to know where and why I was keeping it secret and why wasn't I heading back home with him and why had we come to the early flick? Asking for the fiftieth time.

Told you, I don't know.

Chud still looked hurt and hell, if you had to choose between killing your mother or your best friend, it's a very hard pick.

I'll tell you in a couple of hours, Chud, I promise. But tell him what? I had a nervous feeling now.

My mother beside me on a park bench, as nearby steam growls its presence, a four-foot stone wall built around it. This one's a sigher, not very interesting. At our backs the vast poster portrait of Tudor-style building, imposing gable spires, stripes of dark-stained wood against white plaster of its walls, old grey slate roof. The times I was the loner coming here I imagined the building our family castle, my king and queen parents, me the prince. The immaculate bowling greens laid out before the grand old building were emerald carpet offerings to us, the American Royal Family.

One of our smaller palaces the Green Baths building in art deco design. Named for its green pool tiles, a place kids cram at weekends, it's got a high diving board and uses thermal heat for the smaller pools. Nothing compared with the natural wonders of Waiwera. Though Chud and I loved going there when flooding made our river too dangerous. Mixing with white kids, governed by quite strict rules: Chud for some strange reason seemed to enjoy the rules and even the company of white kids who weren't into fighting and acting aggressive.

Never seen my mother so agitated, not even when Henry was talking himself up to giving her a belting. She is shaking like a leaf.

CHAPTER TWELVE

SON, SHE SAYS. Your father is alive.

What father? I'm suddenly confused though a moment ago I was sitting in yonder building on my prince's throne right beside him, Mum the other side. What are you talking about?

Your father, his name is Jess. He is alive, son. He's alive! And she breaks down in tears.

Oh, Mum. I put an arm round her. But my mind is trying to find a place to fit this information. I'm peering at the letter to see if a photo came with it. My father? The man who, who made my mother pregnant — with me? How can this be? And who is going to help carry me through *my* shock?

Dear Lena

Don't know if you remember me. It's Jess Hines. The American GI from all those years ago. I survived the war and if you ever gave me a thought you may have assumed me dead, killed in action, as I did not write as I promised. I have long anguished over whether to write or let you alone and get on with civilian life like so many millions did. But your face, the memories, refused to let me go.

I got one letter from you. You may have written others but a mail boat was sunk by a Japanese sub and Lord you can't imagine the disappointment, it was like an incident of multiple deaths to men who so looked forward to getting letters from loved ones. I don't mean to be presumptuous there.

My mother gives a silly grin at that.

Conditions in Guadalcanal were such that letter writing was out of the question. But please believe I thought about you an awful lot. Even though knowing you are married and likely regretted what we shared. For that I ask your forgiveness, as—

He must have written something intimate. She read this letter the day before. Knows what's coming and where the embarrassing bits are.

What a hellhole we were sent to after the dream world of New Zealand. The battles took place in steaming barely penetrable jungle. Bitten mad by malaria-carrying mosquitoes — death and terrible sickness in itself, blood-sucking leeches, scorpions, snakes, biting flies and an enemy we hardly saw, only the deaths he caused us, or their maggot-ridden corpses and our own gruesome dead. You would not have believed how swift and hideous the decay of life in that Hell. To think, a proud soldier would actually be grateful to be wounded and invalided home. But that's how we all felt. Wanting to be injured enough to be sent home, never to have to go to war again.

Seven months there I was quite badly wounded with multiple gunshots. Took five bullets. Was flown home with scores of other wounded men. Three months recuperating and I was assessed fit to return to combat duty. Europe this time.

Again my mother feels this Jess guy is writing private stuff and she turns away to read it to herself. Then looks at me and says, you have two more half-sisters, Yank.

A thought that repulses me. I don't *want* two more half-sisters.

He was married, got divorced a few years ago, Mum says.

I feel better: divorced at least.

I've thought and thought about writing to you, asking myself what is the point? You'll either not remember me or not wish to, given you are married. I am presuming your husband came home safe to you and your daughter. But then I thought, don't be silly, you'd be lucky if Lena remembered you—

Dad. Dad? (Dad?)

Nope, just won't take. Wish Mum would stop crying now. People going past looking are embarrassing me. All because of a letter from a man who didn't even send a picture of himself so I could confirm or reject my years-long fantasy on the spot.

Did he send a photo, Mum? She shakes her head. Have you got any photos, Mum? I never asked you about it — about him. Ever.

No, you didn't. And I wouldn't have told you anyway. Not when I thought he was dead.

He's alive, Yank. I can't believe it.

Feels like a good movie spoiled, ended too soon, halfway through the story. It's reality now, of him actually stepping up and saying, Hi. I'm Jess. I believe you're my son. But where's a *photo* at the very least? What if he's not a cowboy figure hero, a war hero, a film star, is just an ordinary person? I ask my mother, what was he like? Yet not wanting an answer.

Through her tears she smiles and says, you really want to know?

What a stupid question. Yes, Mum.

Wonderful. Treated me like a princess.

A married princess, I can't help saying. To someone else.

But she just smiles the more. Says, and look what it gave me.

Huh? Oh, she means me. Well, you're a pretty special mother too. But did you really have to go with an American? And now what do we do? Write back, tell him he's got a son here and ask if he feels like visiting?

Settling back to civilian life was tougher than I thought it would be, she read on. *Seems society and officialdom treated servicemen in different ways. Some missed on veterans' loans for business and housing. Serving in two different parts of the world meant 'papers had been mixed up'. Meaning lost. I moved to Jackson, our state's biggest city, to get work, provide for my family. My wife worked nights, we shared looking after the children. We were arguing a lot. We managed though to save close to a deposit on a very modest house. Then the marriage fell apart and naturally I gave her our savings—*

Mum? Why don't you suggest he comes here as a tourist, with a group? That way Henry won't know, we can arrange to meet like we have here.

I'm suddenly getting excited.

No, she shakes her head. It's over, Yank. He's single now. But I am not.

Huh? She may as well be.

Sure, I want you to meet him one day. But the past is the past.

I haven't had that past yet, Mum.

And you'd like to. I know. Her face is glowing like I've never seen. The colour in her eyes has grabbed some light source and has them burning like pale green flames. She's flushed. And look, the hand holding the letter is trembling. I'm shaken too. He's alive. My God, my father actually exists.

Life is pretty good now. Hoping very much yours is too. Been such a long time.

The rest of the letter doesn't say much, just how America is a wonderful country to live in — for some.

Fondest regards
Jess.

Dear Jess, I began, uncertain at what to call him, but not Dad, and Mister Hines would be too formal.

Not sure what to say or how to start. I can say it came as the biggest surprise of my life to hear from you. Mum thought you had been killed in the war and me, I guess not knowing or hearing anything about you, I invented this person in my mind. Boy, did I imagine you in so many different roles! Actually, I was given the name Yank long before I knew the reason.

I'm thirteen, in first year of high school. Mum and teachers want me to go to university. But I'd like to be a musician, a singer, play guitar too. I'm obsessed with music. It must be from you because Mum is not that musically inclined. Henry — her husband and kind of my father — is a wonderful singer —

Not that I'll be telling him of how Henry has treated Mum and me.

Rugby is a big thing here, most boys and men play the game, everyone goes to games and talks about rugby all the time. I'm not such a good player and secretly glad I'm not. I want to be a musician.

My best mate Chud is the best young player anyone's seen in years. But do I want to be like him? No. He's had a tough life. His parents are terrible to him. But anyway you don't want to hear about that I just want you to know he's like a brother. And if we do meet, he'll not be far away. I know you'll like him.

Seeing you've been here, you'll know what an amazing place Waiwera is.

Saying that evoked all sorts of mental images of my mother and him writhing in sexual union. God. The sights of Mum not Waiwera.

I work a few hours a week at the local post office. The manager, we call her Mrs Mac, is very kind and really likes me. Don't know what more to say. When I get over the shock of getting used to you actually existing, I'll write back.

Kind regards
Mark.

My real name feels awkward, but signing it as Yank to a Yank was silly. Can't even write Takahe, as I'm officially known at school. That name belongs to someone else too.

CHAPTER THIRTEEN

YOU'RE TOO HARD ON HER, Henry, my war buddies kept telling me after we came home. All right for them, they don't have a living reminder resident in their homes. Have to hear his name *Yank* echoing in my home patch. Easy for them to say I'm too hard.

Not that my wife was the only one: a few others had flings too, just no children came of it except when an unmarried village girl had a child to a Yank. No one gave that kid a permanent name reminder.

The biggest day of my life spoiled — felt as if my officer's rank was also rendered worthless. I was the senior man. My heavy responsibility to stand in the meeting house and read out the names of my killed relations and mates, with no sign of my wife, the daughter I hadn't seen, my mother averting my questioning eyes. Responsibility claimed me; I had to stay at the party at least till the last of the formal speeches was over. A sick feeling in my gut.

What a shock. This kid in the house I and my late father built for *my* and Lena's children. What am I supposed to do, celebrate? Sign him into my will?

As for her, Lena. How could she? I could have beaten the bitch to death, not just given her a hiding. I felt like throwing her into a hot pool, and her kid. Lord, I never knew such anger and hurt. All the deaths of a brother, close friends in that war didn't compare to this. If I had been asked to imagine the worst possible thing to happen in life, this was beyond that.

I went into my shell for months, could barely function, not even the big plans I had to improve life in our village were enough to pull me out of the gloom. I even contemplated suicide for the first time in my life. Couldn't speak to Lena and if she'd dared open her mouth — even in apology — I would have put a fist in it. The kid by association was on my hate list. And yet I love children.

Time is a kind of healer. Except my wound felt permanently infected: I couldn't get rid of it, kept festering there in my mind my heart. Even thought I might go crazy — my emotions were like one of our boiling pools, never going to cool.

A man has to work though. The Waiwera Hotel as good a place as any. Got on well with the Irish publican; we knew we were good for each other. I could handle the drunk Maoris. I was soon running the show, the public bar first, then the private bar after hours which was as much social for me and the owner, drinking with hotel guests who legally could drink beyond the hour of six o'clock, and our inner circle of mates, including my close army buddies. But back at home things weren't good.

I just couldn't stand the sight of the kid, the damn name the village had given him, public declaration my wife had slept with a Yank. My public shame personified in the kid's very existence, my manhood mocked by his every living moment. Took years to learn to live with it.

We slept in different beds, Lena and I. Naturally a man has sexual needs but damned if I was going there with her. Found my release in a few other women over the two years of my anger. But I'm no womaniser: I prefer a settled home life. I wanted my kids to grow up in a stable home environment. But in our situation?

One night I walked into her bedroom to find her undressed and lust — maybe vengeance — took over. She just took my breath away. It was over pretty quickly, bordered on savage. Yet I realised I still had a spark for her and that she was mother to our daughter, even if Mata was gun-shy from her very first encounter with me.

Ended up sharing the marital bed again. On far sides of the bed to each other but the inevitable did happen. Not saying I was lover boy extraordinaire. Just that sexual activity did take place and so did another child come about. I called her Wikitoria, after my mother.

Mum lived a few doors up the rise and never graced our house on account of her refusing to forgive Lena. Couldn't blame her. Our girls had open invite to go to their grandmother's, and of course the boy didn't. Nor could he have expected it. Not his blood. To hell with him.

In my mind I'd think, you want your grandparents, boy? Then fuck off to America. My spiteful, nasty side. But we all have one. I hardly ever hit the kid unless he'd done a wrong that couldn't be overlooked. Greed a quality I hated and so if Yank ate more than his share he got some hard face slaps from me. As well he should. Us Maoris are brought up to share. Greedy people don't fit in our community. Funny how I never saw him as a complete Waiwera boy even though he knew no other place. But I didn't have too much of a problem with him — as long he kept out of my way. Not much to ask in your own house, is it?

Lena and I were never going to claim back our marriage, not how it used to be. Pride on my part, no denying. I am a proud man, always had a stronger sense of pride than most. From a little kid I couldn't stand anyone trying to take away or deny me my pride. At school if a teacher talked down to me I'd fly off the handle. When bigger, older boys bullied me I attacked, my own safety be damned, with fists and curses even if I lost a lot of the fights. I did win the wars though. Bullies left me alone after a while. And as I grew I picked off every boy who had bullied me and never let up till I beat each one. Everyone knew, never mess with Henry Takahe. I was never one to look for it though.

Pride, I know, is both good and bad. Maybe I was guilty of being unable — or unwilling — to forgive and forget. But the same confident streak gained me captain's rank in that drawn-out war. Pride in being a Maori with intelligence and leadership qualities who resented his European inferiors getting promoted in other battalions, awarded medals, and damned if I was going to be left behind. Took my complaint to our commanding general himself.

I asked him respectfully, why are Maoris not considered good enough for officer material, sir?

Taken quite by surprise the general said he didn't know such inequality existed, hadn't given it a thought. But since I had confronted him with it, he'd recommend me for instant promotion to lieutenant, just as long as my commanding officer agreed.

But I said, sir, that's half the trouble. The man you're asking to recommend me is the man who won't.

In that case, Sergeant Takahe, I shall make the recommendation myself. But God help you if you prove to be all complaint and no delivery.

I delivered. Ask my men. In every battle and skirmish I led from the front. Good enough for my men, good enough for me. Won their respect, same time I realised we couldn't be the same mates as before: there had to be a separation. Out of which I learned heightened responsibility, as if I owed far more than just the unit under my command.

Pride in being Maori meant we Maori soldiers didn't stand for being called niggers by a bunch of Southern Yank GIs in a bar in Italy when we had a couple of days' leave. We hoed into them and gave the racist bastards a hell of a hiding. Maoris are no Negro slaves, we're slaves to no one. Pride is what you show every person and in your own village it sets an example, indeed a standard, for young people to follow. Pride is what pushed me to cleaning up our community, hounding the town council to install full electricity and sewerage services, so we the village in turn could lift our living standards and with it our dignity.

In that war I learned to appreciate liberty, understand the layers of democracy and how it is worth defending to the death. I went from an ignorant young man just wanting adventure and a fight, to understanding that our German enemy must be defeated at all costs or they would rule the world with an iron fist. We saw their acts of retribution, executing every second male in a Greek village to avenge the deaths of a mere few of their own. Admittedly, we came to respect them as a worthy foe that could fight almost like Maoris, with ferocity and cunning and guile. But to want to rule the world is just madness. And when we found out after the war what they did to the Jews, naturally we felt proud at having done our bit to defeat Hitler and his Nazi henchmen. The Japs, they were more the Americans' and Australians' to deal with.

As for an unfaithful wife, a soldier would rather be dead than come home to what I did. That the guy was American seemed to make it more hurtful. They were our allies, same side. I'd never do that to another man's wife, especially not a soldier on the same side. Never.

Of the kid, all right I didn't know much about him. Didn't feel guilty either. Heard him sing, though, and he was pitch perfect. Normally that shared musical ability might have been enough to get on with the boy. But in the circumstances, it wasn't possible and nor was I inclined. He was in his own world; his mother spoiled him but I was indifferent to what they did. He was not my son.

The kid was inseparable from Chud, whose father Ted was a big-time regular at my bar: a real low character I'd banned more than once for fighting, hated by everyone except the company he kept, same ilk, men not from here. I could see plain as day what the parents were making of Chud, felt sorry for him even if he was Yank's best pal. He didn't stand a chance with those hidings his father and mother dished out to him, all the Kohu kids, poor little blighters. They'd grow up and do the same.

But I couldn't go and bash Ted stupid or next I'd be minding everyone's business. Fix the village problems first, I thought, then I'd start cleaning out the handful of undesirables, as well those shameless women who'd get drunk opposite the pub, Shirl Kohu one of them.

The war taught me a higher sense of duty. I wanted to look after my family and serve my community. Perhaps one day at a political level. Not saying I'm perfect — I have flaws like every person. But in my essence I'm a good man. I trust myself. And the boy was not my blood.

CHAPTER FOURTEEN

POOR NAIVE VILLAGE MAORI BOYS. High school robbed us of our innocence. We cut it physically, sure, but physical didn't count for much in
the eyes of our white peers. Or not in the B class I was streamed to. Even
though I was no rugby player, I came from the robust outdoor world of
the river, our baths, the mountain; everything of life a physical adventure
and experience, a world I'd expected to continue on much the same — till
high school.

The streaming system tore friends apart from starting day. Not one
Waiwera boy got into the A class, only me and one other in B. Most of
the rest were in the dunce H category, including Chud. Low levels ceased
talking to higher levels. It was like we suddenly spoke different languages.
High school shook us rudely awake to find ourselves lost, confronted
by sons of fathers with jobs we'd never heard of. Surveyor. Accountant.
Doctor. Lawyer. Banker. Chemist. Landlord. Pilot. Scientist. Sheep,
cattle and dairy farmers. Businessmen of description endless. Engineers in
different fields. Sellers of every imaginable service and product.

It hurt to see the different *thinking* that rubs off on the sons, what
they talk about, how much they know, how they apply themselves to
study while we, the Waiwera boys, feel like dunderheads straight out of
the backblocks who can't apply ourselves to anything of the mind. Alien

beings of limited ability from planet Waiwera in outer space just a thirty-minute bus ride from high school.

Just a few of us woke up, Chud not one of them. He and the others latched on to a term picked up to blame: the *system*. Being white man superiority, anti-Maori. I'm not sure it was any of that. Three Waiwera boys were expelled for fighting. Throughout the year Maoris dominated in detentions and canings, academically but a few of us and then not at the top level. We'd just arrived like at a rugby match to find better-prepared opponents, fitter and smarter, and in a different game. I might be Waiwera through and through, but I wasn't blind and deaf.

I looked at these people and reminded myself I was a chunk of white on Mum's side and white with maybe a bit of Spanish, given the coppery complexion, on my father's side. If I was going to play this game then I better know the rules. There must be some advantages us Waiwera boys had through our unique growing up.

The very time I needed a father who could help steer me through this. I looked at my Waiwera mates and peers reeling, saw how more and more resorted to fists to even things out. I knew if Henry was on talking terms with me he'd advise me to take the Pakeha boys on with my fists. But he wasn't and I was not a person like that.

If I just focused on my music, got to know my father through letters, I might be all right.

CHAPTER FIFTEEN

SITTING IN THE MUSIC ROOM. Our music teacher informs we're about to hear one of our classmates, Nigel Blake, play electric guitar. We assume he's rich because his parents have bought the guitar, just as I assume being Maori our race is musical and rarely does a white person have the talent.

In an amphitheatre school classroom Nigel has a full set-up for us to peer down on his performance, like cruel judges who have already made up their minds. Nigel Blake is a scruff who pushes the hair length and style rules to the limit, can somehow make his school uniform look like a fashion statement, but doesn't say much and he's hardly noticed.

Well, I don't know how long he played for, only that my own ambition to be a lead guitarist in a band was over. I could never be so good. Never. So was my attitude about Maori musical superiority changed. Music is just music.

I suggested to Nigel he and I join forces to form a band, fearing he might have a better voice than me too. We were inseparable after that performance. At school and neutral places, though, not our homes. Even if I was the more self-confident and probably more dominant personality, his race ruled and my race were the darkies of the country, a minority too. Their right to issue invite, our privilege to receive.

His father was average, musically, Nigel's talent from his mother's side, she of a family of gifted musicians, though Nigel said she was more a frustrated performer and confided he often heard his mother and father arguing over what they had done with their lives.

Nigel's influence on me was big. As I couldn't afford to buy equipment, we messed around after school in the music room sharing Nigel's guitar, and I sometimes got to borrow an acoustic guitar from Toby Taita, who lived up the road from us and could play anything. We used the school microphones and so I got to learn when to be close, to move away, which sounds reverberated, which notes were vulnerable to being easily lost. We'd go for hours till the caretaker told us time to go home.

We went for long aimless walks, maybe into town, or wherever, talking music artists, different styles, our own ambitions. Often after being with Nigel several hours I walked the three miles home as there was no bus scheduled. Would sing the whole way. First year of high school soon became the second.

I ran into jealousy from Chud; he accused me of switching sides and forgetting who his real mate was. Not mates — mate. And why didn't I invite him to the music sessions? Because knowing someone most of your life you know if he's musical or not. And Chud wasn't. Just as I couldn't play rugby. We were in different streams at any rate, so we mainly saw each other on the bus to and from school; post-Nigel only to school.

Out of the blue I got a late reply letter from my father, but with an astonishing surprise: money.

Fifty pounds in the form of a money order, a fortune.

Who better than Mrs Mac to arrange a savings account with the post office? She warned of the dangers of temptation and that I must resist at all costs or the money would be squandered.

Naturally I wrote back to Jess and sent it with hugest thanks and hoped it hadn't made him short. Discovered a selfish, greedy side too when thought of telling my mother was too much in case there came expectation to share it. Told myself, if my father had meant it to be shared he would have asked.

This was my fast ticket to becoming a musician. I withdrew ten pounds and put down a deposit on an electric rhythm guitar. Could have paid in full and still had money left, but seemed this was rare chance indeed to get ahead, young though I was at understanding life.

I would make monthly payments of two pounds for eighteen months, then both instrument and amplification equipment were mine. Now Nigel and I needed a drummer and a bass guitar player. We were on our way, me thanks to the man magnificent in America. Especially when he wrote less than six months later sending *another* fifty pounds.

To have such money enough to send me I figured he must work in the oil industry, or have a good business. I'd write and ask. Though for some reason distractions kept putting my reply off. And I got this sense of awkwardness, as if our relationship was being forced, by his money and the expectation I be thankful. Wrote him a half-hearted response and it took several months to get around to.

Had my reply to Jess been the following year, just a few months closer to enlightenment via countless hours spent analysing with Nigel Blake, I would have written to him about music.

Of the social revolution born of modern music. Of not knowing who started it, just taking my place in the line for my turn to be swept along by a universal force. From Nigel I was filled with this sense that *we owed people*. We, the whole listening, changing world, owed musical artists for helping shift evolution itself.

Little Richard, Nigel said we owed him big-time. He set his own standard that other artists followed. A crazily outfitted and behaved Negro who, Nigel somehow had discerned, dressed and acted like an effeminate clown so white Americans couldn't put a label on him and therefore would let him be. Way ahead of me, Nigel was one of those types with bits of seemingly inside knowledge on all manner of subjects.

Chuck Berry and Jerry Lee Lewis and a few others must have got the ball rolling too. You just picked up on whoever was the dominant figure of your time. So we thanked Elvis Presley; he influenced the world. Every big city and small town in his home country, every country on the planet even Africa, he had an effect. He could have been Jesus Christ he was so important. But with quite a different message.

Seemed impossible that an American singer could change a society so distant and so irrelevant and totally unconnected to his. But that was what

Elvis Presley did: changed tiny, obscure Waiwera; changed Two Lakes; changed our entire tiny nation of two point something million, stuck way down in the lower Pacific — three, four years after the rest of the world had been transformed. Changed Yank Takahe: make that Yank Hines.

Elvis liberated our dancing limbs; pulled away the masks so we could openly express what had previously been vague, sometimes troubling, emotions and thoughts. He said it was okay to show off, good to strut your stuff.

He gave girls permission to be overtly sexual, in dance and in the tone of his sultry voice that said he was coming after them. His photographic images transformed bedroom walls and festooned shop windows and picture theatre billboards.

He informed, enlightened us we'd been hoodwinked about life and social conventions and it didn't have to be this way. Not any longer. We could be whatever we chose to be. His musical phrasing sent us into raptures, me in particular. I could mimic his every note and tone, his unique phrasing. We wore his cowlicks, his confident half-smile; made our eyes project a melting quality just like his to the girls; stood around with legs astride a symbolic world, ready to turn our crooked smiles into sneers of contempt for the older generation, at any peer who would dare mess with us. The man made us cry — and not ashamed in secret, but openly.

He came like a letter from America, addressed *Dear Young World . . . I, Elvis Presley, give you permission to be whatever you want.*

He could have written: *Dear Yank, I, Elvis Presley, give you permission to rise far above Henry's ignoring of you and become a big star like me. Just go out and do it, son. Get yourself all shook up, turn yourself loose. Then watch big Henry reduce to a tiny little man of no consequence. Drive past him in your big limo, park it right outside his hotel, picture his face when he sees who's riding in back.*

The cult of Elvis was on every radio wave, he played himself in movies that seemed to come out monthly, we packed every seat and sat gob-smacked in every aisle unable to get enough of the King, unable to believe such a person existed and yet he was ours, we could purchase him for the price of a theatre ticket, price of his long-player or single records, if we owned a record player, play him for a few pennies on the milk bar juke-box, hear him free on the radio waves.

Single-handedly, Elvis Presley rocked society yet brought something breathtakingly exciting, of true meaning. It felt unbelievable.

Nightly we sat with ears glued to radio speakers waiting to hear his voice, to become what we had no idea we'd been craving deep inside. Yes, even kids. Every growing one of us cheered and proclaimed Elvis's latest number-one hit song on the Hit Parade and had the lyrics off by heart days after hearing it, with numbered hand-written charts on every bedroom and living room wall confirming Elvis's supremacy.

In one fell swoop Elvis unlocked every cell on the listening planet Earth and set the hearing world free.

The magazines told his fans he came from the South, a town called Tupelo in Mississippi. My father came from that same state, could well have similar qualities. Imagine: Jess and Mark Hines, unique father and son combo performing to adoring audiences throughout America. Imagine.

CHAPTER SIXTEEN

A BIG SENIOR MEN'S RUGBY match is on, against our traditional arch rivals, Tanepatu. It's tribal warfare: fights break out in the grandstand, on the sidelines between spectators. Rival supporters break out in the haka throughout the game, itself a mighty spectacle of raw Maori power and skill in ferocious competition. They're actually the same main tribe but it's more like civil war for ninety minutes.

Chud will be at the game. He wants to be a senior men's team member more than anything except get out of his horrible home. Waiwera is not the same with the heart of its population absent; the tourists more or less have it to themselves, just the elderly and our cheerful chatty women guides along with a few penny-diver kids, too young to care how important rugby is to our culture. Rugby is a game even girls and women are mad on. Our men elders become young again, boys' eyes are on fire, retired players want to play again. If I was a good player I'd share the village passion for the game too.

Instead I think about this latest letter from America. Wonder who to share it with — Merita? Decide she's too old for drama and maybe me showing emotion. For Jess has sent yet another money order, this time a hundred pounds. He's set me free. I can buy a car — a car! Pay off my music equipment. Buy my mother something special, or give her the cash.

Who to share this excitement with in a locals-deserted village?

Find my sister at Falls Bath, by herself. Mud-grey water drops from a concrete pipe six feet above, feeding from a larger into the smaller, concrete-encased pool, through a twenty-foot length of eighteen-inch-wide pipe. The overflow goes down a channel that runs, eventually, to the river.

Mata's flushed cheeks say she's been here a while. A rock face overhangs half the pool in a semi-circle, ferns and stunted scrub sprout where they can take root. The noise of the water falling is constant and the enclosure makes it resonate: you have to half shout to be heard; the waterfall can't be turned off. We swim in the higher natural pool too, though some don't like the squelchy mud and sometimes you hit a hot vent spurting beneath. Two piwakawaka — fantails — chase each other and claim my sister's attention for a smiling moment. Older Maoris believe fantails carry all sorts of meanings depending on when and where you see them. Kids just think they're birds.

It's cold and I'm keen to get in the bath to warm up. Tell her, I heard from him again. She's happy for me, knows what how much I love hearing from him.

Why doesn't he send a photo so we know what he looks like?

I already know what he looks like. Proceed to give my description of a tall, lean man, very handsome, thick dark hair like his son's, musical and probably rich. Looks like Elvis.

What if he's not rich and doesn't look like Elvis?

That's not possible.

She tells me she's getting out, so I turn my back. She's nearly a woman now. My sister Wiki is ten, brother Manu seven. The age difference means we're not as close as Mata and I are. Says she has something to tell me.

I'm pregnant.

Oh? Well, you are nineteen. Thinking, Henry won't like this.

He's from my work. (My sister works at the telephone exchange in town, on the switchboard.) From the Far North.

Maori or Pakeha?

Yank, who cares? God, sometimes you are obsessed with who is white and who is brown. Does it matter?

Sorry.

He's Maori. Doctor said I'm nine weeks.

Does Mum know?

Yes, but not telling Dad. I'm leaving home, going to Auckland, start a new life. My sister looks happy. And if your American father ever turns up, you make sure I meet him or else.

I will, I promise her, and with a real sense of anything being possible now.

Will you call him Dad?

No way.

Why not, if he is your Dad? Would you ever call my father Dad?

For some reason her questions feel as if they've caught me. No, I say. Though I might: I've had my moments of wishing.

Moving costs money. Does your boyfriend have a car?

If you can call it that. Might not make it to Auckland.

Arguing with myself, this is your sister and you in the position to give her money, help her get away from Henry. How much? Fifty? A hundred? There goes my own car. But she's my sister, who comforted me when Henry's silence made me miserable. When Henry hit Mum who was it got us out of the house?

You can have a hundred quid to help. Now she has me smothered in sister's kisses. Don't thank me, thank my father.

Thank you, Elvis. She laughs. Or is it John Wayne?

Try both, I say.

CHAPTER SEVENTEEN

WALKING UP NEWLY SEALED ROAD, thanks to Henry. Doesn't feel the same as dirt and stones, slippery mud in the wet, a layer of dust in the long dry. Our town council must be sick of him with his never-ending demands to improve the services at Waiwera.

This is the third trip of surreptitiously carrying Mata's belongings to her boyfriend waiting in his car. Henry won't be happy even if she is legally allowed. He's the kind you have to ask permission to do anything he considers important. Her being pregnant Mata knows would only bring comparison to our mother having me. Me, I still think there's something sad about someone's pregnant kid leaving without saying goodbye. Even if it is Henry.

Houses like fluorescent paint daubs and light blotches appearing in and out of steam drifts, a good sky of stars above and a one-third moon portion. This is the last trip. I shake Lew's hand in the semi-gloom, he's fine looking, very polite, good enough for my sister. I hug and kiss Mata goodbye, she promises to write and thanks so much for the money they couldn't have done without it.

Watch the red tail-lights go past the carved tekoteko figures you can see their rounded head silhouettes in the car headlights, bump over the bridge planks, under the memorial arch, and that's my big sister gone. She was the best sister.

House lights change to smudges. The lit candles old people still use are pencil glows, every light source turned fuzzy, or gobbled up for some moments by the steam. Smell the candle wax on the breeze, drifts of tobacco aroma, see the splutter of kerosene lamp up at Merita's. She raved about Henry forcing the council to install electric lighting, yet often prefers to read her newspaper under the kerosene light, which from a distance throws a different hue, captures human forms and seems to slow them.

Cabbage and mutton smell emit from a steam box. Toby Taita is out on his steps singing like a mournful Negro. I'm captivated by his singing style; it's quite unlike most others round here, I've heard it on the radio. I stand listening till the song finishes. Toby lends me his acoustic guitar — or used to till my father made me rich.

Our landscape strange, eerie, with its human and creature-like noises: someone throttled, a life being slowly squeezed by a terrible force, conspirators whispering, desperate sips of breath like drowning, a geyser roaring — wasted sight spectacular stolen by the dark.

Shuffling figures, giggles, kids and youths, snatches of conversation from somewhere and nowhere, ghostly shapes flitting in and out of existence, someone lifting a steam box lid to take out cooked food, a stooped figure near the big boiling cauldron silhouetted and swishing, I know by the posture, a mutton-cloth bag of vegetables; figures coming and going from the baths keep getting claimed and revealed by the steam. Laughter, always laughter that only the sky can claim.

People in old weather-beaten armchairs and battered sofas on porches, spilled down wooden steps, they chat and smoke and hum, whistle, or just contemplate. A foot taps in time on hard surface to the accompaniment of strummed guitar, Django Reinhardt style, I know it from one of the singers in Henry's group who plays brilliant guitar self-taught, and who gave me a few impromptu lessons. Archie's advice: The key is to let go to the music, kid. The other to stretch your fingers so to find chords and combinations others don't, that's why Reinhardt is so good, because he pushes the limits of finger extension. With his deformed hand too.

Every one of us knows each step of the way, where the ground is prone to collapsing, little lurking fissures recently opened up, hot spots giving warning of worse to come soon, collapsing areas.

Up on the raised level of poured concrete surface and concrete bath tubs, heads and bodies in and out, laughter and talk aplenty; we recognise each other by shape and the dimmest overhead light the town council begrudgingly gave us, three lamps over a two-hundred-yard section.

To the changing shed, built on a working bee weekend by the senior men's rugby team at Merita's urging — she found the money from somewhere. Told the people, among ourselves we can't be dressing and undressing outside in the open like primitives, and can't bathe when it's raining anyway because our clothes get soaked. No windows, just an open slot at eye level to look out of, a place acquiring the odours of our bodily leavings.

A different modesty is required when everyone bathes nude, females covered by a towel right till the moment of immersion, males cupping a hand over genitals. In the warm waters a baby gently sloshed and Sunlight soap the size of its torso rubbed over its skin. Lovely; if we're lucky we'll get a hold and coo into its little innocent face staring up at the chosen kid with a canvas of stars on his head.

Old tattooed crones whose crinkly forms you brush against, who speak in Maori or English, tell stories of enemies thrown off Totara Hill bluffs, the usual of the lost status of captured warriors made slaves. Of the pride we had as a race isolated from the rest of the world till the first European explorers came. Of our beloved original village twenty-five miles away but gone forever when the mountain blew up when Merita was a six year old.

Together, life in its different stages and ages, we stick with each other all the way to the grave.

A gathering of naked bodies in the dark with light from the universe, the nearer moon, maybe someone's lit a couple of candles and put them on the sill of glassless window in the changing shed, and ember pinpricks of cigarettes smouldering in the water-sloshing dark are still a form of light. And all light is love.

Mata and her boyfriend, their child inside her, will be driving through this night. I guess it is day in Mississippi if we're night here. Take our turns at being under the unspeakable vastness of black canopy peppered with stars, smeared with galaxies, being continually investigated by curious bright men trying to understand the impossible distances and epic scale. While we just see without having to understand.

The river gurgles below us, invisible unless it's caught a big full moon, rocks above the surface like sharp pointed heads of people treading water against the strong current.

On weekends, when we use the baths all day, it's any and every kid's job to control the channel flow. We move between the hot and cold, usually getting a little richer with each change: in the river till we can't stand the cold any longer; back immersed in our lucky warm waters while a cold rain hammers down, we sink to just heads showing, sweat chilling quickly on faces, smiles and cheeky grins plastered everywhere.

The overflow cut-out takes away our body grime, runs down to the river. There's the big natural bath too, cooled by a cold-water tap feed, the pipe runs over ground, corroding like everything here. The houses sit perched like on tiptoes to avoid the scalding heat. Or just succumb to the thermal corrosion in pictures of sag, rust, crumble and constructional droop. But as if with guarding eyes down on their children.

And now I have a secret. A reason for my name. Mrs Mac was right, *Yank* did isolate me. Without my knowing it had pointed me, my life, in a different direction. The money windfall has me feeling I'm holding back a guilty secret. For it's a ticket out of here, should I wish. Yet this is my home: I want to show my father the parts of Waiwera he did not see. Introduce him to the cast of Waiwera characters like out of a movie.

Chud once said to me, you're so lucky. Living in Henry's house and him never talking to you.

I said, that's lucky?

Sure. He's the big man round the village. If you were his son you'd be like some of the kids we know whose old man is real good at sport or something else. They can't live up to their father. Henry doesn't care if you fall into a hot pool and die. You don't exist far as he's concerned.

So your old lady, what does she do? Loves you ten times more to make up. And what does that do? Makes you strong, lucky boy, on your mummy's love. Where you get your confidence from. An old lady who tells you over and over, *you're my special boy*.

Chud in a good imitation of my mother's voice, and the exact wording of a refrain so familiar to me it must have stopped registering. Or felt as if it did.

But Chud was right. I just felt so loved. Which did make me lucky.

A whole lot more now my father is on the scene, if yet to appear. What of Chud then? Well, his home situation couldn't be worse. But I'll help make up for it. He's my best friend, whatever he thinks. When we go to America together we'll get good jobs and become rich.

Just watch us, I tell the stars as all around my people laugh and talk, sing too. And the thermal heat never ceases its boiling.

CHAPTER EIGHTEEN

HENRY DID FIND OUT ABOUT Jess's first shock letter to me. No surprise in our tiny community — but surprisingly he did not lay into me, just made sarcastic comment that maybe my true feelings had been rekindled, maybe I'd disappear and go to America.

I think he was just being defensive. Even a little jealous, which kind of pleased and kind of did not. On the one hand it said he still had some feelings for me. But jealousy is never about love, it's about self.

I wrote back and informed Jess he had a son. Not as imposing obligation on him, he wasn't to know, just one of those things that happen. That I had no regrets once Yank was born as a mother is a mother no matter what. Besides, I wrote, you gave me the finest son and if you ever do meet him you'll agree.

If I believed in God I would be able to say, it is all part of His mysterious plan. But since I don't believe, it feels like my life was fated. How many other local women who had love affairs with Yank soldiers ended up having a child? For I am in no doubt whatsoever having Yank tainted me forever in the village's eyes, not just Henry's. I think it inhibited me from ever showing spontaneous gaiety, from going to a dance, dancing at a party. Even my normal desire to laugh felt curbed. I just went into my shell.

In replying to Jess I worried I was tempting fate. Yet his sudden coming to life again did not set my heart racing, rekindle any flames of love or even physical passion. When it should, given he freed in me not just the climax, but the notion such a thing was possible for a woman. Oh, how some aspects of growing up here make us ignorant and blind to life and its possibilities.

Yank also wrote and Jess wrote back to each of us expressing of course his own happy disbelief. Yank and I wrote again, but it was over a year before Yank got a reply. I'm sure he sent Yank money, though I wasn't going to ask my son. He always had a thing about money, a craving.

Or so I thought, till I realised he craved a life better beyond this village, much as he loved it and loved his friends. Like quite a few of the kids, my son wanted out of here. He'd stopped begging me to take him away from living with Henry, but it was still there, just suppressed.

Before every Christmas Yank spent endless hours in the river earning money so he could buy Christmas presents for me, his two sisters and Manu.

Always a most excruciating time. Yank and Henry's present-giving and-receiving ceremonies were done separately: never a present for each other, stepfather and my son. Eating our main Christmas meal was just as awkward, as we could hardly have two sittings. I couldn't see how Henry could keep it up, but he did.

Two photographs of Jess I'd kept hidden all the years; only ever looked at on the odd occasion, just to remind myself. Or sometimes if something in Yank's behaviour suggested his father's genes had come out.

Funny how a man assumed dead had changed three lives, and probably my other children's too. Even after Henry and I settled down into a routine of marriage, of a sort, his refusal to acknowledge Yank's existence kept a certain edge in our house. Henry got on with life, his job and duties towards the Waiwera community; resumed relations with me, but it would have been so much better if only he would have had something to do with Yank.

Like any woman I wanted more than just a functioning marriage. In a few years I'd be forty, with my kids all left home — what kind of life would I have to look back on? Other than raising four kids, what had been the point of my life since I only worked as a fill-in guide, and in the busy season as a receptionist checking hotel guests in and out?

Telling Henry that Mata had left home was almost as bad as revealing Yank's existence. For Henry believed he adored his first-born, when really you have to be there in the child's first years to bond with each other. Mata detested his violence, any violence. When Henry had had too much to drink and was in a mood he'd hit me but not as bad as some of the men in our village thrashing their wives and not as bad as our sensitive Mata perceived. I think her impression got cemented from her first encounter with Henry beating me up the day he got back from the war. Our daughter Wiki and son Manu he spoiled rotten. Doted on his mother too, though she stayed away from the house and never spoke one word to either me or Yank.

Funnily enough Henry didn't explode as expected about Mata leaving without saying goodbye — asking permission more like. He went for a long walk and when he came back presented a sombre figure, later asking about the boyfriend, was he a good young man, what kind of family did he come from. Said, I hope he makes a better father than I've been.

Could have knocked me over with a feather. In fact I said, you've tried to be a good dad with her. Not your fault the war took away your bonding years.

Villagers know each other's most intimate affairs, but damned if I was satisfying anyone's curiosity on the letters from America. And not as if I was the only woman from here to fall for a Yank.

But everyone needs to share things and there was one I trusted: Barney.

A man of routine who took his baths duty seriously, last thing at night blocking off the water feed from the boiling lake to the channels so the baths could cool to the right temperature. His favourite place was the wooden seat by the bridge; kids had to vacate if he turned up and he grumbled at the wet of someone's swim shorts on his seat. Sat there like a real-life warrior figure guarding our entrance. We had carved warrior figures in fence-post form, tekoteko, flanking the road down to the meeting house as symbols of guarding.

Hello, Barney. 'Ello, Lena. He'd give groaning greeting and squirm as if uncomfortable at my close presence, shift position, reach for notebook and pencil. We'd learned to talk without his needing to write it down. I'd come to understand his broken sentences, found the code therein.

After posting my reply to Jess's latest letter I sat with Barney. Below us the sounds of kids in the river, straight after school. Told of Jess's letter: how after several years of correspondence he feared he was falling in love with me again.

Barney pointed at himself to mean he and I might have been an item if he'd been quicker off the mark than Henry. As for the American — forget him. A hint of jealousy in Barney's wicked grin. But a different jealousy to Henry's.

Then he frowned and got out something about Henry being quick off the mark in other ways. But looked away when I pressed him on it. Second cousins on their mothers' side, Henry a year younger but close to Barney's brother Harold (the one killed in the war). A rugby star, representing the province at senior level aged only eighteen, Barney found his own war injury cut short a most promising sporting career.

Henry had always been the more dominant personality, the boy the male elders marked out for a leadership role one day. The same elders who had assured me Henry would grow out of his fighting ways and then I'd see the calibre of the man I'd chosen as my husband.

If only, eh, Barney? I laughed. We might have made a good couple. I shouldn't have said that, for his face got serious and he bunched a big fist and got out, 'En-ry. No good. War damage more dan me.

Not as coherent as that, required me to stitch Barney's words together to make one garment. I found myself sticking up for Henry. He's matured, I said.

Barney's vigorous shaking head, he didn't agree. And there seemed to be something he'd like to say on the matter.

I described what Jess looked like, tall and handsome like you, about the same complexion. I stood and did jitterbug dance steps he taught me. We were laughing. Barney was saying by pointing at the faraway, how this went on while he and Henry were at the war. I thought in chastisement at first, till he burst out laughing and indicated he and the other servicemen of those times also had their share of fun with the opposite sex. Henry too? Of course Henry. Surely you knew? We all did it. It was war.

I was quite shocked. It didn't seem fair. Why was my sexual dalliance of greater sin? Another standard for women of course.

We sat down again and he wagged a finger at me to mean, don't feel guilty, don't let anyone make you feel guilty, let alone Henry. Barney's face getting quite serious then. You are a good person, he said. You are too, honey.

What about the American, Barney wanted to know. He spoke it mer-can. You love? No, I don't love. Not even this much? He held up two slightly parted fingers. Not even that much.

'Enry den? Now that was a question.

You know, Barney, I'm not sure I love any man. Teased: except you, my very good friend. Platonic. He got his troubled look once more but found cheer enough to say he was glad the mer-can didn't have my heart again.

Walking home I could feel something odd — but what? Then I realised my knee hurt — from Barney's hard squeeze saying bye, when I had to get the evening meal ready. Barney made gesture he felt Henry didn't deserve either my cooking, or me.

But there was sexual feeling in his touch.

And I was disturbed because I had a sexual response. With a war-injured man, handicapped? Or a man I knew who'd lost only his speaking ability to that war, who I understood well, as he did me?

It felt like hope and reassurance had touched me. And desire had squeezed through Barney's hand to my knee. Not since Jess had my heart gone so pitter patter. My mind saying, don't be ridiculous, Lena.

CHAPTER NINETEEN

SHE SAID, I'M GETTING OLD, eh Yank? She had me sat out on the porch with back to the view. Old was right — we were eating a plate each of steamed pudding with whipped cream. She kept missing her mouth with the spoon. It was embarrassing.

I took the plates inside and rinsed them in the sink. The tap was corroded, everywhere stank of urine. And her house was being eaten away.

Back out on the porch we saw two groups of tourists follow the red-uniformed guides over our sights; their numbers increased every year. Kids' heads and shoulders poked out of the bath tubs line-up — I could hear their laughter. But that world no longer drew me. I was seventeen, feeling grown up.

Like everyone Merita knew about the letters Jess wrote. I told her I had quite a lot of money in the bank thanks to my father. She said, good for you. Spend it on something that will help your future.

So I told of my paying off an electric guitar and amplifier and speakers, intentions of forming a band.

Music, she said. What Maoris do best. From when I was a girl this village has sent culture groups to America, England, to entertain. When the Yankee soldiers visited here, we wowed them with our Maori songs, our hakas and poi-dancing, showed we could perform modern music originally come out of America just as good as them. Except the Negroes.

Now that lot can sing, and oh could they dance too. Right down there, where the kids play marbles, the Negroes would teach locals their different dance steps. We picked it up quickly but could never do it like them. Poor things, what they had to endure in their home country. Even when they were here some of their own whites treated them badly. But still, they were a cheerful lot and the Maoris took a particular liking to them.

That war, Yank. No one knew anything about why it started. What did we have to do with Germany and its invasion of Poland sparking off Britain declaring war and us following right after? Commonwealth ties to be sure. But a war the other side of the world, when our men had already fought in the First World War? Started by the same Germans too. Not our politics, shouldn't be our fight.

Even to those few of us who read the newspapers and magazines, it was too complex to understand. I didn't think we the public were being told the whole truth at any rate. They say truth is the first victim of war. Same as a marriage breaking apart: truth heads out the door first. All we knew was, our boys got the blood lust and signed up in their droves; couldn't wait to get out of here, experience overseas and fight the enemy.

One minute we're living in peace, just a tiny tourist attraction and a basic people. Next our able-bodied men are gone, the country is on rations, months turn into years and still the fighting goes on.

Your mother was such a renowned beauty, elders from other Maori villages had sent their finest boys to try and woo her. But nothing gets in Henry Takahe's way, as I'm sure you know. In my parents' day it would have been an arranged marriage, as mine was. Lucky I learned to love my husband. Henry gets your mother pregnant with Mata then goes off to the war. I think Henry was making sure no one else could have her.

Though Henry came back a captain and seemed to have grown up, each and every one of those boys had broken off their boyhoods and leapt into manhood before they should. A person has to live through the growing-up stages, or else what was missed out comes back like a sore. Your friend Chud will be the same, mark my words. His damn parents took away their kids' childhoods. You can't do that to children.

Sometimes I wished Merita would remember she had seen my father, pluck a picture of him from her old memory. But she went on about a different past.

Our men served in the First World War, like my husband, even though we had three children at the time. He signed up in his dead brother's name, anything to fight. I would never have dared stop him. Sometimes men have to be warriors, to preserve what is precious. Such a terrible death toll too, thousands of our New Zealand boys, several dozen from Waiwera, slaughtered in those trenches in France, Turkey. The poor French, they lost millions.

But fighting for your country and coming home to the same second-class treatment at the hands of the Pakeha? No good. Most went into retreat, shut down to the outside world of the Pakeha. Some moved, a few got into business and did well. But that type never stays; they wanted a proper toilet, electricity, a job that took them places.

After World War Two, the same thing happened: the Maoris came back to second-class citizen status. Except this time they demanded equality. Leaders such as Henry were not going to take no for an answer. You kids miss all this stuff going on.

What your mother did, if it had happened when her husband was at home, yes, she did wrong. But he was not at home, hadn't been for three years. I'm a traditional Maori woman, does what she's told. But if I had my life again I wouldn't put up with most of it, what a woman is supposed to endure and not say a word.

Newspapers. Ah. That way I learned that on both sides of marriage, sometimes people get tempted. Life is never simple nor black and white. Even the view from here changes. Depends who's doing the looking.

Remember when I told you your high-born Maori ancestors kept slaves and you stood right here calling out to your own people they were all your slaves?

I remembered all right. Bellowing out to a handful of local kids: *Bow down to me, slaves!*

Well, what if you are not high-born? Who does the calling out then?

CHAPTER TWENTY

THE VIEW FROM NIGEL BLAKE'S sitting room, of the lake and the island like a giant woman's breast in the centre, was quite something. A power boat tore a gash in the still waters; a sail boat in the distance looked like a cigarette paper. This was my first time at a Pakeha home.

We sat round a wooden table. Nigel and I had spent hours practising music in the Blake's garage and his father told us we could make it our permanent base: there was no need to garage the two family cars. Hemi our drummer lived in the Maori settlement ten minutes' walk away, his village our traditional rugby rival when teams relived battle days of old, but he was too shy to take up the invite to make Nigel's home our practice venue. We'd have to bring him into the different cultural experience slowly. Tony, the bass guitarist, had no issue but was gone off to do other things.

Nigel's mother appeared, with tea and hot home-baked biscuits on a tray. I barely looked up at her but when I did was struck by how attractive she was. Brilliant blue eyes, dark eyebrows that matched her dark brown hair, very good looking; her son had inherited her looks. Not that I for one moment fancied her. Not a band mate's mother, about the same age as my mum.

Pat Blake was headmaster of a primary school. He loved Nigel's musical ambition and was saying he wished he'd had the guts to do what his son had, instead of following a conventional, boring career path.

But I started to notice Mr and Mrs Blake had no connection between them, and to my eyes she was so attractive he should be unable to take his hands off her. But what would a seventeen-year-old know about relationships between married couples?

Isobel was her name. I felt quite at ease with these people and realised the race divide wasn't as bad as I'd thought. Unless I'd just struck lucky. And surely Nigel wouldn't invite me if he knew his parents had a dislike or disregard of brown people?

Maybe she read my thoughts: Mrs Blake — Isobel — wanted to know if I could show her around Waiwera the same as I'd shown her son. Sure. Would she and her husband like to arrange a visit? Pat Blake piped up and said he'd visited Waiwera several times with school student tours.

Isobel asked about bathing in our thermal waters. I told her our baths were private and visitors were not encouraged. What I meant was that outsiders were barred unless with a local who had to be an adult, as the village jealously guarded aspects of its own life. Not sure if I felt perverted considering Isobel in a swimsuit, a woman in her late thirties. I pictured a rather pleasing sight.

Nigel and I veered off conversational course with his father as we were desperate to try out a couple of Sam Cooke numbers. Nigel was a very good vocal backer too. Back out to the garage we went into our own musical world.

The trouble with trying to imitate a giant is you simply lack his stature. I could just reach Sam Cooke's high notes but with nowhere near the ease. Though Nigel swore I had Cooke's voice off near perfect, a singer knows when he has.

Pat said Isobel would drive me home, as he had work to do. On the way I told her I was moving into my own flat soon, and buying a car. She asked where on earth a seventeen-year-old would get the money, so I explained.

What a story, she said. And you don't have a photo of your father?

No, but I have this picture in mind like John Wayne from the movies. Handsome but in a rugged way.

Like his son, she said softly. Gave a little smile in the dashboard light glow.

I gave one back, the smile that my mother said her special boy would one day use to woo the pretty girls.

And damn me if Isobel didn't throw one back. And an awkward, tension-laden atmosphere came as if suddenly through the air vents.

I worried if my smile had been too flirtatious as we spoke not another word till Waiwera. I asked to be dropped off at the bridge: so your tour will be a surprise.

Thanks for the ride. My pleasure. Goodnight. Goodnight. See you soon? Yes.

Stars out in their glory too.

CHAPTER TWENTY-ONE

WHEN THEY FIND OUT, as they surely will, they'll say, there, you see? Was in her nature to betray her marriage vow of fidelity. Not just the once. The name the knowing gave her was apt, she is a slut and none will forgive her, not this time.

They'll say, poor Henry, not his fault, he couldn't see what she was like, they were just young, not out of their teen years, how was he to know the latent dark side dwelling inside that woman? After what he's done for us: he alone pulled and benignly bullied our village more into line with modern times. We owe him. So does she.

They'll say, leave her, Henry. You should have ended it the day you came home to that shocking news of her disgusting, immoral behaviour — and with a Yank soldier to boot, while you fought for your people, your country.

They'll say and they'll say and none of it will be right. Factually, yes, but what are facts when those looking in are not privy to the private life, to the circumstances that can converge and change things, change people? Seems my lot to be unable to throw off that damned war: it keeps claiming me, or its participants do.

It is not sex a woman does it for — ask any woman. Well, most women. And when she does it while married there are complicating factors, she's desperately unhappy, just wants to be loved, wants her existence confirmed. Maybe I always wanted my existence confirmed.

That Henry's marriage to me is hardly blissful must be obvious to even my harshest critic. We're hardly the couple of the decade. But have I not been the best mother to my children, instilled special pride in my kids so they might grow up wanting to be different, for life to be better than village living? Did I not counterbalance Henry's ignoring of my son to raise a self-confident young man with a bright future? A boy even my antagonists, most of them, regard kindly because my Yank likes himself.

No, a married woman even in my situation doesn't just jump into bed with another man for the physical side. Hardly physical anyway with a man who proves so awkward, if very tender; whose impaired speech means strange moans escape him and so do tears. Sure, there's some physical pleasure: of course there would be after years of being roughly taken a couple of times a week sometimes more by my husband.

Compare to this gentle soul who kisses me softly, touches my face all over, gives his feelings and long-held thoughts through his eyes since he can't express in words.

This man doesn't ravage me. He makes love. As any woman best desires. There is an element of pure sensuality, a little raw lust no denying, once I abandon to the act. But it isn't fucking. I go with him on the same journey; we dance together; the strange sounds he makes I shut out. For a while I think I might achieve — well, climax — the same as Jess gave me or, rather, freed from me.

But Barney had waited too long, he told me afterwards, too many years of wanting not so much my body as me, the person who always had time for him, who judged him not. Not that he ever strung sentences together.

And I was hardly going to inform Henry we were through and go off and live with Barney, maybe marry him one day. Nor was it intended, though, as single incident; that would be disrespectful of Barney's feelings and my own needs. A woman needs to feel loved. Men make a big fuss about quite the wrong thing, as if what happens down there is anything to do with what happens in a woman's heart. Dumb, blind Henry.

If you lined up every eligible male in the village in a contest for looks, physique and intelligence, Barney would win on two counts. Well over six foot, broad shoulders, powerful chest, and noble features mirroring his pride . . . most women would gladly breed with him. Perhaps he had intelligence but it couldn't get past the walls of his psychological injury, like a serious case of stuttering happened suddenly in adulthood.

I urged Barney not to display any of his feelings in public. And not to expect intimacy whenever he felt like it, or I would be jumping from Henry's frying pan. Said I'd give him the signal from time to time. My getting pregnant was not a danger; I'd had a hysterectomy some years earlier.

We sat on the bridge bench the same as we always had, and sometimes on another similar bench Barney had built in a private setting easily explained to the inquisitive, it was on his family's land, I was his good friend and why wouldn't we sit and connect wherever we wished? Not as if anyone thought Barney had sexual feeling. When, really, he was a young man not quite forty.

We knew kids sneaked through the trees to spy on us. We were more concerned they'd step on fragile ground and get a severe scalding than we were to hide anything. Hardly did the deed outside nor at my house; that would be just asking for it. We'd go to Barney's little whare his parents had left to him and his sister who'd later died of goitre (I remember her hideously swollen throat). It was a tiny dwelling, with carved gables, an outside toilet, very basic inside. He wrote on his notebook the word: welcome, with a little smiling face.

The walls were covered in photos, like every Maori house. The two bedrooms, partitioned with walls that stopped short of the ceiling, were never used, as Barney slept in sheets — clean ones — on a mattress on the wooden floor of the main living area.

We made love on this floor bed. He didn't rush me; took his time, a true, considerate gentleman. As a cover for my visit I always entered his house with vegetables in a bag for boiling in a pool, or I left home with a pudding or a cut of meat to cook in a steam box or on his small wood-fired range. We sat out on the porch looking down on the main thermal area so our people could see us and just assume the friendship. As his little house had but one curtained window looking into the living room, we could not be spied on even by the cheekiest kid. Barney had a pig-hunting dog that would growl if anyone came near, a stand of trees one side of the house, a thermally created chasm the other.

Fancy taking advantage of Barney with his war injury: it's only natural he'd respond to the siren's call. That's what they'd say. That Lena was born a slut.

CHAPTER TWENTY-TWO

THE EXPERIENCE WAS BIGGER THAN a seventeen-year-old had words to describe. I knew it had special meaning, even importance: it wasn't just sex.

My first time, but obviously not hers; a mother of two children, the youngest my school classmate and fellow band member. She just didn't seem old, not once we lay together. She had the energy and hunger of youth the same as I did. With experience's teaching and self-restraint, till the differences no longer mattered.

At some stage of this unbelievable happening I had thought I was re-enacting my mother's life: she the naive, unknowing young Waiwera inhabitant, seduced by Jess and the broader world he came from. Me seduced by a married older woman's sophistication and womanly wiles. Yet who was the seducer? Lena or Jess? Me or Isobel?

Showing her around our village, I took her places no ordinary sightseer would get to see. Same places I intended taking my father — if he ever came. Got a few sideways looks from locals, but she was too old for anyone to think that far. Couple of mates did give me funny grins, and I gave my most innocent look back. I guess sluts do it naturally, make deception an art of conveyed innocence when the loins are bursting and the lustful mind has no conscience.

Felt like I was my mother parading her lover for the whole village to see.

I started to worry I'd read her intentions quite wrong for she was full of questions about the place and we must have spent over two hours walking around. The rarely seen area where Barney had built a seat Isobel found scary and exciting: why didn't we open this area up to tourists? I explained it was volatile and kept changing so was too dangerous.

She said, like you perhaps?

I was too inexperienced to throw something witty or bait-accepting back. Just my loins stirred even more. *Me, dangerous? Mrs Blake, what do you mean?* Was her who looked dangerous.

That's where I live, I pointed out as we came right by our house that yet had never felt completely mine. I didn't want Isobel seeing inside as her home was beautifully furnished compared with ours. Promised myself I'd learn how to furnish my own house one day, like the Blakes'. We moved on.

Took our turn of gazing into the crystal clear blue depths of Wharepapa pool, like a million tourist eyes over the years. Its white-crusted silica sides you could see thirty, forty feet down before Hell's black claimed it and sent fast-rising bubbles like warning signals from the Devil's raging domain. Green stain from a bag of greens cooking. Another bag of shucked corn cobs attached to a flax string gleamed juicy yellow in the boiling wet. A woman's smile white in the sun. Beads of nervous sweat trickled back of my neck, or else it was the heat coming off the pool.

On the conventional tourist route we ran into Chud, who wouldn't take the hint three was a crowd. Catch up later, I said, dismissed him. Got a long stare to say our friendship came first. Not today, bud. Chud kept getting bigger every time I saw him, tall and muscular. Like his father, except with a prouder bearing. Poor Chud. But this is private business.

King George Geyser erupted on cue for her. She stood staring as it blasted like a pub full of angry drunks going off. I gazed at her form beneath the blouse, the breasts my classmate had suckled on, the body that had carried Nigel and gave birth to him. Not that I had these thoughts attached to any guilt. But it did seem bizarre.

King George hurtled skywards and my eyes admired the slim ankles, sign of a good figure old Merita would say, long as the calf muscles aren't too formed and weight is not showing above the knee, and look at the hands: fingers must be long, wrists skinny. And when you behold the most important part, the eyes, remember: they are the windows to the soul.

So the eyes might turn to me, I asked, are you enjoying this?

Yes, her blue eyes paler than the sky answered. Very much so, more than you think.

Through the clear blue windows at a soul I'm staring, and trying to figure what I'm seeing, what my mind is trying to understand. My age and her age cannot surely be a match? It is supposed to be confusion meets confusion, fumbling inexperience collides with groping unknowing. First-time teenagers don't know what to say. They don't have to.

But I need her to say something, to define this for me or I'll not be able to go through with it. Hold my hand, walk me through it, or it won't happen. I know it won't.

We're in her parked car up at the redwood grove, fifty years tall, planted by some visionary for the public's enjoyment but surely not what was starting to unfold in Isobel's car. Out her windscreen the soaring giants so far from their native American soil, like massive erections — symbols of pending event?

Farther in, beneath the giants' shade, awaits intimacy, the new knowing; somewhere in there it will take place — *if* her soul reads true.

I could not have recalled but a couple of sentences what she said, not hours, weeks, months later. Had to wait, until my mind caught up with my emotions. I could not tell a soul, especially not Chud. No one, or all its meaning would be lost.

But of course I do recall how it started, how it became inevitable. Of course I do . . .

She said, listen. I am not calling you that name. Not any name. You are someone special and so I wish to start this part of your life with something special. Give of myself to you; who I might have been but did not — perhaps could not — become. Many people are locked into situations they cannot escape.

You in turn must give of yourself, your best self, even your confused self. For clarity will surely come, not now, but afterwards.

That's what she said, nuzzling my ear. I swear the hairs back of my neck crackled.

She told me another thing: Do not ask why this is happening, seek only to lose yourself in every moment.

Of course she knew that I the virgin youth wanted a singular part of me lost in a singular place in her (though to recall only the physical is to miss the meaning) . . . That occurred, somewhere in the tall shadows of giants, a place off the track where we lay down on soft moss and fallen needles and the trees stood like guarding sentinels and birds trilled as if glad for us.

Before we coupled in the act of sexual union, her breath was sweet upon me but not as sweet as her sounds, she dripped them over me, put her mouth to mine and broke me open.

She made sighing sounds and soft moaning, a hand stroked my face while the other snatched at my hair. And she said, this is what I have long wanted to be. Just this. Complete.

In the joined wet of our mouths, her tongue that knew and had teachings for my own. The smooth arc of her teeth, yet feeling every slight indentation. The perfect form of woman to my unknowing hands.

Our clothing came off. I'm trembling. Now touch me. She meant down there. Where man's meaning awaits like some vast wordless learning gained in just a touch.

Down there is velvet damp with scent I know in the instant. Feels immediately familiar, as if I knew it all this wondering time.

There is texture alongside my spread fingers; fine down, thick tuft, and the slick-covered folds and crevices men are made to explore. Electrical charge when she takes me in her hand, sends my head spinning. Her mouth works, maybe she spoke.

Too young to know she is guiding until I am held against her damp place and she rises to meet me, takes me inside. A surging sense of belonging, returning.

I know now what she gave, in being the woman she craved to be. And maybe Isobel was like my mother, the secret longing she must have had, seeking something beyond what she had words for, something beyond her own circumstances. Maybe my unusual parentage, the natural environment, its thermal activity, my Maori background, village innocence . . .

Yet I know she was teaching me love. Simple love. Not so much her own as how to receive and in turn to give back. Expressing like dance, like poetry, as kissing, feeling, clinging, writhing, sweating, thrusting, moaning human animals extracting treasures of the soul from each other. Without necessity for as much as a thought, a learned word or formed sentence.

Afterwards, driving me back to Waiwera, she didn't speak, though a hand did fall for a time on my knee and she did smile. I didn't know what to say. I wanted to, but words wouldn't come and I could tell she didn't want to hear words from me.

Boldly, I thought, she took me over the bridge and through the village, turned left down our road to Henry's house.

Then she said, I trust you. No more needed. She trusted me, which she was right to do.

CHAPTER TWENTY-THREE

IT'S THE TOWN'S BEST DANCEHALL, with new lighting that pulses and darkens and brightens as the light operator wishes and the selected music track dictates. Mirrors pick up all of it but like in a dream, where the meaning shifts and you need an eye to interpret it. Six hundred persons its operating permit allows, being about five hundred dancing and the hundred wallflowers pinned to the walls and glued to the benches that lined them. Looks of hurt and lack of confidence, caught in the stark light even in this darker place, of boys and girls knowing what they aren't before their time.

Not that the dancers care; they are relieved and glad not to be socially disabled, imprisoned in an attitude. Lost they are in rock 'n' rolling, not wanting to miss twirling the partner, catching a hand: lost in the throbbing voice and beat Mister Elvis Presley is giving them. The boys are but poor imitations and self-conscious clones of the world's most popular pop singer, Brylcreemed hair catching the ceiling lights, licks and kiss curls stuck fast to sweating brows. Bodies moving frantically yet with deliberate plan inside skin-tight pants stove-piping into winkle-picker shoes, suede and leather going this way and that on the wooden floor.

Girls are made up to the tops of their beehive hairdos, make-up plastered on by the inexperienced, the unsure, not those who know mascara mixed with perspiration turns beauty into the beast. And there's a certain confusion, a hesitation, as if wanting to be told what next in this gathering of small-town rustics unwittingly at the forefront of an international social revolution, loose skirts flying, tight skirts pasted to rumps and grinding hips, high heels twisting and clacking, straining under dancing's demands. Some just follow the leaders, who themselves lead only by having more self-confidence; others have mouths agape in no less than astonishment at being part of this benign revolt when it feels like a mob knowing not what nor why it does.

Boys are primed to scatter their seed in any pretty girl's vagina, vaguely aware there's never been a time in history with so much chance of succeeding — not just at sex, till now a dirty fact of young maleness punishable by law by social disgrace by damnation, though the act, the desire, the animal urge feels so natural.

Look, the girls are exertion-wet and excitement-damp between thighs and yet unsure of what exactly sex is, other than the dire warning of pregnancy; the dreaded unwanted unplanned child growing a girl's shame; her grubby little secret told against her will. And what if this exciting thing called sex hurts? What does a girl do — *how* does she do — the big It? Why is It so much more important to boys than to girls?

But hell, there are more than a few young women quite comfortable, at home with their bodies, happy to let nature take her course, eager to experience, impatient for a desirable boy's intimate touch. A lucky chosen boy can have his way with her, as she will have hers with him.

The better dancers are smooth in delivery of this primal ritual, postures more upright, timing last-second. Confident they'll make the move, with cocky grins and prowess extended to flashing eyes. Some hog the centre floor, others prefer the reflection feedback in the mirror. Here you go, hon, flicking female partner in a twirl on her toes, connected by single finger digits, she threatens to lose her grip then he draws her back, hips going, on fire with sexual movement and desire set free.

Chud sees his friend Yank is on fire, his feet move in perfect easy time with the beat; he spins his partner, she's one of the prettiest ones in the vast, seething room, but other girls are eying the handsome bastard, wanting a turn with him, to lay best and, they hope, final claim. Lucky shit.

Yank's too engrossed in the dancing — in himself, his brooding friend observes — to notice that the gain of girls also earns other males' dislike.

Chud is flattened against the wall, features creased in frown. Wants to be out there but can't; wants to show he can dance, but something inside holds him back.

He *knows* he's a good dancer, how otherwise if he's such an outstanding rugby player? Yet his feet turn leaden, heart heavy with despair. Waves of self-loathing wash over him, a dark sense of lovelessness grips him. The whole ill direction of his life, his bad upbringing, becomes known now and it's so awful a truth someone has to pay. No person can carry such burden, for it says he does not belong, not here not anywhere except maybe, one day, in the company of others angry like him, filled with hate yet with a wanting so much to love and be loved in return. A geyser rumbles inside him.

Another song finishes; sweating, hard-breathing, breathless dancers smile, laughing with disbelief at what mere dancing can do to the soul. Young women sip air to maintain dignity, knowing dignity will be discarded soon as the next song starts and moves five hundred young bodies to an instinct they know nothing of, despite the self-consciousness many can't shed. Hardly time to exchange names then the next amplified number booms out, wallflowers tightening as the magic wand of music casts its spell over the dancers and leaves those wallflowers frozen stiff, wretched, stranded.

We flail and wriggle and twist bodies and stomp and slide on smooth floorboards wet with sweat. This is fornication in public, with clothes yet to be removed. Statues line the walls as if stuck here forever: every Saturday night, it must be unbearable. Look at poor Chud. I know he can dance. But when he gets here he freezes up.

Think I'm in here, the girl's every look and suggestive movement says so. I push my dance moves to the boundary; I haven't practised this it just comes as I slide into her crotch to crotch and meet no resistance. See her eyes pass briefly through that gimlet look of raw sex on offer and her hair would toss back if not confined to a sprayed net like a fat fish, but her eyes again flash signal like a beacon that her cunt is mine. It's yours, Yank! And I thank Isobel for the cloak of sexual confidence: with love, everything happens beforehand. No need to rush it.

Whipped up, I thrust a leg between her again; she throws her head back, a sex-glazed smile to the mirror, her weight held suspended in my arms; laughing she is, hips still wiggling.

Hauling her to me I plant a kiss on her grinning gob and for some reason in the turn have Chud in my vision, a man wilting before my eyes.

I see a young man who in the old Maori days would have been adopted by a great warrior's family because of his physical prowess, his parents banished maybe killed. Back then he'd not have to prove himself through dancing. Back then it would all have been different.

A pushy girl cuts in on my partner. Move aside, kid, give someone else a turn. Your mascara's running, you look like a drunk clown. Immediately she gives me message simple: I'm yours, darl. All the way to the sack.

Me, I just put on my nonchalant mask, to let her know who's running this show.

Meanwhile the angry one stuck fast to the wall squints round the vast room at the bobbing, sinking, rising heads all aflutter; skirts flying, hips going, five hundred pairs of shoes squeaking and rasping and clacking and clattering on the laid polished timber lengths, wet with sweat, the odd fallen tear; his eyes sweep what he can see of the figures seated and stuck to the walls, nailed to the floor, minds refused permission for bodies to dance.

For all the girl's attention I can see Chud knows they have it all in common, clammed and jammed up like this. Chuddy, Mum's Boyboy, I wish I could play back your life and start the reel again. But I can't.

From just a baby the stunting took place. When baby needed comfort, baby wanted crude sounds to be soothing voice, wanted hands to be soft touch, wanted to stare into big faces all asmile for him, babybaby, baby Chud boy, boyboy. To take deep breaths of the walnut vanilla scent of their love for him.

Boy, every boy, wants mummy closeness, mummy always near, mummy anytime he needs her and when he doesn't need, just in case. Boy wants daddy to talk to him teach him life lessons, put arm round him walk out in public show the world boy got daddy's love, not that difficult, not that hard. Boy wants daddy to take him out into the wild of nearby trees and make them seem the forest, the jungle, pretend to hunt wildest animals, father and son together, bring home the kill for happy mummy to cook for happy family even if father did buy the kill from the meat man.

Boy needed daddy to go swimming, let boy show him spots up river down river, eddies and fast flows, how he can run underwater, swim a hundred yards with the swift sweet current, come with me, daddy, come with boyboy, let's do it together, eh, daddydaddy, let's, eh? Boy needed this. He needed.

His anger requires a victim. Chud moves around like a wild beast prowling for the kill.

Yank has lost himself in the new girl's arms and in the low lighting has been allowed fingered access to her most private place, and such a joyous, nerve-tingling place it is too. (Though he has known better and sweeter and meaningful truth.) Murmurs escape him, like the war-damaged man his mother sees, of meaning to him and her, him and her. The girl's mouth is slightly ajar, like the door to herself opening wider. Like her low intelligence being allowed out to play.

Wild beast can scent his prey, there. Now he is flooded with his other self, he is someone. Now he feels as close to being loved as he'll ever feel. The boy alone no more, he has company of his other self. Look after me, boy. I will, Chuddy. I will. And over the both of them go, two Chuds one in their hatred.

Yank picks up the flurry of movement even in the toned-down light. He senses it must be his friend, always knew the reason why, but hates it no less. We made a vow, remember, Chud? That when we grew up we'd do it different, do things better. You said, may as well lie down and die if life is going to end up the same. Jeezuz, Chud. Jeezuz.

Lost his dance timing in the instant. And the girl looks suddenly dumb.

In the moment before he lifts the punching ante Chud knows — he *knows* a step too far. But too far gone for the rational thought to take charge, no one's in charge least of all himself.

Gone, he just keeps punching. But that's not Chud, it's a crazed wild animal escaped from the cage and attacking what he thinks are his cruel keepers. And his best friend has pushed through the crowded dance floor.

Takes two large security men to haul the animal off. His roar stronger than the amplified songs out of six big speakers. He never raised his voice to dogshit father or lowlife mother. He wouldn't have dared.

They bundle him out down an alley the alarmed and wary dancers have formed for his passage, he's twisting and kicking and spitting, gone of this world. Not that he was ever allowed to be part of it in the first place.

There are enough to know the smoothie boy Yank has lost his body-guard best mate, so the trouble's not over yet.

Outside, outside under the star-filled sky yet giving of no light, several youths have punched Yank to the ground; another has grabbed his girl companion from behind, while his mate thrusts a hand up her skirt feeling for all he's worth and crying out to his numbskull mates *she's ready for it!* As if her whole night has been spent waiting eagerly for her prize boy catch to be beaten up and her fanny felt by roughest hand and mean-thrusting fingers, and being held by the throat is what turns every girl on.

When the moon lights the scene, the fallen youth is blind to it in his slumped foetus curl, this form on the grass knowing he's learned a life lesson. Don't upset the other animals in the pen.

Inside, inside the police cell that natural light has never touched and strongest commercial detergent has failed to rid of the liquid spillings of males in wretched condition — vomit and urine and runny shit and semen, the smell that hurting leaves, detergent can never cover the collected foul body odours, the putrid stink of the banal and less than ordinary masses who find themselves here. Well, inside here, the cops have given Chud a bit of a working over and written it down in the station log book that prisoner so-and-so had to be restrained by force due to his violent behaviour.

And so he's feeling not only unloved and a stupid juvenile who went many punches too far, but hard done by, unjustly beaten by men in official positions who have no right and ought to know better. Angrier, way down deep in him where love should reside.

The door unlocks and the burly sergeant fills the doorway, reminds of Yank's old man, Henry, big and intimidating and frightening to even a physical powerhouse like young Chud. Yet a fatherly kindness there too — if you were the cop's kid. If you weren't in one of his cages.

Sergeant's tongue clicks, my, my, my, are you in trouble.

Yeah, he's known that for some time. Now he wants to die. Probably his whole short life wanted to do that.

CHAPTER TWENTY-FOUR

RAIN PELTING DOWN LIKE A tropical downpour, when Henry finds his old wartime mate Barney sitting on his bench by the river.

Hey, Barney, get under my umbrella. But Barney doesn't move, just sits staring straight ahead, drenched, hair flattened over skull, shirt showing his every muscle, trousers against powerful thighs; he was some athlete in his day, not fair what war stole from such a fine specimen.

You all right? You'll catch cold sitting out in this. Go and jump in a bath and enjoy this wet in comfort. Henry grins, but Barney neither moves nor speaks. Not that Henry expected conversation: what they've exchanged over the years since coming home is friendship and Henry's protection of his mate who lost part of his mind in an incident he may not remember.

At first they thought it was his hearing. It wasn't; it was picking bits of his brother Harold from his hair, off his face, wiping the blood splatters and brain matter from his helmet, fat gore and exploded flesh bits all over a man right down to his boots where part of a finger got lodged in the lace as if trying to knot it. All of that had put the inner trembling in a man and run off with his means to speak properly.

Happened near the end of the war, not that anyone knew for certain it was going to end, just that things had swung all the allied forces' way and monumentally weary men dared to believe they could go home any time soon because of the number of German corpses, thousands of disabled tanks, reports the allies had sacked Berlin and captured or killed Hitler himself.

Barney refused to be invalided home, conveyed to his commanding officer he must go where his brother's remains were hurriedly buried to grieve properly for him. Captain Henry Takahe kept insisting Barney was not in fit state, he must return home where he must surely know his loved ones would help his recuperation. His mates had to restrain Barney from assaulting his commanding officer; a most serious offence even for a man lost of his speaking ability and just lost of his beloved brother, even for a man related to that officer.

Henry took Barney back up to the hill then and let him howl for a good couple of hours. It was agreed to keep quiet about Barney's injury to respect his wish of seeing the war out like a man and for sake of his brother's memory.

Now for the third time Henry asks Barney if he's all right. Finally Barney looks up, wet running from his matted hair but under the shadow of Henry's umbrella, shakes head and points at Henry, words trying to form, wanting to form, but all he can manage is: you . . . you . . . you wrong, 'Enry.

Wrong about what? And why is Barney crying? Or is that rain water running from his scalp?

Henry sits down beside Barney. Tell me with signs, I can put it together. Doesn't know that putting his hand on Barney's shoulder wracks Barney with guilt and he pulls away from the gesture like a man caught eating another man's food. Tucker they called it in the war, which you shared to the last crumb. Same as you were prepared to die for a mate.

Le-na, Barney gets out. Which has Henry stiffen at mere mention of his wife's name and the context not too flash by Barney's expression. For surely that's not hatred an old mate is seeing?

Barney, what's the look for? I'm not feeling comfortable all of a damn sudden.

The damaged war veteran is with risen hackles himself. Jabs at his own chest: you talking to me in a tone like that? I am sure I know something about you.

Barney gestures that Henry hit his wife — again. Henry tries to shrug it away, says, women.

But Barney shakes his head adamantly, not how a woman should be treated. With respect, he tries to say and Henry anyway knows.

Our marriage was never the same after the war, Barns. You know why. Plus, things had changed with both of us. Five years apart at a young age is just too long.

Well still don't hit her, Henry.

I'll try. Hard when you never knew any different.

Henry gets up. I'm going to do stocktake, want to come with me? I'll call the quantities, you write them down. Then we'll have a few beers afterward, just you and me, talk about things. What do you reckon?

Watching the two old friends pass under the memorial archway, by names of their fallen comrades etched into metal plaques that each man puts a hand on, like stroking a dying mate. She is lover to both men.

On the other side of the memorial archway in its centre a Maori warrior statue guards this blessed place with spear and fierce expression, tongue thrust out, daring any stranger to come here with any but best intentions.

A woman smiles in the rain with every best intention for this funny little world that could be anywhere at times, but today uniquely Waiwera. Henry still doesn't know her secret. Not sure she knows her own secret, the one deep inside her that only one man of long ago let speak.

CHAPTER TWENTY-FIVE

A THIRD OF HIS MONEY has gone on the motor car. A Vauxhall Velox, green the only colour in the car yard. The cost of freedom, a young man liberated. Another third spent over the payment period on electric guitar, amplifier and speakers.

School is two terms behind him. He has a job in trainee management at the town post office, arranged by Mrs Mac. Not really him, but it's a job to pay the rent on a flat in town and living expenses. A full life, with the band practising every night and all weekend. Elvis Presley numbers dominate their repertoire. Their looks are clones of Elvis. Though Yank has started to move on from Presley, he's discovered black music through a parcel of single and long-player records sent by his father.

You say you'd like to be a musician. Well, listen to these artists, I think you'll like them. Don't be overawed by the standard they set, these are exceptional people chosen from all of America, two hundred million to choose from. Negroes are born musical. And you'll probably know from school their long history of great suffering created great music. Mississippi is a breeding ground for black musicians. Even redneck whites enjoy their music. Hope you enjoy. Write and let me know. Fondest. Jess.

Now Sam Cooke and Ray Charles numbers have been added to the repertoire, and the sound is proving very difficult to emulate. He practises on the three-hour drive.

Borstal. He grew up hearing the term and took no notice as it's not a place he expected to end up. But when Chud got sentenced, Yank found out from Mrs Mac it is an English penal institution for youths, this country being founded on British principles of politics, including law and order.

He wonders how they put boys of fifteen to nineteen in a place like this? A grim brick building sprawl, coiled barbed wire on high walls, several watch towers where he sees the outline of guards behind glass, no different to a prison. He's seen movie scenes like this. But as a place of residence for his best friend?

He's arrived with three hours of spring wind in his face, singing songs learned from the records his father sent, feeling pretty good. Sam Cooke is still the vocal benchmark, Yank frustrated he can hear every perfect note and subtle phrasing yet can't come close to imitating the man. *Don't be overawed.*

Through a life-weary security check, Yank is feeling overawed at this place. Has to show his driver's licence to a guard, is directed to a door which turns out to be a series of doors, leading to a large visiting room.

Takes a seat at a table broad enough to sit three on his side. The room is filling up with other visitors, mothers and girlfriends, some with small child in unknowing tow. Every adult has a certain look. Not Yank's type, not a one.

He hears the clang of steel grilles opening and closing through the inmate entrance. Jangle of keys as several young men appear the other side and a guard unlocks.

In walk five swaggering young men in blue denim and grey jacket uniform, Chud at first hard to recognise he's grown so much. And his expression is so different. Though not when he breaks into smile at seeing Yank.

Relieved at seeing Chud put on the Elvis lopsided grin they used to practise along with the legs-apart stance Elvis took, Yank stands and Chud comes over and they shake hands.

Afterwards Yank can't remember the first awkward minutes of conversation, of Chud's eyes constantly roving to fellow inmates, or just unable to hold Yank's gaze. Says there's not one boy from Waiwera in here, how he misses home but it's all right here, you get used to it. And I've got a couple more guys to fight to be kingpin.

Has to explain the term. Which makes sense, as Chud is one hell of an athlete and always had plenty of anger to give him fighting advantage — if that's what's important. And clearly it is. (Yank never liked violence.)

Chud leans forward, with the eyes of a fervent door-knocking fringe Christian looking for converts, says do you know how hard it is to be kingpin at age eighteen? Some of these guys are going on twenty, soon be moved to a men's prison. Yank, I'm in a fight every few days. Wonks wanting to take me on, knock me back down the ladder. But I beat them all. You should see the respect I got in here.

To a friend who doesn't know what to say. Who thinks, fighting for the sake of it?

Then Chud says, I bet you got yourself a pretty girl now.

No.

Come on, the girls always liked you.

Yeah, and I like them too. Just in no hurry for a girlfriend.

Chud got a funny smile on. Oh? You happy playing the field? As if he wanted to hear Yank say no. As if desperate for Yank to say no.

Too busy. I formed a band. Told you in my letter I bought a car, with money my father sent.

Lucky you. Chud's face says envy is choking him.

They talk about the different songs the band plays, Chud playing more knowledgeable than his lifelong friend knows he is. Yank switches to rugby, how Chud's team is doing without him (not very well). Chud tries to force back his proud grin. They need me.

Yank wants to say, and you let them down.

Words run out, from both of them. Why Chud grows suddenly animated, over the top in saying goodbye? Out of relief the visit is over. Making Yank promise he'll visit again, but no hurry. You got things to do. So have I. Even in here. Laughing. Moving his weight from one foot to the other, like he does when covering up hurt or embarrassment.

He drives home thinking his friend's life has sort of come to an end. As if the first journey wasn't bad enough, now he's starting a worse one. Makes Yank sad and afraid for his friend.

CHAPTER TWENTY-SIX

FROM A SIGHT MOST DAUNTING the crowd become our subjects, puppets on the ends of our music-making strings, my singing and rhythm guitar, drummer, bass, saxophone, and Nigel Blake on lead guitar. Hundreds of bobbing heads in changing colours cramming the hall before us, The Viscounts, a name Nigel found in a history book about old England.

Us. The band, centre of attention, manipulators of these young people their happiness. Grinning at each other: all ours.

From Elvis we hit them next with a surprise, know they'll stop dancing not knowing what to make of the song, a track from a long player my father sent (his taste is amazing). Pitched at the top of my note range: we argued about dropping it to an easier level. I said no, I've tried that and the song loses everything. Otherwise the song came naturally, like the rasp Negro singers have.

They get like this our subjects, at first open-mouthed at hearing the quite unfamiliar. At it being a no-dancing number when young people like to dance. Looking up at me as lead singer, telling me I had better sing it good, the band had better be on their game, or we're through.

So I just close my eyes and sing in imitation of a song from one of the records my father sent. From Mississippi, America, to here at a dance hall in Two Lakes, New Zealand.

Have to reach the emotional high at the end of the song or our subjects will revolt, they'll riot at the prince letting them down, he shouldn't have built them to this state if he wasn't certain he could deliver. I have to. We have to make them our slaves.

Need a bomb to blow out the noise erupted in here. A part Maori, half white American imitator, with help from his friends of course, has caused a sensation. The prince and his inner court have produced nothing less than a miracle, taken the audience to a place they can never come back from, they're there now, over yonder, where musical giants await. They are saying, we've bought it! Meaning lucky us, the deliverers of another's musical originality.

During the night glorious performing in return for adulation: we can have any young woman we want. Which spurs us young men to greater heights of being desired.

From up on our elevated platform I have views, should I wish, of the big sliding entrance doors, opened to let cooler air in, when I see someone right out of her age group. Framed in the centre, with light behind so I can't see her features.

No need to. I would know her body shape, her presence anywhere.

We're doing a medley of songs by various artists; our subjects, many of them, are singing the words of the chorus imploring a girl to answer her phone. The usual anguish of song lyrics about the hurt and glory of love. The infinite need of humans all on the same theme. And there love is, throwing a smile right over the heads of my subjects solely at and for me.

Where have you been, Mrs Blake? Can hear her in my mind saying, call me Isobel. Yet she won't say my given name. Not that names matter.

In his dancing arms Isobel, singing to her in the tiny living room of his flat, discarded clothes strewn on the floor, curtains pulled. A hundred, two hundred times he's played this number, and still it opens his heart and sends forth sung-along lyrics to the woman of no age, the love she's taught him, how she's enshrined women, taught him woman.

She has come back, to the youth a couple of years more receptive, more open to the learning she has to give him.

Kiss me. Kiss me, the lyrics implore, with emphasis on *kiss.* As if the act itself. Singing it now right into her mouth. Kiss me. Kiss me.

CHAPTER TWENTY-SEVEN

MUM, WIKI AND MANU CALLED in to say hello. Didn't hear the knocking for the music from my new record player. Thank you, Jess. Forgot how good looking my mother was, the long, thick, straight hair and proud features Merita told me carried her noble ancestry. Green-grey eyes and a mother's smile for her special son.

I cast around in case there was evidence of my lover's visit of last night, if there was her perfume scent lingering, anything to say a woman of my mother's age group had been here. My sister and brother naturally casting kids' curious eyes everywhere.

Mum had a new hair styling; I wasn't sure it suited her. It was the village woman trying to go city. Still, now I could see the appeal she would have had to my American father. The explicit details weren't going to enter my mind but I did see some parallels. Now I did.

Wiki most impressed by the amplifier and microphone set-up, as I shifted my gear back and forth between Nigel's parents' garage and the flat to get more practice in. As my kid sister and brother were my audience here I boasted at how well the band was doing, but my mother ruined it: with some help from money sent from America, she said. So I suddenly discovered resentment at this unannounced family call since Mum was scratchy. Wondered why she'd bothered. What if I'd been in an intimate situation? And how would I have explained my lover's age?

All right, I'd developed a miserly side and should have thought of my mother whose patchy income still came from filling in as a tourist guide and doing the odd shift at hotel reception at the Waiwera Hotel.

Mum, I've been meaning to give you some money. But she waved me away. If it doesn't come naturally then don't be forcing it, son. Makes it a different kind of giving.

So now I felt guilt. Especially when she said they didn't have a lot of time as they had a bus to catch back home. I'll take you. Just relax. Cup of tea? Something stronger?

Nothing, thanks. Wiki, Manu, go and buy yourselves an ice-cream or something from the shop we passed. I have something private to discuss with your brother.

Soon as my siblings went out the door, Mum pulled a brown envelope out of her handbag. Here. I want you to look at these.

Sarcastically I asked, who died?

She shot back, might be you in a minute. Open it.

I shook the contents out on to my lap. Photographs. Black and white. One of my mother in Waiwera guide's uniform with a man whose face was darker than hers, the photo must be old. Negro, but not coal black like in a movie. Maybe half-caste. In civilian clothes. I had never seen one Negro tourist in Waiwera. In fact never set eyes on a Negro, period. Just on the movie screen, playing servant roles and over-acting the buffoon for the white masters' amusement.

The other photograph was of — I think — the same man but a lot clearer and a closer shot. A handsome man, languid smile like he was posing for the camera. In a uniform. Military.

Wasn't until I looked up and saw my mother's face, those eyes saying what the slightly parted lips did not need to, that I knew.

This is your father.

But he's a Negro . . . ?

I look at my arm with quite a different eye. I'm the same brown but now I discern a certain duskiness. I have urge to rush to a mirror and reconsider my face. Get the alarming thought of my contempt for Maori slaves of the old days: Negroes were slaves.

This can't be. My father is *white.* With uncanny resemblance to Elvis. Or the ruggedly handsome features of John Wayne. When I was younger my dad was a cowboy — and they're all *white* — with six-shooters blazing, saving my life from Injuns. I've carried this choice of images in my mind for years. This is *not* him.

I think of coal, boot polish, the Devil, evil, all the bad and negative moods described as black and dark, even the night is black and the day is glorious light. A virgin doesn't get married in black. Nothing black is pure. No food is black. Black is what is worn at funerals.

Mum, Negroes are poor.

Because they're not allowed to be rich.

They're servants, waiting on rich white folk — sucking up, more like.

No choice. They got to eat too. Rich white folk, as you call them, set the rules. How would you be if our own white race set the rules? Well, in a way they do but least brown folk have got opportunity to be whatever they want. Just have to try a bit harder. But not the black folk in America. Jess told me that much. It's called a colour bar, son. Don't be looking down on half your existence.

Mum, we're high-born.

Says who?

Says Merita.

Her head starts to slow shake. I think she was making you feel good.

Merita doesn't lie. She said your great-grandfather was a very high chief and his fathers before him. Said his head was so sacred a specially appointed person had to feed him by hand. He kept slaves by the hundreds, like an Egyptian pharaoh. He was like royalty. Why would Merita lie to me? She loves me.

Now you have your answer, son. Believe me. I am not high-born. If I was then Henry would have had to accept what I did without complaint. The village would have taken my side no matter what. My families on both sides are ordinary. Nothing wrong with that. You are what you are.

Well I'm no child of a descendant of slaves. And I'm sure as hell not a nigger.

Her eyes narrow. You'd call your own father that?

Every concept I have of Negroes is in turmoil. I realise I'm prejudiced too. My father sent a Louis Armstrong long player; I'm sure I'd seen the same man in a movie playing the boggle-eyed fool nigger. Jess wrote the man is a genius, a giant astride not just America but the whole world in his musical influence. Why did such a colossus allow himself to be portrayed that way? I am confused.

Where are you coming from with this slave stuff, Yank?

She walks to the door. Stops.

By the way, that was one beautiful voice you were playing. Who is it?

What sort of question is that after my own mother has hit me with a bombshell?

Mel Carter, I answer. Puzzled. Hasn't she given me enough to deal with?

He's got to be a Negro with a voice like that. Some voice that nigger has. I'll call by same time tomorrow. Bye, my special boy. Remember we're only slaves to ideas and attitudes.

Holy cow, I'm half black.

PART TWO

CHAPTER TWENTY-EIGHT

CHICKENS SCRATCHED FOR FOOD IN our dust, ate the worms and blown seeds under the cluster of raised houses, foraged in the woods but always came home to give us eggs and sometimes faithful heads to chop off and thrill kids with a body pumping blood and running round like crazy — and give the family food a couple hours later.

I remember at least two hogs in a wooden pen we threw scraps into and the hogs bumping hard against the timber enclosure, snorting, gobbling up like they'd never ate in a month; they'd eat anything. Their beady eyes we kids could see warmth in, even intelligence, we'd talk or make noises similar so they understood and dang if they didn't answer back.

In fact there were a good two dozen hogs and every household in the shotgun line-up of shacks gave their scraps, picked up from different rural sources: cabbage cut-offs, rotten lettuce and collard stalks, turnips, corn husks, corn mash, corn liquid, unsold bread bought dirt cheap from town bakers at cents a bin. We stole corn from fields, to feed ourselves and the hogs; to us it was the sea, the unbroken vastness we'd never get to experience in liquid, only pictures and imaginings impossible to re-create middle of Mississippi except as a field that made a great sighing, moaning in the wind and we could plunge into it and lose ourselves forever, swim it in our minds, and when it turned back to land we could take a thousand cobs if we chose, the theft not noticed among the millions of plump yellow sweetnesses within green sheaths.

Not that we pined for the sea: we had a river and ponds, a few little lakes; we pined for near nothing except to experience a whole week of full bellies, to gorge every meal for all seven of the Lord's created days on hog fried, grilled, boiled, roasted, cooked in coal embers, we dreamed of feasting on crackling by the big bowl, trotter gristle, even the toe claws, of feasting on the layers of meat, fat and crisped skin unless it was boiled to just like chewing gum, of dining on the snout we'd talked to and been answered back by, kind of sad but sure tasted good, chewing on hickory-smoked ribs, fat-back, carving thick slices of roasted leg, having it cured as bacon and ham hocks boiled for hours with greens, any greens. Our mother salted strips and chunks of it, stewed pork in a chow mein everyone swore was as good as the Chinese cooked; she had curry recipes to turn old vegetables and going-off meat to biting, sweat-forming feasts; we sopped up the gravy with pone bread, our tongues and throats burned and we came back for more. This is what we pined for if we pined at all. Just a week-long belly full of pork.

We ate boiled hog ears that had heard our every creeping movement their way, picked meat from around empty eye sockets from eyeballs melted in the cooking heat, eyes that had once told of a brain, a mind behind all the enormity of snorting, snuffling bulk and hefty animal presence that looked at kids from the far corners of a curious animal mind. We spat out bristles missed in the scraping, we started one side of the hog's cooked head, on the meat round the teeth rows we said was kissing hog lips and sucking on its face. Munched through the length of tail, boiled bone sections of meat, fat, skin combined. That's what we might have pined for living jammed up side by side in each other's faces and lives and tempers and, we grew to see, lust appetites and loves, to just once in a while get to gorge a week long on hog, sweet hog.

The adults went to work in town in old trucks and broken cars, some walked to nearby fields, some stayed home. Kids went to our mother's one-room school class, she was a Jeanes teacher, funded by something called a foundation by the name of Anna T Jeanes who wanted Negro children to get an education even though Miss Jeanes was white and rich and had no children herself, or so our mother said. Was Miss Jeanes helped make our family a little different.

Not saying set on another path, for you are who you're surrounded by, mostly. But she gave us another form of language, structured grammarwise, not sing-song spontaneous like ordinary Negroes. And we had the choice of coded nigger talk to hide and disguise meaning from wrong ears, or speak straight and correctly as our mother preferred. But then it's not a mother's life to live: we each belong to our peers, more or less.

We were raised to be grateful to Miss Jeanes; without people like her we Negroes would have worse lives when to kids it doesn't feel any but what it is, and worse not a word that sprang to mind let alone worse again. Since kids hardly ever went to town what did we have to compare to? We only heard the stories and from time to regular time noticed the missing faces gone to jail or heaven via the violent route or they went north, just about all to do with white folk not liking us niggers and to get better paid work and suffer less racial prejudice.

But really, a kid doesn't notice politics or what truly ails a people even when it's notably us. Guess we were luckier than some.

Far as we knew we ate pretty good, mostly. Pig feet and chitterlings, chicken fried and baked and done perleau style, gopher, armadillo sometimes, tortoise, grits, black-eyed peas, boiled and roasted peanuts, pecans we found growing wild near the river, gingerbread and buttermilk, waffles with Georgia syrup, and in lean times meat grease and salty lard on pone bread.

To us youngsters it was mostly sunshine days and all our spots in the woods, the river, the areas of water we could cool in, explore, hide sometimes; we played under the houses up on piles for Old Miss floods making our tributary spill over, underneath there with the clucking chickens, finding their eggs and listening to adults going at each other with words or humping: we listened in disbelief to female moaning that wasn't from a beating but why we had yet to have idea, we heard men declare *God* in that way and the gasps and groans above us and giggled in imitating what we did not know.

We heard singing, individuals and joined, it meant little, everyone sang even kids did and without really knowing. Like play, we just did it and forgot soon after. Though of everything, it was the singing and music-making that must have burrowed into our young minds and taken up residence there, waiting quietly to be remembered, drawn from like a wellspring when the time came for needing it or just to express.

Mostly we heard nothing but each other and what we could conjure from our imaginations under the dark and cool of floorboards, scare off the rats, get startled by a stirred armadillo, look out for snakes, listen out for a hornet nest, get covered in spider webs, bitten by skeeters and chiggers, just lay there talking to each other or a cast of characters imaginary and real like our oldest friends there under the dwellings.

Guess most the men got drunk on Saturday nights, coon dick they drank, they gambled on Florida Flip, craps, Sissy in the Barn, cooncan; whooped and hollered and sometimes argued and fought with fists, a knife sometimes, gun incidents became lore, like some of the characters did. Most everyone dressed up, they visited other communities, but loved the juke joints best; bought crazy brews from the turpentine stills, got happy and sometimes went mad on it. And everyone danced and sang as if tomorrow was never coming, and for some it never did. We'd see the bodies lugged on to the back of a truck, or hear the stories. Life and death went hand in hand, like they danced together.

We took to the woods to do some real hunting, rabbit, 'dillo, coon, squirrel, turkey, gopher, anything that moved on land or in fresh water, from morning till dark we lost ourselves in there, came home with mammals and birds and fishes, or nothing at all but excuses and cuts and grazes for our mommas and grandmas to tend and lick, say kind things to us failed boy hunters, how we'd do better next time. Or we came home with food for the table, sometimes to spread round a few tables and wallow in adults' praise. Guns we knew early.

And when it rained we messed about in huts and shelters we'd built, made mud pies in puddles, slid down wet clay slopes, or holed up somewhere just listening to it drum on the roofs the millions of leaves and needles, the continuous thrumming on the grateful ground drinking greedily. We stood out in it with mouths opened to let the sky fall in to quench thirst or just the sensation, it didn't matter, nothing matters when you're a child in the endless sequence of growing up.

Our difference was, our mother made us read, made sure we kept up with study tasks set by her pamphlets of teaching rules she kept locked in our little classroom the storage cupboard where the children's books were kept so as drunk or ignorant adults didn't use them for toilet paper, to light a fire.

We Hines kids were told we had extra responsibility on account of our mother being the teacher who in turn owed to the generosity of Anna T Jeanes and her foundation, but we were still what our peers were and couldn't be nothing else, not till later in the years when these things started heading us to what could only be revealed by the written word.

Only a very few families shared our compulsory interest in the written word and not that it made a power of difference in how we lived: our mother got a most modest salary, she taught for the love of it and the debt she felt she owed to the kind white woman to enable her to help lift young Negroes educationally and — she very much hoped — as advantage to her own father-abandoned brood.

Life is an endless dream, no need for remembering as living it every moment is enough. Things happen, sure they happen, and some of it bad even real bad, but you kind of shut it out, does a kid, because childhood is not meant to be painful it's supposed to be joy.

And so it turned out to be. Hell, I don't even remember it actually meaning anything that we lived in the state of Mississippi, let alone have awareness of things peculiar to the South and directly pertaining to us, people of dark skin, colored the whites called us, and niggers and Negroes. We were just kids growing up where we'd been born, learning from our mother that one day a greater, wider world awaited us when it seemed we already had that promised world right in our contented young hands.

Then youth made greater and greater claim on us, we practiced dance steps in the same dust and mud our chickens pecked from, and as we grew all we wanted was to express through dance and song and instrument-playing, express our African origins with feet yet three centuries firm in America. Thus we learned our own steps and movements and means of patterned display. Acquired our own unique suffering too.

Miles we walked to venues, hundreds strong of our own young exuberant kind, competed with each other at any of a dozen styles of dance, but tap in particular. We did whatever work was required to purchase shiny patent-leather shoes with the steel toes and heels, the threads to go with them; we practised prancing and preening the required walks and stances and postures, then got lost in the pulsing, sweating, floor-hammering madness of each other's smooth-moving company every Saturday night without fail.

We danced till the sun came up and Sunday bells were commanding our mothers and grandmothers to church and we had to hurry for fear of punishment — not from fathers as men didn't figure like women did in any of our communities: we weren't big town or city boys, we feared our mothers and grandmothers. Naturally though every year we lost more and more regard even respect for our elders, no matter that we loved them. Rather dance than pray. Bed a fine girl than sit in church listening to the congregation doing shouts, hollering to the same unanswering God, singing like angels to His long-deaf ears, beseeching Him for what He plainly had no intention of delivering.

CHAPTER TWENTY-NINE

Southern trees bear a strange fruit,
Blood on the leaves and blood at the root,
Black body swinging in the Southern breeze,
Strange fruit hanging from the poplar trees.

THE WORDS TO THAT POEM came back to me — to any Negro who knew them — not long after returning home from the war. To find as if we'd never participated, as if we had served on the enemy side.

As if our dead servicemen had died for nothing. As if every lost limb, eyesight, hearing and mind, every disability and constant nagging pain, had all been wasted.

Back to our beloved, hateful South; back to the dominant white populace still the same nigger-haters, and even more hell-bent, most of them, on showing us who was boss.

Came home to strange black fruit still hanging from poplar trees, to white citizens of the country we'd fought for stringing up Negroes, even war veterans, even women. Men who'd not served were lynching good men who had.

How stupid, how naive, how dumb we were to expect things to have changed just because we'd fought alongside our white fellows. Land of the free our national anthem claimed us to be. A lie if you were of Negro extraction, living in a country where any drop of Negro blood was like a tainting.

I should have known, we all should have known, that attitudes of three centuries' making do not change, even given a world war we were engaged in supposedly as equals, defending our country, our beliefs. We Negroes should never have kidded ourselves this war might change things. Not in the South.

We had another war left to fight, against an enemy called racial prejudice.

They gave us the most lowly positions: sanitation, cleaning, dishwashing, lugging heavy ammunition all day, every menial task an army needs but no soldier wants to do. But then we were young Southern Negroes only too glad to be called up for military service so we could get out of Mississippi. To go other countries was an impossibility for any but a rare handful of blacks. Now we were going, even if soon to a war. Felt more like a windfall holiday to exotic overseas lands than fighting another people to the death.

It should have been plain to us when we were segregated on racial lines that war or not, Whitey from the South was never going to consider us even remotely as equals. But we were so excited and anyway so used to only Negro company, we hardly gave the segregation a thought. When they told us we were going to a country called New Zealand, way down in the South Pacific, no one had ever heard of it. We imagined them to be brown- or black-skinned natives in grass skirts with bones through their noses — and likely cannibals. We would have put up with anything though just to experience how other folk lived.

What we arrived to was a modern society much the same as ours, except quite a few years behind. And the majority of the population was white. What a country, what marvelous people, what an experience, as backward as it felt to even us poor colored boys from the South, bars that closed at six o'clock at night, not a shop open past that hour and everything closed on weekends. But friendly, open, hospitable locals who gave their allies warmest welcome.

Including, to our shock, Negroes.

Which we didn't get, not at first: that white people could treat us as equals and their own dark race, the native Maoris, had the same rights as the whites, they played sport together, married one another, had representation at political level, a born right to be whatever they chose. How could Negroes be permitted to drink in the same bars as whites? Back home that would cause a riot, cops would arrest us, a white judge would throw us in jail.

Though we did discern an economic difference between the two races and hear the occasional disparaging remark about Maoris being inferior, the vast majority of whites were like what we'd heard some of our North American whites were: unprejudiced, color-blind. Some of those northern whites were even on our side, so we heard from Negroes who had lived up north.

We found the Maoris a bit like us, more physically robust and expressive in music and dance, and their men were very partial to a fight, which won our admiration as they were not scared of anyone. And all men love women. Their skin was brown to our mostly black and their features more like Mexicans'.

Then a bunch of us soldiers went to this thermal wonderland called Waiwera in the town of Two Lakes. Where I met a Maori woman; Lena was her name. At home she would have been called a mulatto, of more white than dark blood. That she was married made no difference: I was hit between the eyes with love.

Two unforgettable weeks together then war called for real, as we got sent in our thousands to Guadalcanal, to fight a Japanese enemy whose battle tactics in the steaming jungle were stealth and cunning and surprise, sometimes with open, near suicidal offensive. We lost tens of thousands. So did the Japs, except it seemed to have no effect on them. They kept coming at us. Thousands more of us went down with tropical diseases, died of infected wounds — even small cuts and grazes could kill a man.

It was the complete opposite of the glamorous war we had believed in. The enemy popped up from anywhere and quickly disappeared into impenetrable jungle, and yet we knew they watched our every move as they manoeuvred to hit us from another unexpected position. They snipered us till the very last of the usually brilliant sunsets, and snipers' bullets cracked the start of gloriously colorful dawns. We scanned the thick jungle growth, every second expecting it to answer with a bullet bearing our name. Mosquitoes, the other enemy, were constantly making us feverishly ill and killing us. Months and torturous months of real war's reality.

To think I felt relief to be wounded badly enough to get sent home to recuperate and maybe not have to return again. Back home less than six months when I was deemed fit enough for active service and this time the arena was Europe. I didn't mind in the least: I wanted to serve my country and do my bit to win respect from our white counterparts, and it was more new countries, quite different to the Pacific Island jungles and a far cry from Mississippi. I did think of Lena from time to time.

In Europe most Negroes found the attitudes of our white countrymen had softened markedly. Due to, we realized, northern whites' influence with their far greater tolerance, and just from fighting alongside each other and realizing racial difference was plain silly. It was from that experience that I think a lot of us Negroes came home expecting a heroes' welcome and even a small change in how we were treated. Not that on the boat home any of us dared to think an end might come to Whites-only and Colored signs everywhere or that integration of schools and other institutions might come about. Even if the more radical blacks talked of such impossibilities as civil rights and equality for Negroes.

It was not a heroes' welcome. We blacks got to march at the end of the parade in my small home town of Whitecave, Mississippi, where the majority white citizens were in a happy clamor for their boys and noticeably silent when we tail-end black Charlies filed past.

A few weeks later I and a black veteran buddy, Vernon Hill, went to register as voters for state and county elections at the local polling station. We were the only blacks in a room full of hostile white officials and fast realizing nothing of Southern racism had changed.

A big Confederate flag was on the wall behind tables lined with narrow-eyed men who ignored us a good twenty minutes. But damn it, we were determined to exercise our right to vote, bolstered by knowing we had earned it the hard way.

Two forms were pushed at us. These asked the registrant to *read or interpret a section of the Constitution.* Having schooled ourselves up Vern and I wrote accordingly. The man who took our forms gave cursory look and scrawled *failed* and stamped twice: INELIGIBLE VOTER.

Still under the illusion the war had changed things, I informed the official we had learned the quoted passage off by heart so why were we deemed ineligible? Reminded we had served our country in the war.

He told us that his decision was final and to get our nigger asses out of there before he called the sheriff.

As long as I live I'll never forget the waves of impotency that rolled over me in hearing, seeing that man, a portly, plain-looking individual who had control over me, over Vernon. Now here we were being treated like vagrant children. I had the strength to snap the man in half. Vernon, whose boxing skills had won him renown in our army division, could have held his own against several of these people. We were *men* being utterly disrespected and not able to do a damn thing about it.

So began an anger that took a hold of me and sent me plummeting into the abyss for a good number of years.

Walking into that polling station hall I had felt proud, believing I presented a respectable figure, tall and rather fine looking I don't mind saying, a man who carried himself well in the company of friend Vernon, who had similarly proud bearing. Two men who had fought for country, for this state, this Southern county, who had earned we thought the right to be treated as equals. And I knew the official's face, as you do growing up in a small town. I'm sure he knew ours.

But the face looking back did not recognize either of us, except as unwanted niggers who had better see sense quickly. I was close to saying something insulting, even threatening the man with physical violence. But a lifetime of training to bite my nigger tongue stood me in good stead, unless I wanted to be behind bars for years.

In our humiliation we left and found a bar — for coloreds of course — and got soundly drunk. Without my realizing it, something inside me had snapped. In Vernon too, and worse, I was later to find out. He ended up on Death Row for murdering a white couple who caught him ransacking their house. I happened to know it was his warped sense of revenge.

Within the year there was a Negro lynching in my county. The two victims were veterans of the Pacific. I first saw the photos published not in a newspaper but reproduced on a postcard that was circulating in the area, seemingly for certain white folks' amusement. A *postcard*.

It showed two black figures strung up, eyes closed, countless bullet holes in the bodies — as if lynching wasn't enough. Two fellow veterans, Negro soul brothers, dangling from a tree.

On the other side was the normal space to write address and a message, a marked rectangle for the postage stamp. The wording describing the scene read simply: Rotten Black Fruit.

We weren't readers — our poetry was scat-talk — but we knew this was crude play on the poem 'Strange Fruit'.

It began with lines about the strange Southern fruit, then

Pastoral scene of the gallant South,
The bulging eyes and the twisted mouth,
Scent of magnolia sweet and fresh,
And the sudden smell of burning flesh!

Niggers had had to burn and hang to inspire those words. But took a white man to write them, though Billie Holiday is known for singing them; Negroes too close to the suffering can't step far enough back. A Jewish school teacher, Abel Meeropol, composed it — and his race knew suffering. On an unimaginable scale at Hitler's hand, the world found out once the war ended. Our six million were slaughtered over three centuries and less systematically.

Here is a fruit for the crows to pluck,
For the rain to gather, for the wind to suck
For the sun to rot, for the tree to drop,
Here is a strange and bitter crop.

I had seen strange fruit once in the flesh, in my fifteenth year when witness to a lynching my mind stored away in some dark recess.

I met a girl and married too soon, we had two daughters in quick succession, and I only had a series of low-paid jobs. In our small town there wasn't much choice. So we moved to Jackson. I quickly gained employment at a print factory, manual work which was assumed the only suitable role for Negroes, but I managed to work my way on to one of the sophisticated machines, well on the way to learning a new craft, better money. I even dared to think I might have a future.

Till my wife announced she was taking self and kids back to her hometown, Biloxi: she felt we had nothing in common, she didn't like the big city and I think she saw the drinking signs in me — of a weak man going to succumb one day to himself, to the notion of being born a nigger forbidden to raise himself up, excluded from destiny by written laws and custom and therefore justified in turning to drink.

Too immature to think much about my daughters, too much getting by in a strange town knowing hardly anyone, I guess I got fogged up for more years than I care to admit. Lost my way to drink and anything that could be smoked or swallowed to get me out of it, took the momentary comfort of any woman available. I was a man full of nigger self-loathing. Thought I had good reasons why, and they were just too much for a nigger to fight against. After what I had given to my country it had ignored me, denied my basic rights.

Years I wallowed in self-pity. Till I had a dream as real as my own groping fingers for her, Lena being the subject.

CHAPTER THIRTY

TOOK SOME TIME TO ACCEPT it had been a delusion, that I was not the son of a white American hero. Near every song from records Jess had sent went off the band's repertoire and naturally my pals were wondering why. I lied and said the trend wasn't going that way, the Beatles had just arrived. English bands were all the rage.

But, they said, your voice doesn't suit the English band style. Thought they were paying me a compliment saying I sang more like a Negro, that I had a natural bent for black music, it was what I loved to sing and listen to, obsessively.

After a few weeks of misery I adjusted and came down from my throne to mix with the slaves of the world. It seemed my mother had this all worked out with Jess, for a parcel of records arrived from him and though it took a couple of sulking days to even open the parcel, I found a treasure trove waiting when I did. And knowing I was part Negro explained everything, including falling hopelessly in love with the gospel singer Mahalia Jackson's angelic voice. This new batch of recorded artists had set another benchmark, it seemed to me. And a person should know of his own kind.

So I was the descendant of slaves — the people hardly mentioned in school history books, those poor souls crammed into galley ships like livestock, transported from Africa to the Americas. To a life of slavery.

I was not high-born, not descended from a great Maori chief, not the offspring of an all-white American hero. I wasn't John Wayne Junior. Just ordinary Mark Hines of low lineage, a mix of bloods that some might say made me a mongrel.

Eventually I apologised to the band, reinstated every dropped song and added many more, every one of them by black artists.

Pulled out the two photographs of my father and said, guess who this is?

And three said almost in chorus, your old man?

Nigel, who did most of his talking through his very good lead guitar, did not look a bit surprised. Was him who drawled, yeah, well, we kind of figured your voice can't have been just good imitation.

The chief, the king, son of a gunslinging cowboy, replica of Elvis, slave owner, pharaoh, John Wayne Junior, was dead. Long live Mister Ordinary, descendant of a Negro slave.

I met Isobel at my flat about once a month; had an arrangement with my boss to start work an hour earlier and take a two-hour lunch break. My boss, who liked music, believed it was for guitar tuition.

Of late she'd been asking if we shouldn't end this, what with the age difference and even more her son's presence in the band.

But I didn't want to let go. I felt I was growing up more rapidly than the chronological norm; I was being prepared for adulthood in understanding women — yes, the plural, as I intended knowing quite a few more before settling down and marrying. I did want children somewhere down the track. As to what Isobel got out of the relationship, she didn't say. I presumed it was partly physical and something about our chemistry that just worked.

At least Isobel was surprised on learning my blood heritage. You'll recall I thought you had Latin blood, she said. Well, part Negro makes it even more interesting. And on the subject of interesting we moved like dance partners who were old hands and fucked each other to mutual fulfilment.

I think I'm ready to go to America to meet him, I told Isobel. She thought it a good idea, and did I have the money? Yes, I said, another money order came with the records. My father must be quite well off.

With winter coming on and no bookings for the band, I'd have the opportunity to go. So I decided to study up on where he lived as the stories I'd heard of Mississippi were not good, what with the Ku Klux Klan, the horrific things they did to Negroes. Wondering — fearing — how I would be treated.

Hours I had spent in front of the mirror trying to see how I must appear to others. If my band mates had always assumed I had Negro blood, but Isobel my intimately closer friend did not, what then did I really look like? If too obviously of Negro origin then my visit to America might not be something to look forward to, even do.

I drove the six hours to Auckland one Saturday, to see someone who would know in an instant which race I would pass for most. Mata. (And to see my nephew again, just a baby when I saw him last.)

Not giving Mata notice was deliberate. I just arrived: no need to bother about the niceties, not my own sister. But thankful her boyfriend was at rugby.

Ma? (What I called her in private.) What race do you think my father is?

My big sister asked, what sort of question is that? Do you really want to know? Haven't I told you what I thought as we grew up? Surely I did.

Not that I recall.

If she said Negro then I would have to prepare myself to eat in coloured-only joints, be subject to other restrictions and racial prejudice.

Come on, Ma.

I think you look a bit like Dad, actually. And she broke out grinning.

This is serious.

So am I. You look quite a bit like him, especially when he was slimmer.

How can I look like him?

Maybe he rubbed off on you. I don't know. Might be you picked up some of his mannerisms. You certainly sing the same.

This was total confusion. Do I look like I've got Negro blood?

A bit of that too. Mata didn't drop a stitch. But if you stood beside

Henry Takahe, people would say you are his son.

Twelve hours driving there and back to hear this. Still not sure what category the Mississippi whites would put me in. Maybe I wouldn't go.

CHAPTER THIRTY-ONE

EVEN ON SKID ROW, WAKING up on park benches, you have moments of clearer thinking. I knew the year was 1952. In my mind I was the Dodger Jackie Robinson, hitting homers against the all-white teams. Before I'd fallen, before the war started, Joe Louis had been the heavyweight boxing champion knocking out the white men of the world. Told us we could do it too. Our athlete supreme Jesse Owens had stuck it right up Hitler at his own Berlin Olympics: Adolf had thought his kind was the master race till a Negro ran off with four gold medals, one of several Negro athletes who took gold at those games.

I thought of the musical giants — Duke, Cab, Brownie, Dizzy, Oscar, Ella, Mahalia, Billie, Charlie, Ray, Nat — the host of musical giants needing only first names, on the trail blazed by Louis Armstrong and every nigger with attitude who'd had the guts to stand up.

And where the fuck was this nigger?

Wiping vomit off my face, craving the next drink, wallowing in self-pity that had descended to unbearable self-loathing. Telling myself the same bullshit about serving my country only to be treated worse than a dog. Just another nigger drunk succumbed, convinced the system was too big to take on, no chance to make something of myself, eyes scanned for the miracle of a dropped coin, a fluke dollar on the park grass, someone to beg change from.

Then my eyes happened upon a newspaper page fluttering on a bench, like a hand beckoning. Under the headline BYE, BABY. FAREWELL, EMMETT I read of a fourteen-year-old Negro boy, Emmett Till, who was down from Chicago visiting relatives in Money, Mississippi. He had been showing pictures of his white girlfriend to his astonished Southern Negro cousins. Someone had dared the boy to say something fresh to a woman shop-owner.

So this unknowing kid said, bye, baby, to the white woman as he left her shop. Two days later several white men arrived and hauled Emmett out of his relatives' cabin to a car. He was found dead with an eye gouged out, a bullet in his stoved-in head.

Barely able to recognize her son in his horrifically beaten state, Emmett Till's mother decided on an open-casket funeral, *so the world can see.*

Now I had this newspaper page in my trembling hands, knowing I had to claim back my life: I owed it my children, to every unjustly murdered fourteen-year-old.

When I was fourteen myself I had daydreamed of riding around in an open-top car, blood-red with shiny chrome fittings and white upholstery, a trunk full of money, wind in my face and the air full of praise for Jess Hines, success story.

In my nightmares, though, the car wouldn't start, or it would break down in the middle of a street where crowds were about to call my name like churchgoers calling hallelujah to God. The beautiful white upholstery would be covered in shit, or smeared all over with blood coming inexplicably from my hand, so when I tried to wipe it, it only got worse.

I'd sense the vehicle being slowed by a dragging weight and look out back to see a nigger corpse roped to my new car, connected to it as if by an umbilical cord. Now, well into my adulthood, my eyes cleared and I saw the corpse was me, roped not to a fantasy car but to a bottle.

Selma, Alabama, couple years later. I'd fallen again, jumped a freight train, broke and broken again, riding with other nigger losers we all talked the same self-deluding promises how the next town we'd straighten up, get our shit together, the perfectly justifiable reasons we were down, wouldn't any man? We're niggers aren't we, with everything stacked against us?

Then she came back to me in a dream one night, as I sheltered in an abandoned building running with rats of feral and human kind.

I saw a little dog drowning in a river and I jumped in to save it. It stayed just out of my reach and kept disappearing, crying like a baby. We swept by scenery familiar, of my own growing up, past endless green seas of corn fields, dogs panting away summer heat beneath magnolia trees, always someone singing, the cool creek near our cluster of shacks, men drunk on liquor or the emotion they expressed in music, dusty roads, flies and meat going off.

Then we rounded a bend to sight of snow-capped mountains and forest quite unlike anything of my childhood. Ferns and towering trees with a menacing presence, formations written on the land by massive forces. Of course: New Zealand. The train journey to and from Two Lakes on the main trunk line.

Told the dog, we're in New Zealand. I think we'll be okay. Apparently we were for I managed to get a hold of him and he snuggled into me like a human and our wet journey seemed as if a new form of flight.

Next, the dog talked to me about how amazing the mountains were and was that snow we were seeing? I said, sure is. This is another country, kid, and we're in it.

For the next stretch I lost the talking dog, saw his frantic form swept swiftly toward rapids. Certain death. But in a moment the river turned to steaming waters boiling with heat, not current. Waiwera, I said. For some reason the boiling took away my fear for the dog. You'll be all right, boy. You'll see.

Sure enough, the dog changed to a child of about five, a cute little boy; we were high and dry on crusty white ground streaked yellow and smelling of sulphur.

The boy smiled at me. He looked like a quadroon. I said, what's your name? He said some Maori word. Asked did I know Lena? No, I don't know a Lena. Wait — of course I do. My memory, kid, what my drinking has done to it.

Looked where the boy pointed. A woman, completely naked,

emerging from a warm pool. Smiling — at me? Lena?

Hello, Jess. Been a long time.

At first I wanted to explain why I'd fallen down the drinking mine-shaft, to tell of my anger at being humiliated, how I could not face a life of always being at the bottom hardly better off than my slave ancestors. Then she put finger to her lips to tell me don't say anything. Beckoned me to her and we kissed and I started to run fingers most gentle over her shoulders, her neck—

I woke up. A rat running over my legs.

But I'm thinking: this really is the last time, Jess, or you'll die. Or worse, a white cop will put false charges on you and a white judge will throw you in the pen. The starting rate is five years for niggers. See if you survive that, dwelling on how Whitey got you even as you ran from him.

And that dream wouldn't leave me. Took a bit to remember Lena's surname as it was Maori and from years ago. Might be I'd shut it out because it was her married name. Takahe, that's right.

I would write her a letter. Even if full of lies on what I'd done with my life since the war.

To get a reply from New Zealand was unbelievable. She remembered me! Inside the envelope two letters. The second from *a son*. His photograph — what a fine-looking boy he was. All this time, a son. I broke down and cried. With added guilt that my self-despair had cost me my two daughters.

Lena wrote in a very neat hand, her tone restrained.

The marriage survived the birth of my son, she told me. She spoke mostly about the boy — my son too! — how well he did at school, how musical he was, and what a special air he had about him.

I attribute it to you. In fact my life has stayed quite dull since our unforgettable two weeks together. Though bringing up children has been a joy, and not least our — she said it: our — *son. The village gave him the name Yank. In the early days it meant something and of course felt like a knife in the heart to Henry. But we got used to it and it became just another name.*

Your letter arrived as if from the grave. My God, Jess, I still can't believe I'm writing to you.

Nor me reading her words.

My son wrote a good letter, quite articulate for a youth. He must be getting a good education, I thought: I knew many whites and Maoris went to the same schools, that segregation there was largely economic.

I read both letters over and over till I could have recited them. Studied every aspect of my boy's features in the two photographs he sent, tried to get inside the mind behind those dark eyes. My heart sang and sang. My sober heart: I'd not touched a drink since I left Selma.

My God, I have a son. A New Zealand, part Maori son.

Lena did not say what her husband did when he found out. Not something any soldier would like of course. But if ever I got to meet and talk with the man, I'd tell him it's not as bad as white people denying your contribution to the war, their humiliation of your race. Tell him it was war and did any soldier not sleep with prostitutes, local women in the different European countries? New Zealand, for that matter.

But it would have been bad a married man coming home to another's child, no denying that. And sure I would have apologized, if just to respect his manhood.

She asked me not to send photos of myself as she had never raised the subject of his true fatherhood with the boy, not one word. He had been called Yank — an irony when, in the Civil War, Southerners called northerners damned Yankees. (In the Second World War, every American got the tag, as a compliment without the *damned*.) Lena said Yank had this romantic notion his father was a white John Wayne or Elvis Presley, and Negro was the last notion in his mind. Let him mature first, Lena asked.

John Wayne, the Hollywood star we coloreds laughed at for the movie stereotype he was, of superior white hero. Elvis, well he was a Southern boy and his musical roots were greatly inspired by black musicians. We loved him. But I sure as hell don't bear a resemblance to Mister Presley.

I had moved back to a Negro settlement called Piney Woods, on land granted to a Negro slave by his admiring white owner, title locked up in a trust so no one could take it from whomever of Negro descent wished to live there and pay rent. Lived right beside my mother who naturally was glad to see her son seemed to have conquered his booze demon.

Working on highway construction raised one of the same old Southern problems: Niggers just didn't get paid well.

But I wanted to send my boy money. Maybe because in this country money speaks the loudest. Niggers kill for it. And certainly die from a lack of it. I wanted to impress the boy, so he'd think about one day coming over to meet — his daddy? His daddy.

While I was at it, I decided I should send some dollars off to my daughters in Biloxi . . . if I could track them down. Their mother had made less and less contact with the children's grandmother — my mother — and was sure to have moved several times. No choice. We're renters, usually. And desperate dollar-chasers.

How would I find some money?

Desperate people learn inventive ways to acquire the almighty greenback. And they don't have to be illegal, just a little shady. Got enough cash together to send to my daughters and to the son in New Zealand. Felt proud of myself, remembering the person not so far back in the past whose every dime went on his drinking habit.

CHAPTER THIRTY-TWO

HADN'T SEEN HIM FOR THREE years, heard he'd been sentenced to prison. Then he turned up on my doorstep. Chud, the con.

Came home from work each evening to him sitting there, like some alien brute with his size, pumped up muscles in tight-fitting tee-shirt even in autumn. Tattoos on his face, neck, arms. Worst of all, attitude as if inked permanently into him: my place was his place. Like we were bonded for life and didn't owe any standards to each other.

He filled his day waking late, doing press-ups and stomach exercises and shadow-boxing for a good hour. Have to stay in shape, Yank, or they'll get me. They being members of his world, certainly not mine. He walked the streets, sussed out burg possies, his prison language for burglary possibilities. The Chud I'd known had never been a thief. Sometimes he got greedy with food from living where there wasn't certainty the kids would have any. But a thief? Never.

Found we had virtually nothing to talk about, from a lifetime of knowing each other's very souls. Chud didn't take hints about looking for a job; he had no notion of paying rent. His upbringing no excuse — he owed me more than this Chud I did not know.

When he started messing around with my guitar, the expensive equipment, he was on dicey territory. He was incapable of taking even the most obvious hint. And I noticed he looked more like his father, lapsed easily into the same mannerisms as Ted. How ironic, to grow into a man like the one you most hate.

Chud spent his unemployment money on beer and cigarettes, bought not one crumb of food. I had started to resent his presence, even dislike him. But how could I be like this with my best friend?

Came home one evening to hearing his amplified voice and discordant notes — Chud on *my* microphone and a stranger violating *my* guitar. They'd been drinking.

No, I don't want a drink. And please don't use that equipment again, it cost a lot of money and if you don't know what you're doing, you can wreck it.

Who are you? the stranger asked, tattooed snake slithering around his neck. The guy had triple blue dots under his right eye, a practised intimidating sneer.

Who the hell are you? I shot back.

Don't talk to my mates like that.

This was Chud. With his own tone at me. I told Chud, this is me, Yank.

Chud said, yeah, but you can't talk like that to my pal.

I said, it's my flat. And my music equipment.

He said, Yank? You better say sorry.

My best friend a picture of naked threat and menace. I could smell the booze on his breath. He could have been his father. His mother.

Now his pal sidled up, acted all hurt. He might even throw the first punch.

Physical coward that I am, I told them my father had sent money. How about I give you fifty quid to get your own flat?

Chud: How much did he send you?

A hundred.

They looked at each other, maybe weighing it up in booze. Fucken lowlifes.

Had to put up with them one more night, taking over my small pad drinking and getting more and more incoherent. Just like Chud's parents, the other guy's too no doubt. Sleepless hours listening to their snoring; Chud slumped in the armchair fully dressed, his pal on the arm.

Arranged to meet them in my lunch break, after I withdrew my coward's levy. No sooner the cash in Chud's hand when he said, count yourself lucky. It's a bad thing to insult a con. With a look that said, you'll keep.

Came home to missing records and they'd even emptied the fridge of food and two bottles of beer. My closest friend like a figure in a dream: walking further and further into the distance.

CHAPTER THIRTY-THREE

HE'S BACK, THAT TROUBLED BOY, now of magnificent physique and so tall, taller than my Yank. With trouble written all over him. And what are those blue tattoo marks under each eye? They look ridiculous, like a child trying to impress. Spider web tattooed round his neck. If he thinks this is old Maori warrior markings, he's mistaken. Those tattoos were *earned*, their application *endured*.

If Chud is anything he's more like a slave who has surrendered himself. Not to others but to the loveless raising he had. But that's no excuse, not even for him, the boy I know like my own son. We all have to rise above adversity.

He's leaning against the bridge railing, has back to the sounds of kids below in the river, not for a moment the same happy, penny-diver kid I knew. This is a grown man oozing anger.

Hello, Chud. How are you, honey?

I step up to give him a kiss, but he pulls back. I turn the greeting to a handshake. His grip limp for such a powerful man; means something is being said here or something is gone. What do I say? Can hardly ask, when did you get out? We all know he graduated to prison for violence.

How long you back for? He shrugs. Staying at home? He nods.

Caught up with Yank yet? His eyes say yes, but without a warm glow. I bet he was pleased to see you.

Just then his eyes meet mine.

No, he wasn't.

I'm quite shocked. My Yank . . . wasn't pleased to see you? Are you—

He wasn't. Ask him.

I watch him walk off, turn off down the dirt path to his parents' house. Walks like his stupid father, arms out playing Mister Tough Guy.

Barney tells me, acting out the movements, that Chud was a good football player. Boy had it all, he demonstrates: strong tackler, fast, good fend, sidestep, and up here plenty of brain power too, most important of all. But thumbs-down to any suggestion Chud would have made it to the top level. We all know why.

As if holding prison bars, Barney indicates Chud's certain destiny now. Clicks tongue at the waste of talent. A throat-cutting action to say Chud might take revenge, means the parents. He points at a hot pool, imitates a dead body, upraised fingers to say two. I nod yes, a strong possibility. A deserving fate too.

Where you off to, Lena?

Post office, to pay the bills. Want to walk with me?

I crook my arm as I've done for some years now, knowing he doesn't need it, it's only a gesture to say he's loved, to say he deserves respect. I am always afraid he'll give the show away one day and just grab and kiss me as a lover out in the open. But maybe we're such an unlikely pair to be an item we're above suspicion.

Funny thing, I don't fear discovery as much I used to. Yet I know it isn't Barney I want to live with, I'm stuck with Henry and perhaps Henry is stuck with me. Maybe I carry on with Barney to put some spice in my life, trying to confirm I am not a dull person living a dull life.

What happens when you want to break away from what you've been used to all your life? I did it once and look what happened. But who is the person I found back then, the woman Jess liberated? A good-time girl who went back into her shell and has never been seen since? (It can hardly count sleeping with a man psychologically impaired like Barney.) What is anyone in this life if not where and what they were born?

Lena, you know dwelling on such things only gets you mixed up.

I called Yank at work to ask what happened between him and his best mate. Got told why and understood. But I also understood Chud. Determined I'd run into him soon and see if we could have a heart to heart.

When they were little Yank and Chud would play-act as babies, make baby sounds, basic baby words, crawling, wailing. Started by Chud to, I think, claim back the innocence stolen from him.

Chud would act the baby part so well it bothered me. More than once I made excuse to interrupt this play-acting because he was too real.

Lena will hear you out, Chud. Hug you, make things right again with Yank, help you find a place of your own. Before you up and murder your parents one day.

CHAPTER THIRTY-FOUR

THE MORTAR SHELL EXPLOSION TOOK not just his brother's life but the memories leading up to the event. Now and then his mind would give back images, seeming to promise a sequence he could lay his old memory on. But always the pictures broke up and fell quickly away, like a dream just starting to mean something.

All those twenty years Barney did not know how he had lost his ability to speak. He did remember the extremely difficult cliff-face climb that had taken most of the day. A unit of five, under Captain Henry Takahe's command (and his idea), had gone up to silence a machine-gun and mortar nest inflicting heavy damage on the main division. Seven gruelling hours it took to scale the cliff; certain death waiting for just one mistake.

Not a hundred yards away the enemy had backs to the raiders. Closer, they counted eight mounted machine-guns and five mortar guns. Henry indicated the ratio — twenty men to five — with twice-splayed hands; even managed to convey by smile that the smaller number had advantage of surprise. This tiny Maori hit squad aching to do battle.

The Germans were talking and laughing, passing bottles of liquor between them, as five brown-skinned men far from their native soil slithered like serpents towards them.

Then Henry indicated all was on the line: follow my lead. Wordlessly he told them, soon, boys. Soon they are ours.

The sun disappears behind us, turning the enemy into silhouettes. Makes their talk and laughter so out of place, I get the thought: this is what a murderer does in civilian life. He wants solely and singularly to commit murder. No feeling could be more wonderful.

My heart is pumping from the exertion of this last hundred yards, even more dangerous than the cliff, for it would be shameful to die at the enemy's hand after gaining the surprise.

Henry has us fanned out; he is leading from the rear to have the situation tactically covered. We love him as a man, a leader, would follow him to hell.

They cease to be human — have to, with the continual exchange in their guttural language, helmeted shapes passing booze around and laughing — I want only hand-to-hand combat, only a fight to the death: man to man, not mowing them down with combined tommy-gun fire. Though we sure as hell intend to finish off their booze and haka to their corpses, show their entire war-mongering nation our warrior contempt.

I am my fighting ancestor, Kereama Heretaunga, wanting to feel an enemy's life ebb from him. To cut off his head and spit contempt in his dead face, to cook and eat him.

My hatred turns to sweat like a breached dam.

We're used to their machine-gun fire raking the slope; their mortars lobbed everywhere a man might be; their blockage of the only pass within miles and miles of mountainous country. As our small unit nears them they begin a time-regulated firing attack down on our main body's position. We use the noise to move quicker with less caution, close the gap to less than fifty yards. I can smell blood like rose water.

The wind blows our way, stronger up here, exposed. Climbing the cliff there was not even a breath of wind. We can smell the alcohol, catch the tobacco drifts, cordite and smell of hot metal.

One of them turns to take a leak.

And as he stands there, full frontal, he must perceive the uneven shapes lumped up on ground he knows well. For now he yells. The bastard has seen us!

We open fire. Less than our optimum distance and they've chance to hunker down, even as we see them fall, the flailing of arms to the deadening sky, the sudden disappearance of a figure from sitting on sand bags. We haven't got all of them.

Caught by surprise ourselves we become individuals.

I see Henry's arm frantically ordering us forward. He stands up. So my brother and I stand up and we run at a crouch, firing. The night flamed with machine-gun fire our way. I stand full height and fire at the spitting flames. See one source go out, extinguished. And I dive to the ground. Give no thought to my brother nor anyone else.

A grenade explodes in their midst, briefly lit bodies akimbo, clawing at air at life departing. So close we might see their eye whites if light to do so. My brother's arm moves, he yanks me flat and near instantly comes the explosion from the second grenade, his. We hear German screams, the thunder of machine-guns; see the orange-red flames and fire streaks of hundreds of bullets.

Then the distinct thump of a metal object landing nearby. Wet sticky stuff everywhere on me. My brother has gone, he's just not there. I'm wiping away flesh bits and, I quickly figure, shattered brain matter.

Look around to see Charlie Raimona leap into the trench, firing as he spins. Germans fall. Another figure — I think it's Henry — fires into the Germans from the side. Charlie drops. The figure is not Henry, it's Tona Daniels; he's stopped firing. Now uses his machine-pistol as a club, screams in Maori. Screams.

Can't get the gore off me. My mind in blind panic against the unbearable. Not Harold. Not my baby brother. I was supposed to look after him.

But this is a fight for life now, so I've thrown my two grenades. Press close to the ground with the whump, rush of air and ear-splitting noise breaking free of the grenade. The firing at us has stopped.

Get to the edge of the trench and there is nothing but dead bodies. Two wearing our uniform. Take out my brother and that leaves only two of us.

From the side a figure emerges and I turn to fire—

It's Henry! he yells.

Something about his appearance bothers me. But not as much as the wetness soaked into my jacket, through my shirt, blood I know isn't mine.

As if my mind has caught up, I am only concerned with what covers me. Must remove every last gory piece of flesh and brain before it claims me. Something going wrong with my mind: I'm trembling all over. A grown man about to bawl like a baby.

There is a last thought Henry was cowering down to the side of the enemy trench. Then next day I'm being brought back in a jeep, stricken and mute. Disconnected. I know only to grieve for my beloved brother. Know only that I cannot and will not return home until this war is over, filled with guilt and shame that I've have failed in my duty to look after my kid brother.

Twenty years it has stayed there in the lightless vaults. I have made love with Lena at my home and we have done our act of walking, my hand in her crooked arm, to my seat by the bridge. Something is going on in my mind.

At first I think it's a new geyser breaking out, a rumbling, a shuddering it seems of the earth. I turn to Lena and see she is registering no more than the overcast afternoon and, I hope, the quiet satisfaction of our love-making.

Then it feels like my ear has popped, as if finally I have reached the surface after two decades down in some mental place of darkness. For I hear myself say quite clearly, Lena? Did you hear something? When since then I have never been able to speak her name in full, nor many other words.

The shock she turned my way was understandable. I was shocked myself. And soon memories were pouring in like breached sandbags.

What did you say, Barn?

Afraid to attempt to repeat lest it be a fluke, I used the old gestures to ask if she had heard a rumbling like geysers close by?

No, she shook her head. But, Barney? You spoke a whole sentence.

Yes, I had uttered something in full for the first time since that evening in Italy. The evening Henry Takahe hid himself till the danger was over.

CHAPTER THIRTY-FIVE

WE'RE AT MY FLAT, PARTYING hard with our latest batch of female groupies, the band members sniggering to each other that if there is no other reward to being a muso then we'll be satisfied.

Have my eye on a woman about my age, so darkly exotic she can't possibly be from this country, but I'm playing hard to get because that's a band member's privilege. The bourbon is going down well too. A drink I discovered is the perfect means of throwing off inhibitions so I can completely cut loose on the stage.

The girls are pestering us to provide live music, but we prefer to play recorded stuff so we can work our verbal magic on them. Tonight has been another sell-out gig. And a promoter has offered us big city venues. We're on our way.

Still, I dream of going with my father Jess to clubs, low lit and menacing, likely some patrons are carrying guns, an entirely coloured clientele, but I'll be feeling at home with my own kind. Drinking together, talking as men, wallowing in the music, discussing every technical and emotional detail, father and long-lost son.

This woman I'm watching refuses to meet my eyes. I ask around: who is she? No one knows; she arrived with another woman who is all over Nigel and kind of left her companion isolated. (I can never look at Nigel and not think of what his mother and I are doing. But do I feel guilt? No. Just feels strange and I don't think he for one moment suspects a thing. He even suggested he move into the flat with me and I had to make excuse about not knowing how long I wanted to stay here.)

Over I go, introduce myself. Ask who she is — you don't look like a New Zealander.

I am from Brazil. And you?

And me? Don't you know? I'm the lead singer.

Of what?

Of the band. My vanity a little pricked.

Oh, she says. I meant what country are you from?

New Zealand, of course.

My friend invited me only one hour ago. I came down from Auckland where I am studying at university my last year. I hope you don't mind?

Hell no. For she — Giselle — is quite the most beautiful and exotic female I've ever laid eyes on.

We talk for a bit and she soon has me completely under her spell, when normally it's the other way round. One of the perks of being in a band, you don't have to chase hard. Her accent, the teasingly direct eye contact, the private jokes dancing in her eyes, make me aware our women are limited in how they express. And if she's impressed by my lead singer status, she is hardly falling over herself.

While talking, I get a thought that maybe my mother looked similar to Giselle when she was twenty-two, same copper complexion, high cheekbones, green eyes . . . Christ, maybe I am falling for my mother. Ridiculous. I just love Mum and naturally would be attracted to someone of similar features.

She's studying English, visiting Two Lakes because, she says with a slow smile, everyone does. A world tourist destination, yes?

I ask if she has seen Waiwera yet.

Yes. Yesterday. It was amazing.

I'm from there. I could show you sights even more amazing, if you'd like?

Yes, I think next time I am here? Maybe it is worth a special trip, you think? Gives me this come-on smile. I'm hers.

You have to see it more than once to appreciate it properly.

Like people, yes?

She has it all, looks, style, what to say. Did you drive down from Auckland? Bus? Train? She came by train. We chat on, I'm falling for her. The bourbon helps.

We talk tastes: she's been raised on Latin music, but likes blues and this new trend called soul. You do? Yes, very much. I run through some famous singers' names, she knows them, of course she does.

Every Brazilian loves black music; we are a mix of races including Negro.

Then I see something about her features, complexion, and the question just comes out.

Do you have Negro in you?

She smiles and says, do you?

Well. My first response is to deny. Been living that father fantasy too long. But find myself nodding and she nods back and then we're mirroring grins.

In New Zealand I have met only one Negro, a Nigerian studying at my university. I was sure I could see the Negro in you, though of course I thought it impossible. You know you could pass for a Brazilian?

I tell my story. She tells hers: mother half Negro, half Portuguese; father French. Like we're long-lost cousins.

I will show you the samba, the rumba. If you are as you say, it will be easy. If not? Her facial expression replaces a shoulder shrug.

Latin American, Nigel? Like ordering a cocktail: he can whip up any form of music. He grabs my acoustic guitar and starts a Latin beat. Giselle so pleased she kisses him — on the lips. And I'm jealous. He's developed into rather a handsome critter, with his mother's good looks. Warn him with my eyes she's mine — buddy. I'm the guy who's sleeping with his mother. But who said life is rational?

Now, being taught dance steps by an exotic foreigner, I'm hers dangling on a string. Just like my mum. Her dance steps don't take long to pick up and she is a superb mover. Lifts me a few notches, the whole room cheering us on. This could be the war years and I my mother expressing what she always wanted, and filled with lust.

Never have I seen a woman so without inhibitions, not on a dance floor. In bed Isobel gives herself fully. But to dance like this is sex in itself.

And everyone knows it, clapping in time, moving with their own sexual urges. Nigel is lost in acoustic guitar samba beat, we go right into the mood set. Time stands still.

That is, until I see a woman far too old for this company.

Isobel.

Is there something flawed about me that I have gone from hopelessly in love with this much older woman, only a few weeks ago gladly lost in her naked intimacy, to staring at her as if an unwelcome stranger?

But then what is she doing here at this hour, unannounced, a married woman past forty at our party?

A night of mirrors. Nigel's mother gives me the same jealous looks I gave him. Giselle looks too much like my mother. And I'm a born slut, not as if I'm doing it out of insecurity. I'm just a slut. Like my mother who is sleeping with Barney and thinks I don't know. Henry was right: he married a slut. Who gave birth to one.

She claimed her visit wasn't planned. Nigel and I the only ones who cared she was present and for different reasons, and I had to make damn sure mine were not showing. Unable to sleep, she claimed, she went for a drive and saw my flat lights on. Hoped we didn't mind if she dropped by for just a little while and anyway she hadn't seen Nigel for some weeks.

I made the introductions. What the hell. Isobel chatted amiably with Giselle while Nigel and I whispered to the other women to play it down till his mother had gone.

Next minute Giselle walked over and said thank you, I think you will make a good dancer. Goodbye.

Isobel sort of eased over, sipping on her drink with studied interest.

An absolute classical beauty, she said. Something our gene pool lacks in this isolated country — variation of breeders. She's part Negro too.

I wondered where this was going. Isobel stepped closer, so no one would hear.

I told that young woman I'm sleeping with you and intend doing so again very soon.

I'm not in the least flattered.

Saw this woman old enough to be my mother. I'd get Giselle's phone number from her friend. Though when I looked around Giselle's friend was gone too. And my old lover was giving glances I thought too obvious.

She said, you listen here, young man. Our relationship works both ways. You have said it's given you so much understanding. Well, perhaps you'd better ask what I want out of it.

Made me feel my age. Jesus.

CHAPTER THIRTY-SIX

HE ARRIVES LATE AT NIGHT at Falls Bath to find someone in the pool. Can't see who it is, but his name is spoken: Chud? Is that you? Knows the voice. Knows all the voices of her family for all the good relieving years of their loving him. Except Henry.

Wiki?

Yeah, it's me. What are you doing here this late, Chud?

Dunno. What are you doing?

I couldn't sleep. Soaking in here makes me sleepy. My father's snoring like he always does, sounds like a lion or something.

Or something, Chud mutters, aware of his discomfort, being taken by surprise. We don't have lions.

Try sleeping at our house after Dad's been drinking.

He can make out her shape but it has no face. Still, female presence alone stirs something within him.

It has felt like a cancerous growth, telling the boy and now the man: *no woman has slept with me.* Meaning he is loveless, still. Being around females is worse than uncomfortable. When it was girls he just wasn't at ease. Now it's women.

What to say, where do the words come from to speak to them? How can I feel relaxed with a woman? He figures the learning comes from parents, following their example, picking up ways and means of getting on or just being together. That a closeness with a female is a conversation times a hundred, a thousand, linked to form a whole. He knows that his discomfort becomes their discomfort, which becomes his added burden, as if shouting from the mountaintops his inadequacy with the female sex. Hell, he doesn't even know how to say hello, would you like a dance, a date, to talk?

The light bulb popped not long after I got here, Wiki says. Has to raise her voice to be heard above the pounding of falling water.

Chud is grateful: at least he can speak in the dark. You're not scared of ghosts are you?

Nah. That's for kids. You?

Well, sometimes. Walk around here and it sounds like murder being done, hearing the steam trying to get out a crack.

I don't believe in ghosts. How you been, Chuddy? Haven't seen you in a while. You tell my brother we haven't seen him at home in a while, either.

Now Chud has something to give him an emotional toehold, whereas before he feared he was in danger of toppling.

I think you better tell him. He's got too big for his boots far as I'm concerned.

Yeah. I dropped in with a friend a couple of weekends ago and he wouldn't let me in. Said it was his sleep-in time.

He might have had someone with him.

So? I'm his sister. And he could have just told me.

Could be he's got carried away with being the lead singer in a band known all over town?

Could be he's forgotten who his family is.

And his friends.

When Chud sees a woman he desires he dries up. Can barely make eye contact, reads her every worst signal back and never sees encouragement, let alone returned desire. In his mind a woman is an impossible mystery. He fears rejection like a mortal blow to his heart. Like the innocent boy punished yet again.

Still, my bro is a nice guy. Wiki's voice from not quite pitch black: he can see her head and shoulders outline, a bit of moonlight up there, a few stars . . . And he is your best friend.

Not now.

He can see no shoulder strap to say she is wearing anything. The words *naked female* flash through his mind like food scent to a dog. But the human pulls him back saying, she's like your own sister.

He swallows — gulps, more like it — the sinful urge.

You have an argument? Friends do, you know. You'll make it up. You two, I've always seen as one person. You know?

Yeah. *Naked female.*

You getting in?

Is he getting in? What, with a naked young woman, even one he knows like a sister? That urge again, but stronger this time, the warning words as if drowned out by the same water-on-water sound making her, the naked female, raise her voice. *You have never slept with a woman. Felt a woman's intimate touch . . . her skin, her mouth, her sex.*

I was.

Doesn't say further that now he cannot get into the pool. *You have never slept with a woman.* Not I. You. Like the wallflower at the dance, sitting there seething, feeling unwanted. Angry.

When he sees a man, however, Chud's mind is clear, working out how to fight him. Can read every signal, conscious or concealed, as if one of Yank's books lent by Mrs post office Mac. Yank's *friend.* Who taught Yank things, but never took Chud into her confidence.

If other males were books then Chud would be the most well-read man around. He can read cowardice from fifty paces, smell fear from twenty. He can look into a man's eyes and know the courage, the doubts he carries, to an exact measurement. He can tell in a few seconds if a man is left or right-handed. He knows which way the other's best blows will come from and is ready with counter punches written like words on a page.

And how does a man of twenty-one admit he's still a virgin when to other men he's the kingpin, formidable man of iron fists? It must follow that, when he's out of incarceration, without the steel bars every way he looks, women would be drawn to him, his physical power, his scary reputation. They are not.

Can't weep, grieve. He's just alone, in an isolated place, the kid Lena Takahe called Boyboy.

Come on, hop in. We can't see each other nude, too dark. And anyway, you're like my brother.

Life, it has just never stopped hurting. *Hurting.* But can't tell anyone. He would have confided in Yank who used to be a brother, but Yank rejected him, though maybe that was understandable.

Come on, it must be freezing out.

Don't feel like it.

Well I'm getting out and you don't want to be seeing me without clothes.

No I don't. When he does. No, he does not. He does.

I bet your old man snores like a pig, she says.

He is a pig.

You said it.

You know it.

What do we call your old lady?

Can try bitch to start with.

My mother is a saint.

Not what some people say.

Who cares what they say? She's the best mother and been pretty good to you too, Chuddy. You talking about what they call her?

Some do. I don't. She's been good to me.

My mother was and is a very beautiful woman.

Like you.

Thank you, Chud.

Other than the waterfall there is silence.

How old are you now, Wiks?

Seventeen.

Makes her a woman. A year past legal age. You've never slept with a girl, you over there standing in the corner like the class dunce, the unwanted, unloved boy. *This is your chance. There'll never be another opportunity like this, never.*

Love is but a few waded steps from you, in undressed state. That close.

That close, Chud, you can reach out and touch her. Do whatever you like with her. To her. Whatever you like, big powerful man your own village never understood, with your anger, what those shit parents did to you.

Well right now, Boyboy, you can claim one of those experiences. Just grab it, lay it down on the thermally warmed concrete, and *take* what has been denied you.

Hearing the scratching sound of towel against her body, barely visible other than movements and a vague shape, that ceaseless pounding of water.

They have stopped talking. The waterfall echoes deafeningly in the changing area, sound hitting an iron-clad wall with a roof overhang. Means anything he does, no matter how gentle, cannot be explained with words of affection, even a hand on her shoulder cannot be followed with request that they get to know each other maybe differently. Dark frees him from cowardice in the face of a woman, but noise traps him: no move can be innocent without words.

He rises from the long wooden bench, without clear intention, all instinct now. Feels his trembling, maybe aware of fearing — for himself, what he might do, what he is capable of — and makes to walk past her.

Wiki? I got to get past, he says with raised voice. As there is little space between her and the pool.

What? she says. Damn noisy in here. They should have a place for spare light bulbs so least we can see. Might be down here with a freak.

He stops at hearing the word. Did she call me a freak? Or was that the echo effect? Close enough to kiss her, fondle those full woman breasts, fuck her. That close.

Somehow he catches her smile in that barely moonlit dark. Somehow he hears her unshouted words telling him if he gets any closer, well.

Well.

Well what? You dressed yet, Wiks?

Not yet, no. Why do you ask?

I don't know. Just did.

And I said no. Not yet.

So close, he thinks. I could do anything I like.

You must be cold sitting here all this time, Chud. Why didn't you get in?

Chud wondering how he can pick out her words that previously were garbled or swallowed by the thunder of water.

I didn't bring a towel.

So why did you come here, a bathing pool, with no towel? Hmm, Chuddyboy?

Asks himself that: why did I come down here? Guess the same reason I roam all over, not just my village but the township, suburban streets, walking, walking, never finding because I never own up to what I'm looking for.

He says, with more than normal voice, I was just out walking.

She says, oh? How boring. Just walking.

Well, as I can't fly. Grinning, when he knows she can't see it. And he has not moved past her, not one fraction. Nor has she moved out of his way. So close he could merely lift a finger and make contact with her bare skin. Skin he can sense like danger, like love at last, in closest proximity.

Chud?

Yeah?

What's your real name?

What's your brother's real name?

You know it's Mark. Now tell me.

The breath of her words up into his face. The drumming of the water. Beating of his heart. Please don't let me do something bad, he asks of himself, perhaps the better self.

It's a stupid name. Don't want to tell you.

The Pakeha version of my name is Victoria. Know who she was?

Nope.

She was an English queen. You know the one they've got a statue of at Marsden Park. All covered in birdshit. Wiki chuckles. My dad says no matter what you do, how important you are, one day you'll get shat on.

Her laugh a whoosh of air against his throat.

Then she says up under his chin, gee, you sure grew tall. He only has to bend his head and he could be kissing her. Only has to reach out and he could be fondling her.

Come on. Tell me the name they gave you.

Michael.

That's a nice name. Got class.

Got arse, you mean. A sissy name. Doesn't suit, either.

Suit what — this place?

My place. Fucken home.

Whoo, you got some feeling about that haven't you?

Wouldn't you?

Oh yes. Be a nightmare, parents like you had. But still.

Still what? Still a nightmare?

Which turns into sweet dreams. Sometimes, Chud. If you really want it to.

Oh yeah? But he says it without conviction. In fact with a plea, for reassurance. Like a frightened kid asking a friend to whistle in their shared dark.

Yeah, she says. She puts the magic wand of touch upon him, just his wrist, but it lights up the world the universe.

He reaches out — doesn't have to hardly move — and finds bare skin, warm, alive, as soft as a pleasant dream, like floating on your back in that there warm pool.

Wiki?

Yeah?

Wiki.

Wiki who shuts off his words, who reaches up and pulls him down to her. Joins her mouth with his. Joins up his broken life. Mends his heart. Saves his soul.

No more the refrain in his aching mind he has never been with a woman. No more.

CHAPTER THIRTY-SEVEN

IT WASN'T QUITE THE MIRACLE first thought, Barney's recovery. Lena described him as reverting, which seemed to irritate him — connotations perhaps of a weaker man.

The bench seat they shared was bedded right by a large pool of super-heated water that had cut its own deep channel a good eighty yards to the river, forming a snake-like, yard-wide stream of boiling fury. The higher sulphur output made for a permanent stench. No place for sightseers. And yet, as Lena got to observe, a form of life — green algae — thrived in places, just on the fringes of pools, shallows at less than boiling point. She saw them as hopes surviving every one of life's disappointments. As a dream still with chance of coming true.

To be able to converse fully was indeed a miracle. At first. And so too did the love-making take on more literal meaning, for Barney could express in words, take it beyond the physical, articulate the assumed. Tell her he loved her, how much he admired her strength.

In this tree-guarded private domain, he now did most of the talking. She teased he couldn't be shut up. They laughed about it. Talking rugby again (his own remembered games), getting a bit tiresome, but Lena listened patiently. For his ego's sake, for a sportsman's pride too, respect for an old soldier. Or so she thought.

Are you listening? Barney jolted Lena from her thoughts, from a sightless fix on the raging stream, a patch of emerald algae.

Sorry. Forgot where I was. You know how it is. And now you can tell me how it is, yes? Knew she was being somewhat patronising, but rugby bored her and as for the war, her view would always be affected by her experience back then: Yank's birth, the woman Jess coaxed out and she could never get back.

Back Barney went to a grand final game the same year world war broke out. The regained voice had given back his looks, put life into his handsome features, no question. Except a voice is but an echo of what goes on within, Lena was deciding. It is a mirror of a person's character.

Several days ago he had talked a good two hours on his war experiences. Luckily, he had lost it and started grasping at words. She told him to give it a rest, meaning give her respite. Wished he'd just quit talking and try contemplation, make love to her — anything except chatter.

Barney took the hint and headed off while she strolled aimlessly; found herself at Merita's metal mail box, three newspapers sitting there. Most odd.

Merita was not ailing as Lena had assumed, just that the kids had not got into a routine of bringing her newspapers and mail up daily. She grumbled: This modern crop of young people have little respect for their elders. In the old days our word was law. Seemed pleased to see Lena, to get her newspapers.

Smell of urine was strong though the old dear kept an immaculate house, including the dirt floor. Lena visited only once or twice a year; knew her son and Merita had a special relationship. Lena liked to remove her shoes to feel the thermal warmth, the incongruous slightly damp feel of earth underfoot inside a constructed dwelling.

Too chilly to sit outside. Merita made tea, asked how Yank was doing, said what a good kid he was — and I know who's responsible. Then looked at Lena in a curious way.

You remind me of her. Margaret. Maggie we called her.

Guide Maggie?

Ae. That's who you remind me of.

But she was legendary. Lena felt there was no comparison. Maggie's photograph was in most of the older people's houses, Merita's too: a standard tourist portrait of the famous Waiwera guide standing in front of an exquisitely carved meeting house with her equally beautiful sister, Bella. I think you're comparing a rose to a daisy, you old tease.

The daisy who could have been a rose? Still could be?

The old woman squinted hard at Lena, tightened her mouth which made the wrinkles fold over her spiralling chin tattoo, inked lips turn to thin dark lines.

Maybe. But the children came first.

As they must . . . but not every moment of your life, girl.

No one else to take care of them. And they've turned out pretty good, haven't they?

Oh, yes. Specially him. Merita didn't even need to say the name. But what about you? How have you turned out?

How do you mean?

Well, you're not happy.

No. Not sad either.

You of all people deserve some happiness.

Only time I tried look what happened.

I think you're trying again. Aren't you?

So she knew. Lena shrugged wasn't going to bother denying. Merita's eyes were saying no, Barney is not your type.

Go over and look in that mirror, girl, Merita pointed.

But Lena wasn't inclined, neither for foolish confirmation nor to indulge even a venerated figure like Merita.

She was our most beautiful woman, Maggie. Half-caste, we could close our eyes when she spoke English and swear it was an upper-class Pakeha speaking. Her Maori was equally beautiful; she spoke the classical, poetic form full of metaphors. You know metaphors, child?

Now I do. My son passed on some of his school learning. You know they didn't try and teach us that much at the local native school. Thought we were all dumb.

Yes. Dumb and the females assumed to have no personality. Why I married a boring man — so I could shine! Merita's laugh a dry cackle.

Maggie had married an aristocrat Englishman, gone and lived for a while on a big estate in England. Sometimes the newspapers ran articles on this beautiful Maori woman who had adapted so well to upper-class

English life. And now Lena approached the portrait hanging on Merita's wall. Looked at it.

That's you, the old lady told her.

Lena turned, but not to deny. It excited her that someone from this village could go so far beyond her world, back in those times.

Except you're still here, my dear.

With a husband who's a very rough version of Maggie's English aristocrat, Lena said. A husband of much mana who is greatly respected around here, and beyond.

But whose mana didn't stop you from — from being yourself. Would I be right?

You mean my American? Being myself? With him, I guess I was. Not sure who I was back then.

Anything but what you still are now, dear. I got eyes, old that I am. Now do as I asked: go and look in that mirror. Please. For your old Aunty M.

So, she is looking at herself in the mirror. And Merita, shortened of already quite short stature, shuffles up and thrusts up alongside Lena's face the photograph from the wall.

Do you see what I mean?

Lena struggling with being compared.

Same hair. Same proud features that I told your son came from high-born lineage — just to make him feel better about himself. Look at her eyes. Are they not yours, almond-shaped and with dreams of elsewhere? Of yearning to be other than where she was born and expected to stay?

There is a similarity, no denying. Lena flicks between the black and white photograph and her own reflection.

You're not going to tell me she is my real mother. Lena, jokingly.

No, but you could be her daughter. Lena, this can still be your home, without you living here. I always told my children to go beyond Waiwera, unique and pleasant though it is. I saw it in you when you were sixteen, seventeen, perhaps younger.

Saw what?

Hunger. Yearning. Born with a mind, a personality that can never be satisfied, not until you try things, see for yourself. Born under a star that keeps you restless inside. You need to go and seek it out.

I thought I tried, a long time ago. She turns from the mirror. What if I never find it? What if it all means nothing in the end? What will I have then?

Not my questions to answer, my dear. They're yours. But no answers here in this village, Lena. And you always have your children. Now, where did you put my newspapers?

CHAPTER THIRTY-EIGHT

THE MAN CAME UP TO the front desk and asked to book four double bedrooms; he was a local and his guests were overseas business friends. Even though he dressed casually, his clothes looked expensive. He paid in advance with a business cheque, commented that he looked forward to his guests touring the sights of Waiwera.

Lena told him of her fill-in role as a guide, that she never tired of showing visitors around her village, how she always found something new herself.

His cheque bore the name Welsford Enterprises Ltd; he introduced himself as Ralph, managing director. And did she know that for all his international travel he still rated Waiwera's thermal sights as the best he'd seen?

Henry came along just then, nodding formally as he passed, in keeping with his manager's role being taken seriously even by his own wife. He never lingered; it was a wonder he employed her here in his domain.

This morning Henry had woken her early and had his way before he went for a bath. Two weeks earlier he had repeatedly slapped her over something so minor she could not remember it. So, much as he had mellowed over the years, the leopard still had spots.

Ralph said his visitors were from America and a wry smile must have shown on Lena's face for he asked, why the smile, had he said something wrong, did she not like Americans?

She looked up at him, instinctively judging whether to trust the man; found herself chuckling.

Oh, I like Americans all right, some would say too much. On one occasion at any rate.

He was trying to read her face and with his own smile forming. Looked such a worldly man. A few years older than she.

He said, not sure what you mean. And by the way, I don't know your name. It's Mrs . . . ? Looking at her wedding ring, which had long felt a farce.

Lena Takahe. That was my husband who just went past. He's the manager.

Ralph Welsford's face fell. He's Henry Takahe, right? I've heard about him. A fine man. Sorry, your comment about Americans must have confused me, as I thought—

Lena stopped him by holding up one finger. One American, I meant. Back in the war days.

Wondering why she had told this to a complete stranger. He was distinguished, but not handsome. Greying, probably prematurely. Very self-confident which gave him a certain presence. The sort of man who could own several hotels like this, and other businesses, and not bat an eyelid. Not that she knew anyone so wealthy.

And do you regret it? The question came softly, as if for no ears except hers.

She shook her head and gave a firm little smile, her gaze unblinking. No.

Ralph shrugged, said, how interesting. Everyone our age remembers them here during the war. I missed out on military service because I—

Had flat feet? Every man says that. Especially round here as Maori men are so ashamed if they didn't fight in the war. Are there that many flat feet?

You didn't let me finish. I had two children and of course a wife.

Lena said she was only kidding. Told of her being pregnant when Henry volunteered and him not mentioning that fact to the recruiting authorities. She did not mention having had a child to the American. Not yet, might be going too far. Might put him off.

Ralph lingered, even while Lena took care of a hotel guest. When they resumed talking, he spoke of his love of Waiwera gained from a school friend, someone whose name Lena knew.

As high schoolers Ralph and his Waiwera buddy had roamed the place, known every nook and cranny, every thermal hot spot. But he kept me away from the river. Maybe that's where I got my hunger for money from, seeing all you lot making this easy pocket money from the tourists. My parents didn't approve of the inter-racial friendship, wanted to send me off to a private school. Old-school thinkers themselves, born into a little bit of money and a big bit of silly class and race snobbery. That friend, by the way, manages my Wellington branch these days. And I told my parents, just to let them know: you treat people as you find them.

Lena thinking, as you find me, mister, more and more interested.

Figuring that Henry's roaming route as manager would bring him back this way, she said she had better get on with her duties.

But Ralph just stood there. Staring but trying to make out he wasn't.

Then he said, this is one foolish move if I'm reading it wrong, but would you like to meet up again somewhere more private?

The Lena who responded was not the same person of the last twenty years. This Lena got frightened and excited in the same moment and let out another Lena who started sorting through office papers and answered, I don't think you read it wrong. Without the slightest tremor in her voice.

Looked up at him then and in a normal voice said, thank you, Mr Welsford. Those rooms are confirmed and here is your receipt. In handing it over she asked, and where might this more private place be? Let her eyes do all the talking.

But heart now hammering. Hammering. Not least because Henry was heading this way.

Ralph handed over a business card. Call the private number after six, any night.

And your wife?

Long gone.

See you again, sir. Good evening.

Ralph was at the door going out when Henry sidled up to reception. Talkative bloke wasn't he?

Yes, Lena said. You get those. A good friend of Tip Taiaroa.

Oh, he must be Ralph whatshisname—

Welsford, Lena said. Thinking: you were inside me this morning yet barely look at me. Offer not one little intimate touch to say we are husband and wife. You hit me. You root me. It's all the same to you.

I hear Tip's done very well, one of the man's managers. Good on him. Wish we had more Maoris in managerial positions. Walked on, oblivious to his wife's state, of her wanting him to turn around and for once say he loved her. Yet wanting him to walk right out of her life so she might be quite another person again.

Staring after her husband with electric signals and lights flashing in her mind. And the strongest sexual tingling, a feeling she'd not known in — why keep counting? It was back.

Perhaps the excitement has her in heightened appreciation of the stars up there as she walks to an address two suburbs from home. Or she has grabbed them as distraction. Her Maori ancestors used these lights as navigation guides to sail their open canoes across that vast Pacific Ocean; at nights it must have felt as if they were crossing the universe itself, the great heaving force they were riding, times of howling storms, the pitch black, not knowing where they were. Their minds must have been born of isolation and narrow outlook, Lena figured, yet probably gave them the unquestioning courage to leave their home islands in search of other, better lands, with eyes fixed on the heavenly pointers.

But how did they know they would come across land in the emptiness of the Pacific Ocean? Who made the unbelievable decision to just set sail? And surely some did miss finding land and sailed right on south into the freezing Antarctic waters? How many perished? What island did the first voyagers start from? In what altered state of mind did they arrive at these untouched shores? Why did they adopt war as the singular culture, no progress as its consequence? Surely some strong leader must have seen this and could have imposed a change?

She thinks of her own uncharted waters. Of the courage required therefore to turn her back on her tiny home island. Of her husband who never really was one. Of what people think of her.

It's Saturday so Henry will have his work cut out running the hotel.

Wiki is legally old enough to marry and there might be something going on between her and Chud. Now that would be a turn-up for the books, my daughter and a man assumed to be in for a lifelong criminal career. Henry won't approve, has always wanted the best for his daughters, though I always believed Chud had great potential. Well, Mata lives with a most ordinary man in Auckland, though she writes and says he's a marvellous husband and father. Manu is thirteen now and more his father's son. He'll be out late with his mates, a lazy boy and overweight at such a young age with the fatty diet his father has fed him. Roast mutton for breakfast indeed. I never got a say on what my children ate, except on Yank's diet. Now look at him: tall, lean, handsome — the boy I called special because I feared he would grow up troubled by being fatherless and now look at him.

As for Barney, drinking with his old war mates, battering their ears with his newfound means to speak again. Now everything he says bores her. Hell, she wants a man who can talk about anything under the sun. Someone she can express her true self to, ask questions about the wider world and how it works. Someone to discuss the deep emotions with, dreams and fears, real and irrational. The life you got born to, Lena, before you became Mrs Takahe.

House lights of just about every residence occupied by, she well knows, white people. Living in a separate world to Maoris, though the working class are at the same level: usually renting. Pakehas understand money; they live and breathe it according to Mrs Mac, who's told Lena like some friendly informer from the other side. Hell, I'm on my way to meet another man.

Now guilt sets in, not about what is imminent, nor to do with Henry. It's Barney. I used him. I gave him a voice he didn't really possess, deluded myself it was him and that was what attracted me. Wasn't I crafting another Barney from my own imagination in giving him a more lively personality? Even the laughter was more my own since if I laughed so did he.

And what does he love about me, if not my beauty he goes on about as if any other attribute I might possess does not count? Yet he made love more than he made lust, and he is a good man.

But Lena wants more than a good man. Wants a more complete man. Gets her to wondering what kind of house Ralph lives in, how he lives and what are the social rules of the rich? Worries he will find her too unsophisticated, but tells herself: be proud of who and what you are. He must have seen something about me. Remember, you've been compared to a legend of beauty. He ain't seen nothing yet.

House parties she's walking past, so much quieter than the exuberant often volatile parties at her village which too often end up in brawls. Not this lot, they have things under control. Like their orderly lives.

And suddenly, look, a shooting star: make a wish for Yank, his music, his father. The music star Yank might turn out to be. Hope Yank will make up his mind and go to America. I think they'll get on.

She reaches the sign saying the street Ralph lives on. Makes her mind go kind of blank and yet in another way as clear of purpose and intent as those stars are clear in the sky. Her face flushes. A woman she has not known in a long while smiles up at those stars, wondering where they are guiding her. Or if direction even matters.

CHAPTER THIRTY-NINE

I AM OVER A QUARTER Negro. Sure, you are where you're raised — mostly. But nor can genes be denied. From the thirteen photos I now have, I know his face like my own; we are quite similar on closer comparison. He is a darker complexion and his hair is kinky while mine is thick and wavy.

I am a diluted version of Jess Hines, Negro resident of Whitecave, Mississippi, United States of America. I have missed most of my mother's physical aspects.

I've thrown myself into my music performances, less for the audience than as a duty to pay homage to the music. Which gets the audience loving us the more. Often I will not be aware of their adulation, so engrossed in the music do I get. Nigel, now my soul buddy, beat me to that state.

I start to think my music career might have better chance of being full time if I lived in America. Soon develops into an obsession that, if I don't go, if I don't meet my father, my life will be spent regretting it. Anyway I have an emotional need to see him, meet my father in the flesh. Everyone needs a father and Henry denied me even a small taste. Not as if I am going to a father who lives in poverty like near every Negro does in the South. *My* father has money. A lot of other qualities besides.

CHAPTER FORTY

I WOKE UP EARLY ONE morning in my mid-thirties able, finally, to face what my brother and I had seen. We'd buried it in our vulnerable youth, drowned it in alcohol, the both of us. Afraid that even in just acknowledging what we'd been witness to, they'd come back for us.

We ambled several miles upstream, looking for fish in a flood-muddied river. I was fifteen, my brother eighteen, but kind of my father since our daddy left when we were young. The sons who didn't need a father: let him rot in hell.

Got to this woods area the one side, a bridge going out of a small township the other. Dusk was coming on. There were several colored settlements on our way back. Might have some fun on the way home, Josh was teasing, get you con-joined with a wo-man—

When suddenly we heard a clamor of some sorts. We knew white voice tones and their different talk in the instant, even not having had much experience of white folks up close. So instinctively we knew to slip into the woods.

Two black boys of perfect complexion to blend with the shadows, we were suddenly our rootless ancestor slave runaways about to witness something. For it was plain this mob heading for the bridge were in a fury.

Squirrels flowed up and down tree trunks. Birds and insects made a last cacophony to the dying day. Somewhere a hornets' nest droned. An armadillo shuffled right by oblivious to us on its own scent trail. Our mother cooked real nice 'dillo. Tastes like chicken. You had to boil it for hours before frying with onions and gravy.

The yelling got louder, we saw they were pushing someone along in the front, couldn't tell if a man or woman, just the color — black — starkly alone among the white complexions. Blacker than our white-diluted skin.

The dying sun turned the clouds to blood, laying a golden cloak over this pastoral scene. The hollering group such a violation in contrast.

Flowing up on to the bridge, there they stopped. I looked at my brother for a lead but he was staring, had that look of hooded eyes, glazed-over eyeballs, and he said, Gawd help us, I think it's a lynchin'. Let's get closer, he said.

Close enough to see it was a woman.

I asked my brother how come they lynching a woman?

Josh said, I don't know. It's our color I guess.

Our grandmother had witnessed her share of Negro lynching and told us why they choose a bridge: same as a tree represents Christ's cross, a hanging taking place over water is symbolic — water being used for baptisms, as well the bridge representing death's rite of passage. The great crossing over, Grandma used to tell us with those wide frightened eyes in recalling. It was plain exactly what was unfolding here.

I could hear Grandma saying in her old-style talk, it be a passage to deys own salvation, de ritual of murder.

She meant to a place without sin or evil, since these are embodied in the victim God created as a born offender for His white subjects to punish.

In dey minds , Grandma said, dey doing God's will in putting out a life over His good water. That's how Southern white folk think, that dey got God-given right to done murder us.

They keep pouring on to the bridge, seemingly a leaderless ooze of excited humanity. But ringleaders there somewhere in the front, or just behind the victim, whipping up the frenzy till it turns, till it curdles like butter cream in the sun. We know that much.

Up front a struggle, not a heaving mass of flailing bodies and loud outcry, no gunshots to warn or calm everyone down. Just a yelling, whooping movement of people around a silent few of fixed purpose pinning the woman's hands behind her back, putting a rope round the neck.

The non-human's neck.

And she stands there, moving not, close enough to see her fixed stare it's almost serene, but not close enough to know if she's with awful fearing or gained that Negro resignation: a state impervious to the physical harm and assault on dignity. Every nigger knows it, even before it's our turn to experience it. Pick it up from the older niggers. Dream of it even before we experience it, the state of being nigger.

Looking back, the whites are close enough to see one thing they have in common. It's spread like a single broad brushstroke across a painting. Not wiping out their expressions, no. This is the portrait of Indifference. Total indifference to nigger pain, empty hearts for our suffering. Indeed, we can see the joy in the faces.

Oafs then, buffoons and village idiots, slow-witted galoots, men reduced by their bigotry, suddenly turned to a frothing state of not quite frenzy, the next stage before; missing-tooth grins, close-together eyes with knitted brows declaring low minds working away simplistic and venal behind each skull. Smiles as broad as the river flowing below, that yet never reach the eyes.

HAYNG THE NEEGGER BEECH!

We hear and see this like runaway slaves watching one of our own captured sisters about to be strung up. Our African sister wears a long dress. Of tight, tiny floral pattern, sold cheap at general stores everywhere, cheaper from traveling salesmen, cheaper still from a thief.

We brothers look at each other with same thought: how is her last flimsy bit of dignity going to fare as she droops from the bridge with dress lifted up? She might have nothing on underneath, and then what'll they say, what will howl mockingly from their sneering mouths? It's sure to be sexual reference, one of their verbal themes being niggers' genitals, our dangerous sexuality, that we're animals of no self-control.

What does God think of His subjects acting like this, to a woman?

We don't think: that could be us. It just is us.

The woman is lifted suddenly in the air over the railing, by sets of strong pale and sun-burned male hands. The rope's looped through the gap in the concrete, she'll be crying out any second, another futile calling to God to come please save her. The sun is dying fast, bleeding all along the bridge line.

I'm thinking, even before she calls Him, He ain't coming, sister. Motherfucker God ain't never coming.

Then she's pushed.

Hands have reached up from behind and shoved the Negro woman at feet and backs of her calves. So she slips clean down in a short descent yet so rapid it's not till the figure jolts to a halt — the crowd gone utterly silent — bouncing a couple times, I think she bounced, that realization takes the place of the lowering sun. Faces hidden in their own shadow yet we see them clear as clear: evil in the massed flesh.

I don't think she screamed or made any sound. But not sure my ears were hearing anything then. I was in that process of shutting down before the pain got me.

Now, like a hundred years later, from out of the darkness I see her head is at an angle and her dress did not end up over herself to expose the last of her twitching thighs and shuddering feet, catch the forcibly ejected urine running down slender naked legs; it flared briefly from the short passage of air her weight had forced under it. But dignity stayed where she'd intended in dressing this morning.

She is just as if out walking and paused to cock a curious head at something caught her eye. Unaware of the craning heads above her looking down with gimlet eyes and broken-out teeth in portraits of grin, smile and grimace, chuckle, soft glad moan and satisfied sigh. Looking down as if at a big fish spotted below and everyone rushed to look, wanting to kill it. Or to confirm it's already dead.

She does sway, a grandfather clock pendulum swing slowing to her last moments. The river flows as rivers always do, this one given of symbolic justification from God in heaven no less, that He is truly pleased with His white subjects and their work over His good water crossing.

A wooden cross rears up a dim silhouette against the darkening sky, bursts into flames like a symbol of the sun commanded back. White hoods appear of men announcing membership of some strange tribe. Countless arms rise in salute to the burning symbol of Christ's last living place. When it would have been their kind that killed Christ.

Our nigger minds are reeling, our brains are on fire. Our young age has no references to grab at and hold for dear life — it is empty air we're groping at. I'm thinking, I can't take this, my mind is going to break.

We watch till the last has dispersed and still we stay there, in case. Trembling like shivering owls. The body hanging suspended is so still.

Sure enough the headlights of a police car come slowly on to the bridge. Another police car comes from the other side, roof lights flashing and yet of same unhurried progress as if at a funeral cortège.

Car doors open and close, two torches identify each other with a little quiver wave of light spears. Then the beams sweep along the lower bridge and stop.

Illuminating an apparition. Of a strange fruit dangling from a concrete span.

PART THREE

CHAPTER FORTY-ONE

I FOUND ONE OF MY bosses in upset state in the office shed on site, when I had gone to ask my next instructions for the earth-mover machine I operated. Not the Albert B Romney I knew.

Into nigger mode the instant of seeing he'd been crying, I asked the ground at his feet where he would like me to go next. Expecting anything from being yelled at to him punching or kicking me because that was how it was.

More and more I found such treatments insulting to Negro manhood, as my involvement with civil rights became more fervent, even if in an underground capacity helping distribute newsletters and organize protest marches. I should be glad something was making Albert B Romney miserable, yet I wasn't. What sort of man would feel that?

He and his partner Jake McRory, both men of average intelligence who yet understood the fundamentals of this earth-shifting game: that it was to drive men and machines to the utmost every hour every day, and to work men beyond paid hours, machines past manufacturers' best-usage recommendations. And when things came inevitably to occasional sudden halts, with busted engines, working parts pushed too far, then to blame the men. Machines sat dumb and useless and with most operators being Negro, easier to assault, abuse, deduct from his pay, hurt his family with total forfeiture of owed wages, fire him on the spot for negligence. Or put him on the next available machine and work hell out of both. And if any fired man came back demanding his pay, stick a gun in his face and ask to be reminded of how much was owed.

Our contract was to build a fixed distance of levee the east side of the Mississippi River, another contractor completing the other side, spring and summer months best before the flooding season risk increased. A crew only thirty strong, we sometimes did achieve the impossible, if for no thanks from our hard-nosed bosses.

Including a man said to be a member of the Ku Klux Klan — and he was crying?

Something made me ask, everything all right, boss? When usually I would never be so impertinent. He told me to come inside the office, he had coffee brewing.

Jess, he began as he poured the black liquid into my metal cup, then his own. Y'all got family members outside your own you truly love?

Yes, sir, guess we all have those. You meaning like, cousins and nephews, uncles and aunts?

Yeah. And nieces too. Well, I lost mine on Saturday. My brother Elmer's girl. Took her own life. Nineteen years of age and she doesn't want to live? She was like my own child.

Tears started rolling down. I knew out of habit to show him I was looking away, but decided the hell with that and took eyes back and kept them there, steady as a machine working a delicate line, seeing he had made such a personal confidence in me by crying openly.

You're a good worker, Jess Hines. You never stand around wind-baggin' and complaining. Just do your job. And you saw death in the war. Think I don't know you're a veteran? You must have seen close buddies die in front of your eyes. Did you?

I sure did.

Does a man ever get over it?

Boss, depend who the man is. How close the bond.

We was close. In fact, Jenny-May said she loved me more than her own daddy. I guess on account of my brother's drinking, being twice as bad as mine which my ex-wife said was bad enough.

My boss gave this weird grin. Guess from not used to talking to a nigger like an equal.

Like to offer my heartfelt condolences, boss. Admire you still here on the job, I do.

Appreciate it, Jess. Last time I felt like this was losing my best hunting dog, got ripped by a wild hog up in the hills back of where you live. Died in my arms carrying him out to the truck. You hunted Pushaw Hills?

Yessir. As a youngster, before I discovered dancing and girls was better.

Nothing better than your dogs bailing up a hog. Working the hairy beast into a spot it can't escape from. Don't know many white men love dancing like you niggers. The girls, well, sure. They a different hairy beast. We all men, even you guys. Grinning knowingly, like two old buddies doing chick talk. Motherfuckers hung like mules. You born that way, son?

Born with what I was born with, boss. Don't know if I'm blessed or just ordinary. Never did the womanizing thing.

He pointed. I could tell. You used to be a drinker, right?

Yessir, something bad.

Ain't bad if you got charge of it. Drink is the cheapest ride from a man's true troubled soul there is. My niece she hated it, my brother's drinking. A beautiful girl she was too, very sensitive. You failed to notice a new dress or shoes she was wearing, she'd run off to her room and sulk. Old Uncle Albert here learned to go after her when I overlooked her female vanity needs, say sorry and what could I buy my favourite niece to make up? Was going to pay her wedding costs myself. Now, she's gone. Just gone.

His tears spilled openly, no pretense at playing a-man-don't-cry, he just cried.

Well, naturally I got up and went round the table and took him up and just hugged my boss. Hell, like he said, some things we're just men the same are we not?

And he took it, my gesture, for what it meant. Just a simple gesture of a human to another. In a few minutes, a few hours at most, things would be back to the same: he'd be yelling at me, I'd be either pretending not to hear because of my machine noise, or falling over myself to please him.

Half a foot shorter than me, the man I was hugging yet a strong man physically. What he was mentally — this unfathomable redneck normally a nigger-hater — I do not know. Me comforting was nothing new: our Negro women had been mammies to their children ever since we got here from Africa, our house-servant men intimate confidants to hear their masters' every secret even the most awful. Been taking these people in our embrace a long time. Wiped their baby bums and wiped their adult eyes, blinded our own when they committed murder, never blinked when the murdered was one of us. Though never was it the other way round, that they had comfort and unseeing, forgiving eyes to give us.

How did she pass on, boss?

Hanged herself. My brother found her in the garage, called me up screaming. I drove like a maniac over, had to cut her down. Just nineteen years young. Had to slap my brother out of going for another bottle of whiskey: not this time, big brother. We owe to be sober, give this innocent a proper farewell. All day yesterday at the funeral parlor preparing her for tomorrow's funeral. I find my brother's so much as sniffed a drink, be his funeral next.

I'm so sorry, boss. Almost called him Albert.

Have to make a speech, in church. When I'm no God-fearing man even if I been raised on hellfire and brimstone. Knew too many crotch-grabbing preachers and money-making shysters to believe. What kind of thing would you say, Jess? So I can see her off right.

I suggested he talk about the troubled spirit in every person, male and female. Just like the beast dwells in each and every heart. And who of us knows which can take control of our minds, when we get caught with defenses down, in a time most vulnerable. Or succumb to the weakness every person carries, even the strongest.

I appreciate your advice. I tell you, seeing a hanged body is not a pretty sight. You know, the neck stretched, eyes bulging, a God-awful color.

Almost languidly I said, no, sure ain't a pretty sight. In my mind seeing that lynched Negro sister. And looking at my distressed boss recalling what he saw of his beloved niece. Passing before my mind's eye endless line-up of Negroes hanging, like strange fruit, from a vast plantation of poplar trees.

A course you niggers are more used to death than we are. Guess you get kind of immune to it, do you?

Feels like we are immune, sometimes, boss. It does. Down to my fawning nigger talk, so to tolerate the sublimely ridiculous.

I figured that. I loved that girl something special, I did.

She leave a note, boss? Make us understand better when they say why. But sadder when the why is just plain misdirected thinking.

Hines, you done read my mind exactly. She didn't leave a note, not even to say farewell to her favourite uncle, or accuse her daddy of drinking away her life by being too drunk to see his girl in trouble. You got children your own?

Wondering for one split second if to mention my son in New Zealand, real enough in my mind to proudly claim. But the rule was, you never get too close to a white person, hurts less when it turns sour as it always does. That river of difference is wider than Old Miss.

Got two daughters live in Biloxi last I heard, I told him.

Like that, huh? Been a while since you seen them?

A long while, yes.

One of the nigger curses, you find it hard being daddies 'cause you can't be husbands.

I heard that. Yeah. What slavery did? You know, being sold and traded, moved everywhere, split asunder my momma used to say of my daddy and her own, grandfathers too.

Could be, Jess Hines. Could be. Albert rubbed his chin. He was not an attractive specimen, mostly in need of a shave, pot belly from the beer he and his partner drank to quench their day thirst. The harder stuff at night.

And could be it's just the way your race is.

Then Albert looked at his watch, said, I thank you for sharing this moment with me, but the show must go on. You can move to helping Larry. And listen, how many times I have to tell you, make that machine scream in reverse, it's when you lose so much time going backwards on slow. Let's get going now.

Sure thing, boss.

CHAPTER FORTY-TWO

THIS IS NOT A VILLAGE — it's a dump. As I move from the sealed to a dirt road, muddy from rain, in front of me a cluster of shacks in a pine clearing revealed in a dawn sun. People moving around, yet to notice me.

I have been to a place kind of similar, when I was about ten and went with Mum and her friend to a funeral in a remote Maori community way up in the bush. Her first cousin had been beaten to death by a drunken husband. We got to this ramshackle settlement, found the meeting house down the end of a pot-holed dirt road, a neglected building that in any Maori community is supposed to be its heart, proudly kept in pristine order.

We weren't greeted in the traditional way with respect and formal welcome. Instead made our own way past groups of drinking men calling out lewd comments on Mum's good looks and what they'd do to her given a chance. Kids my age and older gave me the evils and held up clenched fists. I heard Mum tell her friend for once she wished Henry was here; he'd sort out these ugly violators of Maori culture and human dignity. But she was determined to pay her cousin last respects.

The corpse looked like it was: beaten to death. A woman near the coffin told my mother she better not stick around long or someone would scratch her pretty face to ribbons. Mum said to her friend in not the quietest voice, I think they're inbred.

At the community dining room we found more people drinking than preparing food for guest mourners. Mum paid her customary contribution and took us out of there. We drove out over a rutty dirt road with houses that bush grew right up to, strewn with rubbish and car wrecks, dangerous dogs running loose, untended toddlers roaming loose. Mum crying for her cousin having to suffer in death as she did in life.

Well, this place here looks worse, even with the sun rays split ten thousand times by the pines and birds in song, a woman singing as if at church.

Chooks run loose, mean dogs growling at me get told to stay, snorting pigs in crudely built enclosures suggest the source of an awful stench. This is just after six in the morning and kids, black as night most of them, are already up and running around in the puddles from last night's heavy rain—

That is, till they see me. And all movement halts and so does human sound.

I must look a sorry sight, desperate for a shower or bath, clothes I've slept in and bits of straw all over me from the hay barn I dossed down in last night. And the blinding realisation these people are seeing me as a white person. Me, a *white*.

Men who had been standing around scratching genitals, picking noses, honking and spitting, smoking cigarettes are now frozen poses staring at me. At this ghostly figure arrived with a suitcase. My utter dislocation no doubt showing like any neon sign in the towns our bus passed through.

In my worsening confusion at going from one town to the next, I'd missed the Greyhound bus due to arrive in daylight hours. I always knew the two and a half miles from Whitecave to here could be the hard part, as there would surely not be taxis in a town with a population of 1700. I planned to hitch a ride or just walk. The bus I did catch arrived just before midnight, dropped me alone in a strange town with a suitcase and no hotel showing an open sign, no lights showing life. I had stuffed up. Wandering the few streets wondering what to do then after a while a truck pulled up and two men demanded to know who I was.

Had my lie ready. I'm from New Zealand — where's that? Well, it's kind of close to Australia. A country they had heard of. Told them I was on a mission for my dying father to say goodbye to a man he made close friends with during World War Two. Lives in a place called Piney Woods. Waited for the explosion.

Which almost came — literally. A gun came out the driver's window. The passenger sighting me down a rifle barrel. That's nigger country, he said.

My father did tell me. But he is dying and they were like brothers.

With a nigger?

Yes, sir.

After checking me out by torch light and it being declared I was definitely what I claimed to be, with my accent, and fact I passed for white in their eyes, they took me to a barn nearby so I could delay my arrival to a respectable hour. Warned, don't be boasting about no nigger friend of your daddy's, not round here. Others might not be so understanding.

An older man takes a cigarette from his mouth to ask, can we be heppin you, suh? You must be lawse.

Somehow I get his way of speaking, that heppin means helping and lawse means lost. Kids are shouting my presence, that *a white man is here!* People pour out from the high houses, up on log foundations; they spill down wooden steps, leap from verandas, and quickly surround me. In the crowd a large woman exclaims, *Lordy be!* Everyone is open-mouthed in disbelief. A kid says, *It's a ghost!* Though I can't feel hostility.

A hundred times I have planned and rehearsed this, introducing myself at my father's village, to his Negro community. I intended to say with great pride, I'm here to meet my father. His name is Jess Hines. Thought I'd be coming to a neat suburban community, colored-only, with oaks and elms and magnolias like in the library books I'd pored over on the South, and that my father's house would stand out as one of the best, if not *the* best. I wasn't expecting a mansion, had read up on the vast economic differences between blacks and whites, that here in the South they lived segregated. But I figured on a dwelling fit for a Negro of pride and, I had just presumed, of ambition; a man still going places, despite the racial obstacles.

Instead I can't speak. The trees are ugly pines. House is not the right description for a single one of these raised shacks. I'm trying not to show disbelief, hoping disgust is not betraying my forced effort at smiling. The smells are so bad I fear violent retching or throwing up. Somewhere the putrid smell of rotting meat. And about one hundred ebony-skinned people staring at me in shocked silence.

Is this Piney Woods?

It surely is. Looking me more than up and down, every set of eyes trying to slot me.

I think you got the wrong Piney, son.

Is there another Piney Woods in Whitecave?

Nope, this is it. You sure you got the right state? Maybe a different county? Lots of places called Piney Woods, like they got three towns called Cairo. Who you looking for? This is a coloured community.

Man by the name of—

I am suddenly so overcome I cannot say my father's name. Everyone's waiting for the announcement. I wish my father would appear. This is ridiculous, madness itself. What was going through my head to come all this wearying, confusing, life-changing way without letting my father know?

A woman steps forward. Claims my voice with her smile.

Well, if you sure this is the right Piney, then we bid you welcome. I'm figuring I know who you looking for. She looks to my right, at a figure closing quickly, though I dare not show alarm or defensiveness, even if at an intending attacker. It would look bad, and like I was scared. I know the rules of manhood.

The woman beams at me. But I cannot reciprocate, just too dislocated. Not a child moves nor any other adult. The woman has hands clasped together, head cocked at an odd angle, as if I am a spiritual apparition. Never felt so alone. The approaching figure is now in my peripheral view.

Then I hear my name — not that I'm very familiar with it.

You can't be Mark, surely?

My first thought is, I'm called Yank.

I turn and there's the man, the face I know so well from photographs. It is him. Recognition instant, yet an apparition himself: as if he doesn't belong here either. As if this is but a pausing place on his way to great achievement, a resting place on a great life journey. It has to be.

For he is all over with pure presence. Tall, fine looking, dark but not quite ebony.

Are you Mark?

The voice is rich — richer than I expected. I must have either nodded or said yes. For his face breaks open with smile that could light the darkness here, darkness not of skin complexion nor night but the place these people have been put: at the bottom of the heap.

Jess?

Mark? Are you Mark? Oh God, but this cannot be happening. I don't believe this.

Did you say Mark . . . ? Lena's son . . . ? From New Zealand?

I can only nod to his checklist. Relief coming over me like imminent fainting spell. I have been saved by this imposing figure, better looking than the photographs, familiar yet a complete stranger. I can hear the years racing to meet right here in the woods-shaded dirt. Yet see his confusion, even a little anger at my stupid surprise arrival.

I'm sorry. I should have let you know.

No. No, he cries. Grabs me in his arms.

Father oh father, I was told you died, that you were killed in the war. You were the unmentionable in the house I grew up in; I had to invent you in my mind. Till one day you sprang to life in written words. You weren't the all-American white hero I assumed: you were what is standing before me now. Tall, dark and beautiful. These years of exchanging through letters were never real. No flesh, no real meaning.

It was worth it, every moment of doubt and confusion and fear about coming here: in my own father's arms for the first time.

And everyone is cheering and clapping and whooping in happiness for us. That woman's beaming face. A son has come home.

CHAPTER FORTY-THREE

THIS IS NOT ME, YOU got to understand this. He is close to pleading, yet I do understand. My father is on another journey, this is but temporary abode, and now I'm here maybe we can share that journey. I don't care he lives here, not now. We are one in our happy disbelief, father and son united. And with the community all excited it transforms my perceptions.

Sure, this is poverty like I've never seen. But there are million-dollar smiles and everyone wants to touch me, make funny comments which I don't get the humour of but nor do I expect to. The laughter is enough: it convulses them, bends them at the knee, they rock on heels, slap hands, thighs, fling pink palms skywards, black faces shine with a sheen of sweat from the humidity and heat already got up. The children touch me gingerly, as if expecting an explosion; run away as soon contact is made, giggling. Led by the woman, several adults start up singing and immediately others set up a rhythmic beat of complex hand-clapping. Kids twist and contort into dancing, feet slipping and sliding in the mud. I have the urge to move and to sing with them.

They praise the Lord and thank God for sending me to my daddy. The women are calling out tasks they must do to prepare for a celebration. My daddy is speechless with joy, keeps touching my face, feeling my hair, stepping back to behold me.

The woman introduces herself with a hug, she smells of sweat yet not offensive. I'm Marion, the preacher's wife. Tonight we gonna have a big party to welcome you, young man. You've come home, son. Jess's boy done come home.

Up these steps to my father's house. He starts apologising. I guess for where and how he lives, inside a dark, near windowless dwelling, same simple as Merita's house but without the sulphur smell. Reminded I forgot to say goodbye to Merita. My eyes adjusting to the lack of natural light. What if there is no bathroom for my first shower since the hotel in Atlanta? Surely electricity for an iron to press fresh clothes so I can look smart?

A light goes on above my head. My father's hand arrives on my shoulder. Where did you sleep last night? How did you get here so early? Why didn't you tell me you were coming? In heaven though a man is at seeing you, he adds. Like I been hit by a train.

He turns me around. He's a good two inches taller than me and this is a Negro I'm looking at — I've seen pictures of men who look like this, might have seen one or two in movies, not the pop-eyed coal-black servant types that ridicule the race — this one is proud and handsome, and I am half of him, my music owes to his genes, to those people outside. Music that's born of the American Negroes' suffering. Me, I have not suffered, only had to endure Henry's silence. Unlike them, I got a free ride on music's train.

His teeth keep breaking out gleaming white, his chuckle has a timbre, his lithe muscular body won't stay still: a man so different to any I've experienced. A black man.

Spontaneous, that's the word comes to mind. My father and all those people I can hear talking, laughing, shouting, singing outside, they are the same: of and in the moment.

I tell him of my worsening confusion and doubts as the journey went on, my long ship voyage, the mix-ups, bussing right across America, a hotel stay in Atlanta and me confused and scared at big-city life. Of last night's Greyhound midnight arrival.

Two white men, you said?

With guns. Told me some woman called I-Spy saw me on the street, called them to check me out. They didn't want to wake the sheriff.

Be like waking the Devil himself. I-Spy thinks she owns the town. Threatened you?

A rifle out the window. The other had a pistol on his lap. But I didn't feel in danger.

Jess chuckles. Sorry, hearing the way you talk brings back memories. That accent. You give my name?

No, I said. They didn't ask.

Say who they were?

No, they did not.

He went back to smiling. Hey, now look at you. Standing right here in the flesh. My boy. My son. This is a miracle. But you must be tired.

Too excited to feel tired.

Ain't you saying it. Me too. You wanting to get cleaned up?

My nod hesitant. I'm thinking outside toilet, like Chud's, could be a rainwater tank shower.

Right this way. I follow him past a small, timber-slab dining table and a strange mix of blue velvet-upholstered chairs, four. There's an embroidered white lace cloth sat square in the middle of it, a decorative vase. Now a floor-to-ceiling bookshelf, not something I grew up with: my books school or library loaned, or lent by Mrs Mac. I've been in worse homes.

Yet he's saying, sorry if I led you to think I was wealthy, lived in a fancy house. Stops at a closed door.

Wanted you to think well of me. See, I had a problem with drink. It didn't like me. And I didn't like myself. Went places no self-respecting man should go. I'd give up, and time and again it would claim me back.

Then he looked at me different. You wouldn't have a problem with alcohol by any chance?

Smiling, I tell him my mother thinks so. But I don't wake up craving a drink if that's what you mean.

Good. And your momma, how is she, what does she look like?

People say she's aged well. I can't tell. She's my mother. Thinking: and your old lover. And my father. Unbelievable.

Still looks the same young and beautiful the photo she sent. Oh, man, someone tell me this is just a dream.

We stare at each other, shake heads, grin then laugh.

Through that door, son, you'll find the bathroom. Take your time. Rest up on the bed over there while I drive to tell the boss some lies to be off work. Don't be shy to go and say howdy to the neighbours.

Walk into a bathroom as good as the hotel in Atlanta. I think my father is a man of many surprises. I'm in a daze.

CHAPTER FORTY-FOUR

MY FATHER CAME BACK AND asked what story I had forgotten to tell him about why I was visiting Piney Woods. Turned out his bosses are one and same who came to check me out, pointed the gun when I told them my destination. Jess said only years of practice at *hovering* around white people enabled him to overhear the pair's story, recognise me in it, concur that I was the son of his closest wartime buddy. He told me how lucky I was, that they were Klan members.

And you work for them?

Klan means less than ordinary men pointing the finger at Negroes that they are lesser. I just never mess with them. The odds are stacked all on their side — at present.

But no elaboration followed.

Piney Woods community put on a big celebration. An assortment of beer and hard liquor soon had everyone primed. They sat on stoops, cut-down oil drums and log cut-offs, spilled off outdoor tables and benches, a happy chaos. Kids ran up and touched me like I was poisonous, ran away squealing, stood in groups staring, made me acutely aware of not looking like one of them. Meat grilled on metal racks, over coal fires, came out in pots boiled on stoves inside. Kids ran hither and thither on shouted instructions from the women. Women outnumbered men. They all sang and danced to flaming cinder torch light: it felt like Africa. Felt like a party at home, of Waiwera Maoris in celebration.

Kids danced with adults, fat people floated and pirouetted on air, the muscular and the skinny both, sublime pictures of blurring feet, twisting, straining, snapping muscles. Limbs cut loose and seemed to multiply, feet drummed complex patterns on the dirt, art was made of coordinated arm and torso movements, bobbing heads had their own rhythm like self-contained little drums.

I could have been the prodigal son returned to a home he'd never been to — no glorious deeds needed, I was just their son. Women kissed and hugged me, danced sexually at me, moved and swayed like mothers teaching me, came on like wild prime prospects out to woo or claim, grandmothers used me to transport themselves back to a young vital past. Fires and flaming torches lit us like ancient camp fires. Little kids fell asleep in mothers' arms. Older kids made perfect imitations of every slick movement.

Lord, they sang better than angels, like life-trained choir members of highest order. Individuals put on star performances, instrumentalists pounded and plucked, strummed and stroked, sent sound rushing like scent through the pines — I swear I heard the needles set off like a billion tuning forks.

Voices learned from cotton fields and prison farm chain gangs and windowless cells and cold rented rooms and grim bars and seedy clubs and ceaselessly cruel existence . . . all stepped up smiling ready to do the next song.

Marion, the preacher's wife, stood up and sang like Mahalia Jackson. Turned everyone silent and closed eyes and keened every ear until she was done. To cheering, clapping and whooping she hip-swayed over and teasingly thrust herself at me like another person of ungodly ways. A group sang mighty praise to God that resounded in the treetops and questioned the hearts of non-believers.

Men, dressed to the nines, came strutting down shack steps like from a castle, a glorious mansion, and pranced into torch-lit centre ring like black peacocks, preening in sheer white suits, white shoes, black suits, white shirt, black bow tie, and Lord did they dance. My father one of them, all in white.

The people cut loose on their worn, hard earth, a little softened by the rain. Like free spirits broken loose from their chains. Roots they call it.

Throughout Jess and I kept staring at each other, and the drunker I got on different spirits and the people, the more emotional I got. I cried. He cried. We all laughed. All sang. Made music and percussion from timber pieces, broken broom handle, cut-down pool cue, bits of metal and leather and rolled-up cloth, blew brass horns, strummed guitars, pounded bongos, plucked banjo, flying hands across the keyboard of an accordion. And we partied till near dawn, till like one of Henry's breakfast servings came fried chitterlings, pig intestines back home, sheep innards the Maoris called terotero. With pone bread served up with laughter and big-bottomed women making sexual tease.

Jess introduces me to his world, away from the township on the highways in every direction. In his older model Chevy we go down side roads of endless plantations worked by Negro labour. Along tree-flanked dirt roads accompanied by constant radio music and Jess's beautiful voice sometimes singing along with a number. The passenger keeps throwing his father looks of disbelief.

At hearing and seeing a man who is a foreigner, half-Negro and yet my father. My *father*? His sing-song voice, how he can go from straight talk to near incomprehensible Negro-speak. Find out where my throaty laugh comes from and my musical ear.

Assailed by endless fields of corn we drive for hours as radio announcers proclaim the virtues of their competing stations. The foreign-born son is in music heaven.

We go to pool halls and smoky cafes and food joints, to hang out as he calls it, and for a father to proudly introduce me as his son from New Zealand, to those he feels will take us at face value. Fried chicken, pork ribs, collard greens, grits, burgers our staple diet, from diners and fast food joints patronised by one race. Blacks. Coloureds they call it.

Other than from a distance I do not see one white person anywhere we go. I have not yet adjusted yet to the *Whites Only* signs, still wince at seeing *For Coloreds* stencilled above commercial establishment doorways.

Yet my father's cheerful disposition never falters; he clicks fingers in time to every song on the radio, to music in his head. Hardly a word on racial segregation. When he must know it's new and profoundly disturbing to me, that actual laws are written to exclude him — us — on account of race. This is America?

I've grown up worshipping a false idol. In the land of the so-called free, a nigger for four weeks. How can that be?

He refuses my offer to pay for anything. At nights we hit juke joints, fun houses where near anything goes, a brothel a dance bar . . . live music so good I am fearful for my own mediocre talent, inadequate in comparison. My father tells me it's a timing thing, every black person born with a metronome inside, a born tonal quality and the life situation being the biggest factors. It will come to you, he assures, it's in your blood. We living here have had lifetimes of rubbing off on one another, our influences come from every corner, from small rural towns to big-city ghettoes.

I hear singers of impossible off-beat timing. Voices that fuse in with the bass drum beat as if one and the same source. Witness obese dancers who can spin on a dime, move with speed and grace, what my father calls panache and fling and deadly movers.

One night this old guy is revealed from a pulled black curtain in a circle of spotlight. Alone, he has a foot drum set, mouth organ on attachment to his shoulder, guitar and a microphone. And a totally hushed, expectant crowd. His stage name is Satan, and his performance of blues and soul is virtuoso. I say genius. My father says America has such talent in every second bar and juke joint.

I wallow in music and drown in booze. Get drunk on coon dick, made from boiled beef bones, fermented grapefruit and corn meal mash. Smoke weed with my father and get to walk through the doors it opens to higher musical appreciation.

From Jess I learn how we all owe the influence of country and western music. We talk about Elvis Presley's influences being black and country music. The pair of us in a duet Elvis number as pastoral Mississippi goes by out the car windows. Jess does not believe the man is a racist. But Elvis can't go public on having coloured buddies, not in the deep South.

We get home in the early hours, sometimes after dawn, sleep till noon and wake to a friendly Marion offering to cook late breakfast, or lunch, chastising that Jess is leading me astray. They have a close bond. Though her first is to God, a Southern Baptist God. Mostly we eat lunch on the run with Mississippi scenery, do pool halls or a river swim afternoons, go all night on music and me on booze and weed, my father just the smoke.

Most show no surprise that I am Jess's son. Must be I'm melding into the human scenery more. Every day I make another adjustment to the idea that I'm one of them, despite my accent and upbringing on another planet. That I am a Negro.

One day he takes me to a cemetery. To his mother's grave. Your grandma was a teacher. She got high on written words.

Inscribed on her headstone the words: To Miss Anna T Jeanes, her Foundation, for lifting me, lifting others. Luana Hines 1899–1962. Beloved teacher of colored children.

This is my grandmother. Glad she is not the stereotype of a cotton field worker, a housemaid.

Plantations of sorghum, corn, soy, peanuts abound. I learn Negro sharecroppers have been forced to walk off their cotton-producing land because machinery has overtaken their manual labour. Negroes toil on every plantation, with whites in charge. Comparing to home would be meaningless. We are too much the warrior people to have known, let alone suffered, such extended suffering.

We go to a Toe Party, where men bid on toes of women hiding behind a curtain. Trick is to judge beauty and form, personality somehow, on just a pair of feet. The buyer obliged to buy drinks all night for his chosen female. Or hightail it if he's bought an ugly damsel.

Sometimes a coloureds-only sign brings out the proud Maori in me. I want to do something back to show how wrong it is. But each day, by the moment sometimes, it grows on me: being nigger. Learning there are quite different rules.

We're at this jive joint one night and we hear word there's trouble brewing. My father steers me into a dark corner, and soon three giant Negroes walk in and go over to a group of younger men.

A huge fight breaks out, bodies fly everywhere, knives flash, I cower at hearing gunshots. The trio leave. There are two dead bodies on the floor.

My father takes us out the back way, says it's the other side of life as nigger. We turn in on ourselves, take our hatred and frustrations out on each other black on black, ever since our ancestors arrived in chains and got bought and sold like cattle.

I pick up some of the jargon, but no intention of using it: in power, jenk, bookooing, woofing, pickin' de box. I discover colour discrimination: skillet blonde is a very black and therefore less desirable person. I'm a quadroon, being quarter Negro; the one-eighth mulatto category is the most desirable pale status. Seems we're all prejudiced.

Jess delivers weed to the lumber camps, owns up how he made the money to send me. I say without it we'd never be together, have become quite partial to a good smoke too. And the liquor curse might have been exposed, for I am drinking every night till the early morning.

We visit other coloured settlements, clubs, bars of every description, even his hairdresser, an experience in itself of humorous exchange and hair-cutting like dance performances, staff and customers teasing each other, that way they explode in laughter and body movement. My father cramming in much as he can.

In the woods shown woodpeckers, squirrels, a shuffling armadillo, animals from my school books and American movies. We never run out of things to talk about, mostly Jess telling of this place, how life is for a coloured person and it's certainly not much grim telling, not how he tells it.

Our visits to Whitecave town are few and brief, to buy groceries at the coloured store, Jess to do his banking: banks can't have a colour bar as *For Coloreds* would mean black-owned and to his knowledge no Negro owns a bank. Yet he says it with that grin you wouldn't think of challenging, a man certain his wishes and dreams will one day come true.

Then you see the reality, of every store queue giving priority to whites not blacks. How deferential, even subservient, they've been made. I see how unlike Maoris Negroes are: no Maori would put up with being treated with such contempt for a second. In our country some whites are scared of Maoris. We are the warrior class and let none forget that, no matter the ones with the least money. We have law on our side, do Maoris, and rights. But then this is not my home country. I must not compare; history and sizes and complexities are too different.

Church spires are visible everywhere in the township. These are people of God, yet I must be wary or they will harm me. To be a Negro citizen of this country, I must know the boundaries, strict limitations and always my exposure even in going about daily business. But just can't quite get myself to believe it.

Jess fears getting known to the police and the local self-appointed moral guardians as a civil rights activist. He did go up to join the 1963 March on Washington, a quarter-million Negroes with tens of thousands of sympathetic white northerners. Martin Luther King made a famous speech that day from Lincoln Memorial steps, my father said.

I have a dream that one day even the state of Mississippi, a state sweltering with the heat of injustice, sweltering with the heat of oppression, will be transformed into an oasis of freedom and justice.

Quoting this on foot as we near a bridge and small town across from a river we followed for several miles one cooler afternoon. Where my father tells in haunted voice that he and his brother witnessed the lynching of a Negro woman, off that bridge.

I was fifteen. My brother eighteen. Got me started on drinking that very night, he recalls.

Where was I at the same age? Safe in Henry's house, told every day by my mother how special I was, receiving — from this man — money which fast-tracked my music career. To my knowledge my country has never had a single lynching.

I don't want to be any other race but Negro now. A member of my father's race so I might right some injustices. Do not want to go home. Have become my father's son.

CHAPTER FORTY-FIVE

ALL DAY HER STOMACH CHURNED with nerves, both at what she was doing — having another affair — and the night itself. A social event quite outside her experience, a dinner party.

A dinner party? Never heard of such a thing. In Lena's world lunch was called dinner and the meal at night was tea. And never did you combine the evening meal with a party, except a late-at-night cook-up of pork bones and vegetables boiled in a big pot for the drunks.

All week anguishing over what to buy, a dress, skirt and blouse, what about a jacket, how did she know what was appropriate? Could hardly ask the shop assistant and look like an ignorant Maori, had to walk the streets for hours before even finding what seemed to be a suitable store.

What if she wore the wrong thing? What jewellery should she buy, since she didn't own a single piece other than the wedding ring Henry bought her a thousand years ago? And what did people do at a dinner party, according to rules the experienced knew and outsiders were going to be exposed for not knowing? Felt like being set up to fail. But damned if she was going to make excuse not to show. To hell with other *dinner party* guests if they were going to look down on her. Might do some looking down herself.

She got the taxi to drop her off a couple of houses short of Ralph's.

Now she was here. On the well-lit stone-patterned driveway of a sprawling two-storey house which she was several times used to by now, yet back to perceiving like a mansion denied common folk like her. God, had she been here, and not to admire the architecture either.

They'd hit it off sexually, like she had with Jess; except this was better because everyone prefers their own kind, she realised. Ralph a New Zealander and never mind the white status. A person is more at home hearing her own accent, the same references, and he had a down-to-earth personality she liked. As for his library, she fell in love without knowing she had such innate need.

Changed into her glad rags at a friend's house, where the taxi picked her up. Bev, separated recently, had no idea what a dinner party was either. Just don't get caught, Lena. And be proud of who you are.

Easy to say. And how should she explain her marital status to the other guests? By removing her wedding ring, for starters. What would she say? What to talk about when she was a stranger of another race and culture? How different did she feel, really, to whites or any other shade of race or creed?

Ralph met her at the front door. He was dressed in jacket and tie, smart trousers. She had chosen a beautiful dress on the advice of a very understanding store proprietor who knew dinner party etiquette, though Lena didn't dare ask what she should do. Took a good chunk of her careful savings over the years to buy the outfit.

Kissed Ralph on the cheek, in case of noticing eyes; panicked hearing the hum of conversation inside. You look absolutely ravishing, he said. But she was scared out of her wits.

A blur of names and faces. Women in outfits that must have cost a fortune, and covered in expensive gold and diamonds; such confident women who seemed so formal despite the smiles. The men seemed to have made a social game of verbal wit: drank spirits and wines, perfectly at ease it seemed — and Ralph had assumed she needed no looking after, damn him. There was a surgeon, a lawyer, several in businesses Lena never knew existed.

The women tittered and made as if men were naughty schoolboys best with their own company. There was a ritual between these women that Lena wasn't getting. A clamminess spread over every square inch of her skin as the minutes felt like hours, full of conversation she couldn't get and to which she couldn't respond, with wit or even just normal reply. The social gap was just too wide.

Ralph teased her about fear being all in the head, what a hit she had made with everyone, even the venom-spitters normally renowned for preying on the socially weak, as he put it.

And why?

Because you were yourself. You didn't have the social recipe to follow so you made up your own — and what a dish you served! Laughing, pulling her close, eyes flicking to upstairs.

Was I really okay? Lena relieved, still not sure she had made a good impression. Not at this dinner party with white people, especially people of class.

You were jumpy as a flea.

You too, your first few times coming to Waiwera as a teenager. You told me: you were scared of the rough Maori kids who turned out big softies.

Exactly. Perception, neither more nor less. Your account of being a tourist guide with a bunch of thick-skinned Yank tourists was a classic.

Surprised myself, Lena grinned. Inspired by our famous Guide Maggie — she felt the equal of kings and queens, paupers and beggars, all.

I know who she is. Tip's parents had photos of her in their house. Beautiful woman. Reminds—

I've already been told. Lena cut the compliment short. Don't want to get a swollen head. I thought, none of you jewel-dripping glam dames has ever taken a party of tourists over a thermal wonderland in their own backyard. The funny bits I just added, to ease my nerves. Not as bad as I thought. Though Janet did ask me who I was writing a letter to when we were eating.

What a cheek.

She said, holding your knife like a pen just isn't done in the company. Hoped I wouldn't mind a friendly piece of advice.

Ralph looked at her hard. Were you offended?

To start with.

What changed your mind?

She looked me in the face and her eyes were kind. And she put her hand on my wrist.

She's a good sort, Janet. Her father is a plumber.

A plumber? They clean blocked toilets.

Among other things. He's a very successful one, has big commercial contracts all over the country. But Janet grew up in an average Kiwi working-class home. She's taken on airs, but harmless enough.

Lena quite taken aback.

Now, beautiful exotic woman who has been living right under my unknowing nose all these years, read what my eyes are saying.

She smiled. I see a man.

Yes, that. And a man who is falling for you . . .

I see that too.

And you?

Ralph, sometimes I think this idea of love just confuses me.

Doesn't have to . . . not if you let yourself go.

And so she did, and the loving was better than good. But of love itself she still did not know.

CHAPTER FORTY-SIX

THE SINGER IN ELEGANT WHITE linen suit finishes his flawless ballad to thunderous applause, raised glasses glinting and smiles gleaming in the smoky semi-gloom and that whooping and shouting and hand-clapping Yank has now got so used to.

Thank you, thank y'all. Now, I'd like to introduce a young man all the way from a place called — New Zealand! Give a hand to Mark Hines, and know he one of our own, brothers and sisters. Sitting with his daddy right down there. One of them war babies came home to roost.

Titters everywhere. Look at my father, he smiles and says you go do it, son. And up I go.

I ask the band if they know a Mel Carter number, learned from a record my father sent. More nervous than I've ever been, I think this is my entry ticket or ticket home. Singing to a black audience in their home territory? Have to remind myself I am of the same stock, sitting right there smiling up at me.

Piano takes the place of strings to open, a big bass sets up the beat, drummer a soft clash on tin, nice and easy; my turn now, glad I've had a few bourbons. Nothing matters now. Just the song. Doing my job. Living in the moment. Time to go, Mark Hines. Just let go.

Hit it. African ancestors at my shoulder and out there before me, a throng of history behind me, smiling: you do it, African brother. Do it.

Sing of nothing being able to satisfy this longing in me. The audience lets go a smile with sound. The band unobtrusive, guess they can see I'm a little nervous. Just focus on the music. When the time comes to step off the dive plank, I just do it. Like diving from Waiwera bridge. I owe it to everyone, not least to the man who began this style of singing, the great Mel Carter.

See only my father when I walk down to his table. But everyone is going *off*, and Jess is up and turning me around back up on to the stage. Asking the band leader can we do a duet, by Little Joe Hinton.

My father starts. I'll follow. We've done this a few times back at home to his record player. He takes the first two lines. I take the next two. Peas from the same pod, and why not? It's what we are. The audience comes on the ride with us at Jess's urging, every chorus line and heart-aching word.

Afterwards, for me, the drinks and compliments and welcome homes have me dizzy. He's set this up; we go from joint to joint and each time I'm introduced and invited to sing. Jess either joins or leaves me to it. I don't want this night to end. It's changing me. Or my father's genes are laying claim.

Driving home, sun soon to come up. Drunk on the night as on the alcohol. My father in animated re-enactment of Cassius Clay taking out Sonny Liston, the big bear, to win the world heavyweight boxing title; Jess telling of mixed confusion and joy at the champion's name change to Muhammad Ali, his religious belief to Islam, that it told white America they had nothing to offer him nor any Negro living in this oppressed land. How it upset the older, more conservative Christian blacks who couldn't understand a Negro converting to Islam, yet inspired most of black America to stand up like he did, be black, be proud—

Interrupts himself to say, we got company. On a country road this hour, bearing down on us? Police.

Turns to me. This is what I been warning about. But hoping like hell to never happen.

Guess the booze has dulled me a bit, blunted my capacity to fear. For I ask, can't we just keep driving at legal speed?

Be our lives at stake. You hear me?

I hear him all right. But we're not doing anything wrong.

He turns on me. I been at you since you got here at what you're in for! Ain't about right or wrong — it's about *survival*.

I'm not looking at the same man of nearly two weeks' knowing. Not near the same man. So I say sorry. Jesus, I'm sorry. And sobering up fast.

Don't say anything unless you're asked.

They cops, or—

Cops. Two sons of bitches, taking up the road side by side. One's got to be our beloved Sheriff Gilbert. He'll know you're here. Knows me. Let me do the talking.

One big uniformed brute at my downed window, another of large girth at my father's window who he greets: morning, Sheriff.

Where you heading, boy?

Piney. It's me, Jess Hines.

That your place of abode, Hines?

Yessir.

And your passenger? Peering, like he's about to put his head in to check me out up close.

A visitor, Sheriff.

What parts?

Near Australia, Sheriff.

Near? What, north? Make it Asia somewhere, correct? As I recall, nothing west but ocean, south is oceans something fierce. East is all ocean too, if I recall my geography right.

Little country called New Zealand on the east. About twelve hundred miles of ocean between. I sailed it.

Oh? Well, is this the fella I got told about, got seen by — We-ell. I'm told your dying daddy sent you here to say farewell to — That you, boy?

He calls my father boy. The ape in uniform my side glares at me.

Get out of the vehicle, both. And do it nice and slow.

Nice and slow two unarmed, law-abiding niggers get out of our car, to morning's first low-glowing smile spreading on the horizon right ahead.

What we done, sir?

I am not liking this tone my father has adopted, it is not manly, it is fawning. Just look at his face, the muscles have slackened, he's gone into damn slave mode.

Put your hands on the roof — both you sons of bitches.

I'm forcibly assisted by my ape, while the big gorilla has balled fists on hips and a smirky smile at my father doing as he's told, like any smart nigger.

If my father lifted his head he'd see his son trying to get silent direction from him, but his face is side down on the roof as crude hands pat me down, same my father. I am a passive person but not liking this.

Okay. Stand up. Bring him round to this side, Wes.

Now the dawn is swiftly melting the shadow from the highway, turning it golden. I'm manhandled round the front and presented like a captive to one Sheriff Gilbert. Stay humble, Yank. This is America. The South.

My friends tell me they found you wandering after midnight.

Yes, I nod.

That's a vagrancy charge on its own in my territory. Loitering with intent.

No intention meant, sir.

His eyes widen. He pushes his hat back. Did you receive a invite?

Answer with my expression: To what?

To speak.

I give him astonished expression. He gives me a backhand swipe like a bear lashing out. I stagger, nearly lose balance. In the moment of looking up at my assailant see my father's expression locked grim, eyes hooded as though in some form of sublime resignation.

Jess says, he doesn't know nothing about our ways, Sheriff.

If I took myself to India, do you think I'd better learn up on Hindus and sheikhs, before I went?

He's just a young man, from another country.

Sure he is — in the company of a nigger. Could be one *active* nigger, we been hearing, right, Hines? Who don't like his own state, the lawful way we do things here. No sir. This here could be a nigger who wants to *revolt* against time-honoured law and order, as practised and enforced by law-abiding white folk. Tell him, Wesley.

Son of a bitch civil rights man, you better not be walking all over *our* civil rights. We got our eye on you, Jess Hines.

To my ears the cop said beech and civil rarts. To my eyes both are thugs on the state payroll. And when the sheriff pulls his gun on my father, to my mind they are officially employed gangsters.

As for my father, I can hear his chains rattling. A low price bid on his fawning, lowered head.

Risking another swipe, I ask, officer? With respect. But what have we done? Why did you hit me?

The gun swings my way. You might like to compare to being shot?

I say, for what? Thinking, you can't do that, you have no right even to threaten it. In my country he'd be in big trouble.

Nigger-lover motherfucker got some mouth. He steps forward. Steel against my forehead. You say that one more time and we goin' bury your insolence in a goddamn coloured cemetery.

He swings the pistol back at my father. Along with the nigger your daddy back home in Zealand loves so much.

I know no one like this.

So I, the nigger slave, say, I'm sorry if I offended you, sir. Truly I am. Can not, will not, look at my slave father.

A smile starts spreading like the dawn with its spilled gold over us, all four, and he says, now y'all talking like you should — with respect. He says lak for like, and breaks up should into two parts, drops the t in *respect*. But not the sneer the smile has formed, he doesn't drop that.

The gun goes back in its holster. He looks at his deputy as if in need of assurance he is about to do the right thing. At my father with his glazed eyes all humble at him.

Then he says, Jess Hines, I were you I'd drop this civil rights bullshit, and just take care of your overseas visitor and settle down to being one obedient nigger who knows his place. That be God's will too, case you forgot.

Genesis 9: Ham's son Canaan shall be the servant of servants. Shem will be blessed.

I asked him as we stood on the road flooded in morning's glory, who is Ham?

A biblical black man, so they claim, who came upon his father Noah drunk and naked and so Noah cursed Ham down the ages. His descendants would be servants of the descendants of his two brothers, Shem and

Japheth. You not learn religion?

Not in our house.

You didn't miss much. My mother didn't believe either. Her reading set her free she said. But it was all around us, still is as you've seen. You all right?

I guess. You?

Know what you were thinking. Saw it in your eyes. But that's how it is, how we've survived. It's that, or take a warrior's stance and die proud.

He'd read my thoughts of swelling up Maori warrior pride. I shrugged and said, well.

His lip curled to a shape I'd not seen.

He said, you can't apply ignorance or arrogance of wet-behind-the-ears manhood to a situation three centuries old. You can't, son. And if you do then I'll whip your ass right here on the highway so we send you back on a stretcher, swear I will.

Up he stepped to me, two inches taller, lived of a different life.

Motherfucker know-nothing New Zealander who may as well be white like they are, if I have to suck dick to live till the day we can truly proclaim victory, then suck dick I will. But I don't have to stand for my own son making judgement on my ways of staying alive when his own life was wrapped in the cotton wool of his soft-ass history. You understand? Because I've been to your country, and it ain't nothing like this.

. . .

I said, do you understand?

I did then. He was trembling with anger. Which is I said sorry and truly meant it. Truly.

Why I put arms around him and felt a grown man sobbing in my arms as the sun shone down from a beautiful Mississippi sky.

CHAPTER FORTY-SEVEN

IN HEAVY RAIN HENRY AND Manu walked under one jumbo umbrella grinning at keeping the wet out; it ran in streams at their feet down a sealed road with gutters and underground storm water as Henry told how he kept at the town council till they gave in.

We could be wading through mud and stepping into ankle-breaking potholes, eh, son?

What's a pothole, Dad?

Made his father laugh. A hole that forms in a dirt road. As kids we used to sail little boats in them, out in the rain without a care. Gone now, thank goodness. I reckon we'll have the baths all to ourselves this morning.

And so they did, five to choose from, the channels rag-stoppered by Barney, good old reliable Barney who could now converse though with moments of lapsing back into the shocked silence caused by that incident, which Henry never forgot, not anything of it, and had a suspicion Barney now remembered. But what matter now, all in the past never to be seen again.

The rain hit their naked bodies hurrying out of the changing shed, blotted out any house lights that might be seen this seven o'clock winter Sunday morning hour, the sun yet to rise — not that it would bring much more than a dull grey light the first half hour.

Sweet shock of contrast. Sweeter moment of father and son linked by the same vessel of water.

Wash your back, Dad?

Henry turned, lifted his weight to accommodate his son's gentle lathering. Rain hammering down. Man and boy's hearts pitter-pattering with love. River below them a swollen muddy rush.

No other bathers appeared. They sang a song. Father as always told his son he had a fine developing voice but if he was harmonising to lower his volume to allow the lead to dominate. Let's swap parts. Sang as Henry washed his son's back, part of the ritual.

They walked home. Henry said their roast mutton leg would be just right. Manu wondering if to say what was on his mind. He would.

Dad? When I told the kids in my class we ate roast meat for breakfast, everyone laughed and said *no* one eats roast meat for breakfast. Are we the only ones?

A question Henry had fielded before, from Mata and Wiki. Yank was sure to have wanted to ask the same, but in the circumstances . . .

Henry said, people have different customs. Maoris come from a feast or famine culture so, like some dogs, say Labradors, we eat more than we need when food is around. Wasn't in nature's game plan for food to stay plentiful. That's why I'm fat. But contented fat. As you well know, people around here can sit down to a plate of pork bones, spuds and watercress at five in the morning. It's how we are.

How you are, Dad . . .

He looked at his son, almost the same height and still growing. I'll eat your share then?

Not this morning. Manu grinned, bumped his father with a hip. Henry bumped back. Manu exclaimed at being briefly exposed to the rain. His father pulled him back with a big strong arm.

Out of nowhere Henry heard himself say, wonder how your brother's doing in America. Saw Manu's surprise, the cover up.

Lucky him.

Oh, it won't be all beer and skittles. Not in Mississippi.

Silence. They passed growling mud holes side by side. They teach you about how Negroes are treated in America, son?

Only a little bit. American history. But mainly about the Civil War and their Constitution and laws and stuff. Glancing warily at his father.

Wonder what they'd think of this place, Dad.

Clearing his throat Henry said, well, a few did visit here, during the war . . . as we know. Coughed again. Lucky us who get to stay here.

Manu gave his father another kind of glance.

Dad? Do you think about Yank much?

Why I just asked the question, I guess. Sometimes.

No, I meant another kind of thinking.

The past again, son. It rolls up on you before you know it, then it's moved on like a missed bus. Can't change how I reacted, if that's what you mean. You've been giving it some thought?

Can't help it. He's my brother. Yet you're not—

His father. As if I ever stopped thinking that every day.

But, Dad, it must have stopped. That's what I figured.

Guess it did. You wake up one day and realise the subject no matter means much, if anything. Maturity, growing up. That and more.

You've been a good dad to me.

And to Wiki. Tried with Mata but missed those first years. What do you think your big brother is doing right now? I think it's an eighteen-hour time difference, so that makes it one yesterday afternoon.

You know this?

Well, if my son's got a brother in those parts. Mississippi, from what I been told, is a place back in time in how they treat Negroes. Least here the whites have come to respect us and we have the same rights. I'd knock down any man of any race who showed me disrespect. Hope you would too.

Manu, being partly his father's son, nodded yes, he would. Threw a knowing grin at his father, snuggled in closer under the arm. I guess he's getting into the music over there. At his father again, uncertain.

Negro music, Henry said. They call it black music these days. Boy, does he love his black music. From a little boy he had an ear for it on the radio. I think he secretly liked my singing and I know he loved listening to our returned servicemen. If he gets famous, might be he remembers me, eh?

He sure will. Manu was smiling, but that could have meant many things.

CHAPTER FORTY-EIGHT

THE CROWD, HE REMEMBERED THE crowd, the noise, the weight of collective demand, individuals yelled out criticism of individual players, or dismissed the whole team as useless. The different creatures spectators and players were. Yes, he remembered that.

The opposition's supporters against everything the opponent's team did even the spectacular; two thousand and more jeering, laughing at any mistake, howling in delight if one of their boys put a big tackle on an opponent. Men against men, like war. Screaming like apes — not that this country had any but the human kind — when a fight broke out. Sometimes the blood lust spread, and scraps and even a mass brawl would erupt in the grandstand, on the sidelines; women fighting too.

Women too: how would he ever forget his mother that day, supposed to be his finest eighty minutes and she decides to have an all-out fight with another shameless bitch right in front of the full grandstand — no. Must bury that memory.

He remembered the power of the massed group, the Waiwera community, how if they did not yet approve of a player, consider he had proved himself in battle, no matter what he did their response was muted, no edge to it, no claiming of a beloved warrior son. No rushing their decision, quite the opposite, and nor could they be fooled: you either played well or you didn't. Today being the final, and him having started back only four games ago, they were wary. He knew why: he was a *convict*, once a star centre till jailed for violent offences; a nutcase thereafter, a lowlife like his parents. The young man of promise should have pursued rugby, been embraced by its spirit of self-control in the interests of the team till he grew out of his problems; that had worked for other troubled young men. The beauty of team, of close community living — your burdens got shared and the noise and clamour dissipated them. Years before, if he punched an opponent, the group would cheer and scream to *finish him!* But that was then. Before he went and made himself a criminal, hitting people.

Grown far too big to stay a back player, Chud moved to blindside flanker in the forwards, his job to tidy up, be a feeder not a runner, a tackler but not a destroyer like the openside loosie of whom everything was expected. Nothing fancy, though every game could have its moments. Just be there, get the ball back, race behind the back line, pile in and support his tackled player, hunt for the ball, impose physicality, drop back if the defence was crowding and a turnover looked likely, be there to take a kicked ball or right beside the fullback as a back-up, or a rear guard if the opposition had closed in.

In the lineouts he was an occasional surprise jumper to throw the ball to, wished he got it more as he was athletic, had spring heels, big hands, muscle and mongrel when the opposition applied dirty tricks. Except they, the people, did not want Chud's old response, not now they didn't. They wanted a new Chud.

So when a punch dug into his ribs, Chud had to wear it, despite wanting to tear the guy apart. The spectators, village judge and jury, were silent awaiting his reaction. So was the referee, even more importantly — being sent off would bring the blade down as far as his supporters were concerned. More: he was going out with their beloved Henry Takahe's daughter and most were skeptical at how long that would last. Such a young man to have a bad past too.

The punch was so hard it felt like a rib was cracked. He lost the take and fell to the ground, trying not to writhe in pain. A man doesn't do that. On his feet again he rushed for the action — the other side were in possession — saw his man, a picture in his mind of his swinging arm connecting with the bastard's throat. Especially as he was grinning at Chud. Grinning, the arsehole was.

At the last moment Chud veered off his target and made a beeline for the ball carrier, to make a legal tackle. Threw himself at the man's knees, stopped him dead then reversed the man's forward momentum, drove him back.

In the tackle he ripped the ball away and like a good number 6 looked for someone to feed it to. There: the openside flanker in the coveted number 7 jersey, the position requiring a tireless, heady, fast player devastating in the tackle. And as he watched the number 7 race in for the try, Chud hoped for approval as the man who fed the ball.

They roared. He heard his name called. Not as much as Archie Tua's rose to the skies, but they knew his contribution, the self-discipline it had taken not to take revenge the dumb way. Now he could listen out for just one voice calling out she loved him. Not for being a warrior, but for being a man.

She was urging him, go and join your team mates, enjoy the adulation, you deserve it. He did consider it but said, rather be with you.

Their flat was quite bare as they were not long moved in. Had money just enough to buy basic furnishings and both were saving hard. Not that it mattered how spare the home surroundings, not when you were young and in love.

Wonder how my brother's doing? You two better make up when he gets home.

We will, Chud said. I miss him.

Well, she said, giving him a look.

What you said that night at the bath. Well.

She laughed. Because you weren't taking a pretty obvious hint. Told you, I'd always more than liked you.

I thought like a sister.

Correct. Until the like-a-sister turned into a woman.

You're only seventeen.

Old enough.

Well.

Smiling at each other. The first female he neither feared nor loathed. The first female he had ever physically touched. The first he had ever made love with.

CHAPTER FORTY-NINE

WE'RE IN THE NEXT COUNTY, my boy and me, at a big club on the outskirts of a town called Irene, and my son's eyes are popping at the sight of this outlandish crowd. Pimps and hoods, a range of shady characters, and women loud works of art. I grew up with it but young Mark has never seen its like. Everybody showing, I tell him. People got nothing else but clothes and attitude to express, the language we evolved with its own rhythms and shades of meaning. Southern niggers can talk a bear out of his fur coat.

Outrageous cats in sable coats, wearing shades indoors, suits that sparkle and so starched you can hear their crackling coming from outside. Big afros a style not long in, array of hats, from little skull caps to creations two foot tall, our race acquires jewelry like credit coupons against the life we live, we strut like cocks displaying plumage. Every pimp has his favourite whore or two in attendance. Every man has eye out for woman flesh. Every mean-looking face is on someone's payroll to watch his back. That's why guns are checked in at the door, minded by two giants. There's numbers guys and roving gamblers, dudes just out of the pen; I keep eye on the drug dealers: some psychotic on their own product might pick on my son, think he's white. Funny how he doesn't look white to me. I just see a son.

It starts with a woman come over to our table asks my son does he want to dance. Later, honey, I tell her. Me and my man got breeze to shoot. She don't like the rejection. Goes back to a group I don't like the look of. But hell, the music's calling me, us both. Me and my boy.

You is what you is. Cain't nothing change that. The singer up there has his eyes closed as he delivers. Hear my son say, this country spills over with musical talent. I feel ordinary in comparison.

Don't be, son. You is what you is, I quote the song. I heard you sing and you got talent. And not because you're my son. I got a black ear for quality.

Least the woman and her group let the song finish before they send their panther representative over, tall he is too, threads hanging off him like bark. He puts a paw adorned with chunky rings on the table front of me.

This your pet Klan boy?

Easy, brother. This is my son, my own flesh and blood.

Look like you adopted it. The guy at Mark who is naturally taken by surprise. I should have warned him.

We cool, brother. Just here to hear the man himself, Big Boy.

You here, sure, like any nigger. But he — points at Mark. He from another planet. Planet called White. You ain't no nigger, not even a mulatto, he says to Mark. The hell you doin here?

Same boat as you, brother, I answer on my son's behalf, starting to get mad. Same stormy sea we all on. I hope you reading this situation, my man. Put the menace in my tone.

Up on stage the saxophonist is doing a solo riff and he's good — if I wasn't with such distraction. Don't mean no disrespect, I say, but this here young man is my true son, I swear.

I seen albinos darker than him, says the guy. Goes back to his friends.

See what we made this life about, son? We made hard fact and harsh consequence of what's not important. Like you and I being strangers in their territory, even though we black the same and barred from the same establishments, beaten by the same white cops, found guilty by the same white prejudiced jury, jailed by the same white judge — and what these niggers do? Why, they check us out like Southern highway patrolmen out to bust us up, even kill us. For being the exact same color in exact same situation as them?

Another man comes over, huge he is. Hey, I say.

Hey, big guy says back. Your boy the palest goddamn nigger we ever seen. Then turns to Mark — spins, actually.

Say something, bitch.

Before I can intervene, Mark says, I'm hoping my father and I are not going to get hurt because we got different skin coloring and got raised in different countries. We're still father and son. Doesn't seem fair it's upsetting you.

The man stares. Glances back at his buddies. Back at Mark he says, tell me something about where you come from, white bitch.

So we are near in that place of no going back. Got my gun in the car.

He says to my son, make one mistake and you and this homo daddy of yours goin get hurt.

Mark says, my mother is a half-caste Maori — that's a race of *brown-skinned* people, the *natives* of a country called New Zealand. My mother fell in love with this man in the Second World War. I'm the result of that love. Between a brown woman and a black man.

My son shows guts. He says: Maoris are a ferocious warrior class, who used to cook and eat their enemies. They kept slaves. Like Negroes were slaves. But my mother's ancestors ate their slaves.

Dude doesn't know what hit him.

If you like, I'll do a Maori war dance right out on that floor. *Haka* we call it. You want to see it?

You disrespecting me I'll kill you, fucker.

I realize the band has quieted to background, instrumental music. So can be heard my boy telling this bullying fucker back, just trying to answer your question, friend.

Back the big man goes to his buddies.

You got them confused, I say.

They going to shoot us?

Not in here. Anyway, what we done to them? It a crime to exist, for your skin to be paler than theirs? Guess you light up like a Christmas tree wrong time of year in their eyes.

If I was a real white, would they dare?

Just then it is announced, Big Boy just about here. Like the Saviour is coming. I smile at my son, till the antagonist comes back.

You just a Klan boy acting English, he says to Mark.

If I'm Klan then I'm calling the cops. Get you charged with threatening.

This is my son saying this, the naive boy from a whole nation of them.

Say what?

You heard. If I'm white then I'm calling the cops to be on the side of one of their own.

I get to my feet, aware this could blow right now. My son follows suit.

We leaving now, I tell him. With our heads held high.

My father is angry as we drive back to his county.

When whites oppress us, he says, every nigger accepts it like God's decree. See one of their own who's not dark enough and they want to hurt him. In every town and city it's black on black and still we don't get it that we been turned against ourselves. Ain't no one talking revenge against the ones who been hurting us for centuries.

That's the ultimate act of destroying a people, pitting us against each other. You still want to live here, son?

Had my moments of doubt, I answer. Tell him how seeing the musical talent has me ready to give up on my dream of being a professional musician.

Listen, don't be worried, he says. It's going to take time to catch up on the influences we grew up with.

He starts demonstrating Big Boy Shand's singing style as the Southern night throws flying insects against our screen, and nigger menace stalks my mind.

CHAPTER FIFTY

THE FRAMED DEGREE ON THE wall, declaring graduation Bachelor of Laws with honours at Canterbury University in 1953, was like some proclamation of the man's higher status to Henry Takahe. The floor to ceiling law books on two walls, several paintings, a piece of metal and stone sculpture, wide desk that made definitive separation between lawyer and client. The ceramic pen holder, leather-cornered ink blotter, a paperweight of a bronze bull, another of cut glass weighing open a thick legal file. Framed photographs of his two rather pretty daughters, two fine-looking sons, in a way more approachable than the man himself. Proud sire of a brood of four who had — he'd tell each client as if in intimacy — all graduated, two in law, another in commerce, the fourth in accounting. James, Sarah, Jonathan, Annabel.

And there his wife, in colour, as if a breeze blew under her carefully cut and groomed locks, brunette, straight white teeth, married to this man who had his life his destiny and every client's fate under control. With a bad news update to give Henry Takahe about his tribe's petition to government for the return of their seized acres.

Had no standing in law, he hoped Henry understood that.

When Henry didn't. Not with all the fees paid out to this point and Richard Upton still edging for the final account to be paid, asking of the tribe's financial position. Henry's thoughts anyway wavered between Lena leaving him and Upton, the man before him.

Henry stood up.

Richard, Henry said, a warrior tribe needs more robust legal representation than what you are offering. We are ceasing all use of your services forthwith. Goodbye.

Driving home he was back to thoughts of Lena. Smiled, rueful, to think what in the past he would have done to unfaithful wife and lover: glad he was past that stage. What did violence ever achieve except in self-defence or to bring drunks under control as his job still occasionally required? The war he'd fought in, that was justified. But not belting his wife; slowly it had dawned on him this was wrong. Funny — it was contact with American hotel guests whose values had rubbed off, their horror of a man committing any act of violence against a female, that started to change him.

Thinking of Americans, news had told of race riots in several American cities, Negroes up in arms at yet another act of police violence. He wondered how Yank was getting on. Not exactly feeling guilty but certainly a man could have done a lot better than completely ignoring the boy. That stupid pride thing again. Maybe a man could get to know him in adult years. Henry hoped so. Though not holding out for making up for those years.

As for the mother, that name slut seemed a prophecy, if he wanted to take prophecy from it. She'd been sleeping with Barney, of all people. The slut confirmed — till he calmed down. Understood his own love-making efforts were selfish, for his own ends, that he had been a diligent husband in that way if no other. Realised war had taken away his ability to properly love a woman — any woman. Taken a lot of other things from a man too.

But he was still here, wasn't he? Still standing, still doing right by his community, as the elders had groomed him to do? Maybe the war had taken Lena's ability to properly love too. Could be she kept seeking what could never be found.

Still, a man couldn't dwell on stuff like that. Instead, he hoped young Yank was getting on all right. It was a tough country and Mississippi, as the world knew, one of the worst states with its prejudice against Negroes.

Kid was never a fighter, but he has got something courageous in him. Won't deny him that. Takes guts to get up on stage and sing. People's worst fear is public appearance. Must have taken guts to put up with my attitude those years, too. Good on him. And good luck with meeting his real father.

CHAPTER FIFTY-ONE

THE HOSTILE CROWD BECOMES A gauntlet we must walk. Of white faces in ugly contortions, citizens of this town yelling to go mind our own town's business, swearing and cursing, spitting, eyes veined red with hatred, glazed hard in the fires of bigotry. From children coached in prejudice to unknowing elderly who never asked a question of themselves in all their closed lives, they are screaming for our blood.

Cops are spaced in front of them with their own glares and sneers at us. *Nigger shits,* nigger of every contemptuous name in the limited verbal repertoire of a species who have beaten, shot, locked up and framed a million times those of dark complexion and Negroid features.

The police FORCE. Big, strapping, paunch-bellied, muscle-swollen, bristling with arms and hardwood and steel restraints, their badges showing membership of a gang with special powers and a list of exemptions from crimes they commit. Look at them: spilling over in frustration at no excuse, yet, to inflict their force upon these violators of their fixed assumptions.

As we march on.

My father has been dignified, all lifted head and set walking pace saying hardly a word in our march from the town outskirts, holding up placards demanding an end to every discriminating practice and act of injustice, singing *We Shall Overcome*, symbolic songs of protest unknown to me as likely the only foreigner.

The mad courage of this public protest by a hated minority in a town infamous for being the bombing capital of the western world, a last bastion of Ku Klux Klan who have blown up Negro churches and the houses of civil rights protesters just like us, murdered Negroes at will, with the tacit backing of city hall and police.

Like at Whitecave, I see church spires, crosses, constructions for folk to gather and pay homage to God. I see His true believers, bulging eyed, wanting unholy death for all of us who are not their own.

We pass within touching, spitting range of the Klansmen who my father recognises and points out. They've got a certain look, he says, forced by the din to speak in my ear. Mirrors of a community, men who snarl and ooze hatred, women who spit venom and verbal missiles at us, who scream like banshees, shriek like witches let loose from the Dark Ages: *Die, neeggahs — Die!*

Die, rot in he-ell, drown in your own sewers, burn in Satan's eternal inferno, a plague be upon you, you're monkeys not humans. On and on the insults and dire dark hopes spew forth, like some self-chosen exorcism of evil, except to them it feels like goodness and deepest desire for racial purity expressed.

I need not ask what I am doing here. It is simple: I am one of these people, marching. They are of theirs, howling at us.

Like molasses down the centre of creamy, frothing white, we pour into the town square. Our orderly column under instructions to remain passive, surrounded by a maelstrom of yelling, screaming, spitting whites closing in as if trying to crush us through greater mass and infinitely greater fury. Like God's avenging angels soon to wipe us off the face of His good earth.

Now an expectant hush upon the crowd as we arrive. Then a great howling, cackling collective laughter breaks out, like let-loose patients of an insane asylum.

And we on the inside soon see why: the statue of the confederate soldier on a marble plinth has live guards — in striped uniforms. Toting billy clubs. And black like near every one of us, excepting myself and a handful of whites come down from the north to join the good fight.

Go on now, fight your own like y' always do, neegahs! Tear each other's throats out! Save us the trouble! Y'all soon be joinin 'em, if you ain't in your graves!

Word races along to us that prisoners — Negro prisoners — have been brought in from the notorious Parchman Farm Prison to guard the symbol of white supremacy, that statue of proud Southern soldier fighting Negro liberation, prepared to die rather than see slavery abolished back when this country was torn in two over the issue. Knowing the marchers will not turn against their own, least not prisoners, yet hoping to see us break ranks, wage civil war against one another.

A police van arrives and cops with large dogs on leashes spill out the back, changing the tone of the crowd to a throaty glee. Canines bark and strain as pale-complexioned humans bellow for them to tear us to bits, rip our throats out, gobble up our black balls, feast on nigger meat. As if especially trained to attack only dark-skinned flesh, the dogs froth, mad-eyed with want.

When my father asked if I wished to join in a protest march I was afraid, of course I was. Not just afraid but embarrassed, at joining a cause when I'd not earned my stripes — the kind you get from flailing by whips.

Marion Williams, the Piney Woods preacher's wife, started to sing up front at the feet of the statue. A Negro spiritual, a Christian song in praise of God, near drowned out and yet the singing could be discerned; I only had to stay fixed on the figure of the big woman on the stone steps and move my mouth to her silenced lips and know our voices were ringing from great soaring mountaintops. That's how it felt.

How I felt, a Maori, here a white man in most folks' eyes. But son of this man beside me, putting arm over a son's shoulders. His voice was shouted down too, but I could feel the vibrations of his vocal cords enter my body, strengthen me. Lift me.

They told me, too: this may be one of the last times, my son. So make it a time of true courage. True love, for each other, for suffering mankind.

My every instinct sensed this, though mind refused to give it words.

Not that we felt the mob would turn on us. Not with the national press here, with the heavily armed National Guard in large numbers, and supportive fellow whites down from the north acting at last on guilt and a sense of duty to fellow American citizens. Still I sensed something of a final process under way that, no different from any inevitable event, would take place.

Might be why I had to keep wiping at my eyes, with no real reason to shed tears, while the rest were still singing and smiling and rocking gladly as they did.

I looked at my daddy and it was as though he had moved a distance, even as he had got so close my arm reached partway round his waist.

Even when he smiled down on me, from his loftier stature born of this Southern experience, by the war he fought for this nation, by the love experience with my mother. That too, all of it pouring out of him, this feeling of certainty he was saying goodbye. Not now, not this minute, nor this day. But sometime, soon.

CHAPTER FIFTY-TWO

SHIT. THAT'S WHAT JESS SAYS looking in the rear vision where he's kept vigil from the first day we sat together in this car. Starts shaking his head.

Tells me, don't be turning around. Moments later he says, motherfuckers. They trying to come alongside.

Turns the mirror back to my ownership as I'm driving, at his earlier perplexing insistence. Here they drive on the opposite side to what I'm used to.

Without being instructed, I speed up. The lights drop back, but not by much and they surge back at us again. I'm wondering again why my father has given me the wheel.

He says, son? I never wished so much not be a nigger in the South with my only son not born and raised in this godforsaken state of Mississippi, this peculiar nation of men who claim us the most free on God's earth, when no black person is close to free.

I ask, is it that bad?

Jess says, worse than that. This is not a following, it's a mission.

Right outside my window the headlight glare becomes a vehicle as it comes alongside. I see the outline of a person that turns into the face of a man lit from their interior light, I guess deliberately. His features are a white man's. Wearing expression only from the South. I know that already.

He could have been in that gauntlet today of Negro-hating white folk.

My father in urgent movement the other side, rustle of clothing, clack of metal against metal. Can feel the energy coming off him like heat rays.

To my left the man looms up stabbing a finger, eyes bulging. Same as we've seen in daylight today, made worse by the tiny glow of eerie light in their vehicle. No sign of a gun — yet.

Putting distance between us for however long it takes them to surge back at us, I get this thought: I am my mother's blood too: Maori. I am Maori. I am also Scots, a bit of Irish. They were warriors too. They knew oppression. Since when did they stop being warriors?

You driving.

I sure am.

You driving.

What I'm doing.

Cross the centre line.

What?

Get into the other lane.

You what?

No one else but us and them on the road.

And you'll be doing — what?

You keep saying what. Please, just shift to the opposite lane.

You for real?

Please, Mark. Motherfucker rednecks not going to be popping off at my son. We got to get you back in one piece, same state you arrived. Your momma, son. The least I owe her is to get her son back alive. My son too.

Just cross into the opposing lane?

Yeah.

And if someone's coming our way?

Got a mile of straight out front. Be all over by then.

What all over?

He looks across, repeats himself. You driving.

I accelerate and shift the wheel hard down to go other side of the road. Different feeling entirely on the wrong side of the road.

Good. Now let them come again.

You fucken crazy?

Mark, we keep talking and my fear's going to take over. Let–them–come.

I ease off the speed. Jess is turned away, though I know he has a gun. I had never seen a gun, not in anger, just hunters' rifles, till I came here. Never even had a dream I shot someone. Done everything else: flew, breathed and talked underwater, scaled tall buildings with bare hands, all the heroic impossible. But guns never figured.

Suddenly my father disappears, diving over into the rear seat. Window winder far side going down at speed, letting in engine roar, our own tyre noise, the night, this life some have no choice but to lead.

My father says *fuckers!* Now you got the *man* to deal with. He speaks it as wid. Adds, man and his *son.* Says it like the word sun. Like brightest light of all, lighting our way on this dark night.

He utters other things, a stream of words in a language of here, his own, not mine. I am what I was raised as. I don't have to understand it. I am not Negro, coloured or black. I was raised a Maori.

If I am not myself first, I can never be of and for my father.

In the rear vision my father rises up like any ambusher. Like any runaway slave turned the tables on his pursuing white masters. Your turn now! Three hundred years long of waiting for this moment.

The Maori warrior in me screams from one thousand years long. I yell, *Klan motherfucker bitches!* Like an angry black man would. Like any man with pride.

In then out of their flood–lighting headlights we go. Air pulses and reverberates from the downed window where my father hunches looking just over the sill.

Hit the brakes!

So I do: hard enough to make an abrupt slowing and bring our pursuers into line with my father's readied weapon.

Shoot them! Cut off their heads! I scream. We'll cook and eat the scum! The Maori warrior coming out.

Everything gets crystal clear. As if I'm gazing into our deepest Waiwera boiling pool at every silica bump, like sponge growth in a boiling medium meant to make life impossible.

As if the algae my mother says are miracles of life on the edges of boiling water have found ways to survive right inside the monster.

That's where we are: inside a boiling hellhole still alive, still with intent and cunning and our manhood still intact.

Gunshots, one-two-three.

In the mirror the headlights wobble, veer violently. More shots from my father's gun. The vehicle shape lurches then disappears, headlights like a rearing, careering wild animal going down.

Gun it!

Down the highway we go, beams spreading the night, insects like tiny avengers sent to slow us, splattering the windscreen to make wet organic mud. Silence upon us. My ears echo the shots.

Then the shaking starts. At the knees and spread up to my trembling hands.

I think my daddy has just killed two men.

I say in a throat-catching voice, Pops? What now?

Don't know why I call him that, just can't say Dad or Daddy.

He gives ghost of a satisfied smile — no, a righteous smile. Heaves a sigh with sob in it. My life — our lives — just changed. Soon be a wanted man — men.

A wanted nigger, along with his nigger cohort father.

I think maybe hell does exist: the living version. Yet feels like heaven, it surely does.

CHAPTER FIFTY-THREE

WE PARTED NOT EXACTLY FRIENDS. He threatened me with violence at my saying I didn't want to return home, be running away like a coward. He told me I had no choice.

Through contacts he had put different licence plates on his Chevy and he drove me to Atlanta, where we stayed a night in a modest hotel, went to a music club; I got drunk, he got stoned.

We said our strained goodbye in the morning, nothing else to say, not when it was all taken by the doing and Jess wanted me out of danger. I took a taxi to the bus station, so fearful of being nabbed. Though I would have been prepared to fight to the last alongside my father. Jail would have been a living hell.

DOUBLE MURDER! newspaper headlines blared as I waited for my bus. Two known members of the notorious Ku Klux Klan shot dead by unknown assailants. Suspects believed to be driving a 1961 model Ford Chevy. The two bodies found in mangled wreck off Highway 54 to Whitecave suffered gunshot wounds to head and chest. Possible suspect believed by police to be involved with civil rights protests. No person or persons has yet been named.

I waited for my bus to take me out of there, starting the long journey back to the safety of my homeland, my tiny country with its affairs so minor and petty as to be farcical in comparison. Yet when I got back there, was never more pleased to be home.

I found ways to follow events back in my father's place of raising. Day after day, for two months, I read every newspaper end to end, occasionally finding mention of the crime and knowing they had a name: Jess Tobias Hines.

Mrs Mac made telephone contact with a library in Jackson, Mississippi. I didn't say I drove the vehicle the night of that double murder, though maybe she guessed. The library in Jackson said the fugitive was still on the run. No mention made of a New Zealander.

Things had changed at home — greatly, in my mother's case: she'd left Henry and gone to live with a wealthy Pakeha businessman. Told me she didn't know what living was till he opened her eyes, how it wasn't so much the higher quality of life money brought as much as the knowledge. Like his library, which she was coming to enjoy more and more.

I told her of my Mississippi experiences. A day later she called me to come and look at some amazing poems written by Negroes, years back, one by a Richard Wright about a man coming upon the remains of a Negro who had been lynched and burnt. She read to me, sitting in her new man's library, of a man being tarred and feathered, and *cooled mercifully . . . by a baptism of gasoline*. Till it was set alight.

Then I got a letter from Marion Williams, giving me the bad news: my father's capture. She enclosed pages from an American weekly magazine, a vivid write-up by a white man who saw what happened — a colour piece, the newsmen call it.

Murder in Mississippi
by Bradley J Heath

The word would have hummed down the telephone wires, whizzed back and forth over his head. The wires, the wires would have sung with directions saying exactly where, which part of town it was and every gory detail of what had taken place. Excitement and gladness conveyed at near the speed of light—

As fast as a murdered man's soul departs?

Quicker than the forced, violent passing of an innocent life?

Hanging from the cross bar of that same telephone pole, his body would not have brought to mind a black Jesus, nor suggest an injustice had been done, nor a genius or good man had been wrongly put to death. Those who gathered saw simply a corpse with human features; killed justly, they believed, because he took the lives of two good citizens, two fine men with a name for caring for their community, for looking after its morals and its virtuous white ways. Never dare mention, in the South, their ritual of wearing white robes and hoods with eye slits, of chanting hate-filled mantras mixed with God's name, like flavoring sprinkled on babyback pork ribs.

He was just hanging there, clothes shredded from him, blood that had run down his legs caked by the drying wind, a prevailing wind from the south transporting dead leaves and clinging insects and other things powerless against its force, carrying smells and odors along its way.

That wind swirled over his blood, blood that used to flow into his member when he was sexually aroused. The mob had cut off his offending manhood with a knife, severing penis and testicles clean away. They cut off his ears to deafen him, perhaps to his own screams — or the sounds of their evil deed.

You'd think that 1965 should be more civilized than 1905. Back then, after a Negro lynching, the pastor of a church in this same town said: *The failure of the authorities to maintain law and order made the lynching necessary for the infliction of justice.*

But a rope's a rope. This one was half-inch hemp, looped by deft hands to form a hangman's noose.

They broke him out of jail against the lame protest of the sheriff they all knew, had all gone to school with; whose children played with their children. He sat in church the day after, no doubt, with some of those men who had taken the nigger's life. None would consider it murder.

Are they so different from their forefathers fifty years ago? Words from another Southern sermon, uttered in those early years of our century: *Last night a sifted band of men, sober, intelligent, of established good name and character — good American citizens — did this hamlet a powerful good. They did remove the life of an inferior member of the Negro race by God-ordained means of lynching.*

Today's victim swayed in keeping with a wind that would not let up. The smallest of movements to and fro was witnessed by the townsfolk, by those who had rushed from outlying hamlets and small towns, all connected by telephone and culture and outlook. Ordinary American citizens.

From the telephone pole where the figure hung, the wires looped from pole to pole and ran alongside roads, as far the eye could see, to dwellings near and far, sending the news: something *good* took place last night. Keen eyes could see the dust trails of vehicles hurrying to the town, the occasional puffs of dust kicked up by horses carrying men of set mind and cruel ways.

A crow landed and gazed for some time at the shape below, or at the mass of human shapes, more arriving like a stain spreading on good tarred Southern ground. It dropped on to the corpse's shoulder and started pecking at an eye. The crowd's exclamations and glad cries scared the crow away like a soul fleeing too late. People wondered if the bird got an eye, strained to see if an empty socket confirmed the theft.

But the dark gash midway down the body took greater claim. They had shucked his manhood like whipping the insides out of an oyster.

Someone cracked a joke about a de-sexed nigger being a tamer beast. Laughter like a vast broken cask spilling every drop of goodwill to all mankind.

They did this —

Bradley Heath wrote as though to me, Yank, personally

— to someone's father, someone's son. To a fellow American.

He went on:

That day at the village circus, a Negro woman dared stumble across the railway tracks, howling, bringing gravel stones rolling down with her as she sagged at the knees, from imbalance or grief. She wore a dress of rough denim and the polka-dot scarf that niggers call a rag. Flauntin' the rag, they call it — in other circumstances, not on arriving at the aftermath of a murder.

By natural courtesy, before they could consider her *only a nigger*, the crowd cleared a path, closing up again after her like a change of mind. A boy asked, face mischievous and foot raised, should he trip her? No, his elders said. *No, you better not, kid.* But they could have said yes just as easily. Besides, she'd not yet run the gauntlet.

Maybe she was a freshly made widow, this
woman vexed amid a crowd not her color, not her
species: looking at her husband hanging up there
like a sight not even the lowest can get used to.
But already she looked too old to be his wife, or
his lover. She looked more like a mother might.
Except surely she'd be calling out, *son! Son!*

Then she saw the unimaginable absence of
loins. Oh, Lord, did she see the ugly wound. And
she screamed, a sound from some place deeper
than any present had ever heard.

Jess had written me.

*My dear son . . . what a joy it was having you . . . what a brief time it was and
yet momentous, in a way only a Negro would understand since we live that life daily,
so many of us. Epic, even when we are most ordinary, dramatic, even in living life
most mundane. Tragic, more often than joyful. I have never succumbed to indulging
after I beat the demon drink. Yet tragedy would now appear to be happening to me.
I have another term for it, however: standing tall.*

*I have become infamous and yet there is no mention of you, other than I had an
overseas visitor residing with me. None at Piney Woods is talking, not to the police,
now out to take another of us down. Good old Marion, the preacher's wife, she's got
them all sworn to silence on the subject of Jess and his boy. And two dead rednecks
have no tale to tell.*

*Nor do I have any regret, except that you were caught up in it. But now you
are safe in a country that is blessed. Though I know the Maori people have some
problems, they are minor in comparison.*

*I had to threaten you to get on that bus, I'm sorry. Or you would be on the run
with me. It is the strangest feeling to be wanted for murder when you served your
country killing the enemy.*

Who are my enemies? This is the question I have asked and found answer for.

*An enemy is he who denies me my dignity and deprives me of my basic rights.
Just as I would deserve to be so described should I act against others in an unjust
manner. He is my enemy who judges me on the color of my skin and not, as Martin
Luther King has said, the content of my character.*

The men who died that night are one and the same beast who might have killed us at the club, when those hoodlum niggers took dislike to your pale skin. Klan members or mixed up and fucked up niggers are one and the same. We should aim for higher things, always.

But it is not the fight you were born to. You will have your own, more tempered fights but struggles for good just the same.

Who knows how long before they catch up with me. I stay on the move, have grown a beard and look disheveled like I did when I was a drunk. You would not recognize me. No, perhaps you would. I like to think you would.

I have no money for you, only my deepest love. I thank you for coming into my life before circumstances would have it end, possibly, in the near future. Guess they'll string me up as an example to other niggers, another strange fruit hung from a tree.

Will write again. But, if you don't hear from me, know my love for you is three centuries strong. Listen out for me singing for you, as if you are the baby I'm putting to sleep with gentle Negro lullaby.

Your loving father, Pops.

Marion wrote:
Then started the sniggering, from a low note rising to a breathing and form of giggling only they would recognize of their own kind.

I screamed: What have you done to him! How could you DO this?

This is of your daddy hanging there, God bless his soul, God give him peace and suffering no more. The newsprint photographs I enclose with my apologies, Mark, but felt you must see them. Make yourself stare at them so you will know never to be such a person who would do this to another human being of whatever race or creed.

Then I heard — and soon saw — a man about sixty, of age to know better and kinder, drawl in voice loud enough to gain a hundred or more in his coarse net: He won't be raping no white woman again.

Again? Not your father, son. He'd never do such a thing to a woman. He respected women.

A hundred and more chorused: He sure as hell won't. *A murderer too. Killed two white men he did. Know I've met many a fine white Southerner. This is just a certain type all too prevalent down these parts.*

The other hundreds took it up as a resounding echo. Which got another whipped up, this time a woman. I spotted her on account she was tall and she stood out because the good Lord did not exactly bless her with good looks, far from it. Made ugly, I think, by her thoughts, her sick moral state.

She said: I'm thinking . . . ! *Then she bellowed:* I'M THINKING, *folks, that this here nigger woman would like to join him?*

This is me she is referring to. As in joining your poor daddy strung up there like curing meat.

Up dere in heben!

Using how my generation's parents used to pronounce words. Up dere in heben.

Oh, Mark, it was like being in a cave echoing with their howls and low moans, those who murdered your daddy.

Out of this pack a man toting a pistol like a short spear started forcing a way through to me the nigger woman stupid enough to turn up. They were making way for him, parting their own seas for him to walk through clear to me.

The one with the gun got to me, ordinary Marion Williams in a state about a murdered Negro taken like that, and he pointed the thing at my head.

Y'all wanna join him up dere in heben, nigger bitch?

He was roaring in amusement at repeating that scorn, trying to elicit another outbreak of laughter, some kind of approval. But the mob had already tired of that one and they just stared. They went silent in the instant that gun barrel pressed cold upon my temple flesh.

You his momma? the man asked.

No, I answered. I am the preacher's wife, of his community, Piney Woods. I'm begging you to give a man his last piece of dignity — I beg you. He fought for this country, was wounded, endured years of war hardship, endured racial hatred just like this in the hope that, one day, black people would walk free — and you did that to him?

It was accusation of, I knew, a deed already owned. Caught the crowd for a few seconds, they moved this way and that like the wind had picked up hard and shook them a little, moved them a fraction physically, not at all in their fixed minds.

The gunman just pushed his weapon harder against my temple, his lips peeled back in some kind of grin.

I told him: So you do it. Fire that bullet right into me.

He said, I will if you don't depart from here.

I am not leaving until this man is given his dignity, I told him, quite ready to join your father in heaven.

Now this was daylight and cowards don't operate in that medium. They soon melted away. The gunman spit his departure in my face. I flinched not. Let his liquid run down my face.

Soon other Negroes emerged, like always, out of the shadows to quietly cut down Jess's body, give him dignity in his last. Lord, my heart was broke in two, for I loved that boy, your father.

CHAPTER FIFTY-FOUR

I GUESS MEETING JESS CHANGED my view of Henry: made me realise how your birthplace, your culture, can make you.

Henry's changed too: lives by a higher code of conduct these days. Since my mother left him we've talked, though we'll never be close; how, after all those years of his silence?

He never mentions my mother, though I hear on the grapevine he accepts she was quite unlike the usual Waiwera village person and they were never suited. He's not the jealous type, not about Ralph's money at any rate. And as he can't see the changes in my mother he'll not know what a happier person she is. To my eyes she was always beautiful, but I swear living with Ralph has made her even more so.

My sister Wiki intends to marry Chud one of these days. Chud is different — like the boy I grew up knowing so well, but now a man. Though I'm not sure he can overcome his parents, both still drunks, lately in poor health. Seems to me it's similar to being black in America: the odds are stacked against you. But who knows, if he tries hard enough, he might make it.

Isobel and her husband have split up. She came and said goodbye, and we made love one last time, though it was not the same. She moved to Auckland. Her son has left the band, gone to Auckland too, formed his own group. We were moving in different directions and anyway he is the superior musician.

Whenever I am with Giselle, I say a little thanks to Isobel for her teachings on how to really love a woman. I've taken Giselle over our steaming acres many times, and always I find something new. A fissure that has widened, our old circular bath finally succumbing to the collapsing terrain around it, now a dry hole. Always we call in on Merita, who has mind enough to pepper Giselle with questions about her country and compliment her beauty. Compares her to my mother, puts them on equal footing. Says she is so glad for my mother going and living with Ralph, look at the change in her. I agree. My mother is a different person. My special mother.

Merita, still going strong in her eighties now, says my mother has finally realised her potential. Confesses she'd sweetened life's bitter pill by telling me my Maori ancestors were of high birth. Now you're strong enough to accept being ordinary, which is not such a bad thing, eh, Yank? Merita points out what I'd noticed already: that Barney, his voice regained, won't shut up, and is all too fond of an audience. But it takes all sorts to make a village.

When I come across Henry back in Waiwera we'll have a chat, a beer at his hotel sometimes.

I can hear Marion singing *Take my hand, precious Lord*, which she told me in her letter she sang as my father's body was taken down from its wooden telephone-pole cross. Who am I to say her Lord did not take up her plea? If God didn't take heed then the folk assisting with my father's last journey would remember the good woman's vocal tribute and her courage too.

Maybe one day I'll follow the dream and go to New York. Go to Whitecave, find out where my father is buried. Call on the good folk of Piney Woods, especially Marion.

He lives on in me. I'll have children, name the first boy after his grandfather. A girl I'll name her Jessie.

I'll listen out for your lullaby from time to time, Pops. Three hundred years in the making. So glad you came into my life too.

Your son, Mark.

BETWEEN THE WORLD AND ME
RICHARD WRIGHT

And one morning while in the woods I stumbled suddenly upon the
thing,
Stumbled upon it in a grassy clearing guarded by scaly oaks and elms.
And the sooty details of the scene rose, thrusting themselves between
the world and me. . . .

There was a design of white bones slumbering forgottenly upon a
cushion of ashes.
There was a charred stump of a sapling pointing a blunt finger
accusingly at the sky.
There were torn tree limbs, tiny veins of burnt leaves, and a
scorched coil of greasy hemp.
A vacant shoe, an empty tie, a ripped shirt, a lonely hat, and a pair of
trousers stiff with black blood.
And upon the trampled grass were buttons, dead matches, butt-ends
of cigars and cigarettes, peanut shells, a drained gin-flask and a
whore's lipstick;
Scattered traces of tar, restless arrays of feathers, and the lingering
smell of gasoline.
And through the morning air the sun poured yellow surprise into the
eye sockets of a stony skull. . . .
And while I stood my mind was frozen with a cold pity for the life
that was gone.
The ground gripped my feet and my heart was circled by icy walls of
fear—
The sun died in the sky; a night wind muttered in the grass and
fumbled the leaves in the trees; the woods poured forth the
hungry yelping of hounds; the darkness screamed with thirsty
voices; and the witnesses rose and lived:

The dry bones stirred, rattled, lifted, melting themselves into my
  bones.
The grey ashes formed flesh firm and black, entering into my flesh.
The gin-flask passed from mouth to mouth; cigars and cigarettes
  glowed, the whore smeared the lipstick red upon her lips,
And a thousand faces swirled around me, clamouring that my life be
  burned. . . .

And then they had me, stripped me, battering my teeth into my
  throat till I swallowed my own blood.
My voice was drowned in the roar of their voices, and my black wet
  body slipped and rolled in their hands as they bound me to the
  sapling.
And my skin clung to the bubbling hot tar, falling from me in limp
  patches.
And the down and quills of the white feathers sank into my raw
  flesh, and I moaned in my agony.
Then my blood was cooled mercifully, cooled by a baptism of
  gasoline.
And in a blaze of red I leaped to the sky as pain rose like water,
  boiling my limbs.
Panting, begging I clutched childlike, clutched to the hot sides of
  death.
Now I am dry bones and my face a stony skull staring in yellow
  surprise at the sun. . . .